PELICAN BOOK

DIVORCE MATTERS

Jacqueline Burgoyne is Reader in Applied Social Studies at Sheffield City Polytechnic. Her research and writing are chiefly concerned with couple relationships, especially divorce and remarriage. She has completed a study of remarried parents with David Clark, a study of unmarried couples, and is currently looking at the ways in which people's working and family lives are interrelated.

Roger Ormrod had a large family practice at the Bar until 1961 when he became a judge in the Family Division. From 1974 until he retired in 1982 he was a Lord Justice of Appeal dealing mainly with Family Law appeals.

Martin Richards is a Lecturer in Psychology at Cambridge University. His research and writing concern parent–child relationships. Together with Margaret Dyson, he undertook a study of the effects of divorce on children for the D.H.S.S.

DIVORCE MATTERS

JACQUELINE BURGOYNE
ROGER ORMROD
AND MARTIN RICHARDS

PENGUIN BOOKS

Penguin Books Ltd, Harmondsworth, Middlesex, England
Viking Penguin Inc., 40 West 23rd Street, New York, New York 10010, U.S.A.
Penguin Books Australia Ltd, Ringwood, Victoria, Australia
Penguin Books Canada Limited, 2801 John Street, Markham, Ontario, Canada L3R 1B4
Penguin Books (N.Z.) Ltd, 182–190 Wairau Road, Auckland 10, New Zealand

First published 1987

Made and printed in Great Britain by
Richard Clay (The Chaucer Press) Ltd,
Bungay, Suffolk

Typeset in Monophoto Sabon

For no effect of tyranny can sit more heavy on the commonwealth, than this household unhappiness on the family. And Farewell all hope of true reformation in the state, while such an evil as this lies undiscerned or unregarded in the house: on the redress whereof depends not only the spiritful and orderly life of our grown men, but the willing and careful education of our children. Let this therefore be new examined, this tenure and freehold of mankind, this native and domestic charter given us by a greater lord than that Saxon king the Confessor.

John Milton
The Doctrine and Discipline of Divorce, 1643.

CONTENTS

PREFACE

Although public concern about current levels of divorce often generates a good deal of journalistic comment, academic discussion of its causes and consequences tends to be highly specialized, addressing itself to very specific issues and audiences. Lawyers continue to debate the legal and procedural implications of rising divorce rates in various academic and professional forums. Counsellors, doctors and the helping professions generally are concerned about its effects on individuals, families, and, of course, children. There has, however, been relatively little reflective consideration of how marriage itself and our customary patterns of domestic life, have been affected by the rise in divorce rates and the meanings we attach to divorce.

This book is intended to redress the balance by providing an overview of divorce in Britain. As might be guessed, the authors originally met through the divorce industry, participating together in various conferences and seminars which focused on the problems of rising divorce rates, and this book has grown out of countless discussions with those in the front line – lawyers, counsellors, teachers, doctors, social workers and many others including the divorcing themselves. We felt it would be helpful to draw together some of the more specialized and partisan debates that have punctuated recent public discussion as well as, where possible, to convey something of the first-hand experiences of those adults and children directly involved. We each bring rather different, but hopefully complementary skills, experience and assumptions to the project and this, the final result, has been a genuinely collaborative effort. Although Jacqueline Burgoyne was initially responsible for the first drafts of chapters 1 and 3; Roger Ormrod for 2 and Martin Richards for 4 and 5, wastepaper baskets overflowing with earlier drafts remind us of how much we have each now contributed to the final result as a whole. The last chapter in particular embodies the fruits of this co-operation. As our separate areas of specialist knowledge and distinctive perspectives began to overlap and fuse we realized that collectively we had suggestions to make about possible ways forward and these are set out there. Although the final chapter is deliberately partisan, the material which precedes it is presented in as impartial a manner as possible. This has not been easy, simply because it is a subject which generates strong feelings and creates divisions – between 'guilty' and 'innocent'; women and men; expert and client – so we have tried to point to the sources we have used, especially where our conclusions may seem controversial. We have also included a list of further recommended reading.

Several long-suffering friends have also read and commented on various drafts and chapters. We would like to thank David Clark, Frank Field, John Hall, John Haskey, Brenda Hoggett, the late Iain Johnston, Anne Ormrod, David Pearl, Sarah Smalley, Daniel and John Stoddart for their patience in offering comments and criticisms. The final version seems to have been typed a great many times and we are grateful to Jill Brown, Brenda Chatterton and Sally Roberts for their efforts in this direction.

1

DIVORCE IN ITS SOCIAL CONTEXT

In the years following the end of the Second World War marriage, parenthood and a way of life that revolved around home and family became more popular and attainable than ever before. In the wake of improved housing, higher average standards of living and a greater psychological investment in domestic life, the institution of marriage became a cornerstone of this transformation. Today, not only will over 90 per cent of the population be married at some stage of their adult life, a figure a good deal higher than for earlier generations, but the vast majority of adolescents anticipate, probably quite realistically, that they too will eventually settle down, marry and have children, albeit in a more precarious economic climate than their parents' generation.

However, in the last twenty years trends in divorce have also generated much public discussion and, at times, personal alarm. Our first reaction is generally one of fear about the pace of change. At a personal level, there are now very few of us who, directly or indirectly, have not had experience of the kinds of personal changes which must be endured when a marriage ends. At a public level, some of the almost hysterical debates about what the popular press has called 'divorce-crazy Britain' suggest a profound unease about current levels of divorce, as well as patterns of family and domestic life more generally. Yet in the course of our research, reading, reflection and discussion during the preparation of this book we have also become increasingly aware of the sources of continuity in patterns of marriage and divorce and of the ways that change – political, social and personal – is resisted. For example, as we shall indicate later in this chapter, even the rapid increase in divorce which characterized the later 1960s and 1970s has to be seen in the context of the stable rate which has, so far, been the pattern of the 1980s. More significantly, as will become apparent from our discussion in this book, many of our observations are accompanied by inaudible but deeply-felt sighs of exasperation that in some areas, such as women's rights or the legal procedures of divorce, so little has changed, and that any alterations that have been made have been largely piecemeal and based on short-term expediency.

Our analysis must, therefore, encompass both of these responses to contemporary patterns of family life. On the one hand, most of us see divorce as a disturbing phenomenon whose sudden increase we appreciate both from public discussion or personal experience and for which, both individually and as a society, we seem so ill prepared. At the same time, many individuals who try to make sense of their marital crises do so within a very limited framework of conventional explanations and solutions which stress the apparent naturalness, desirability and normality of one particular pattern of household and family arrangements. For example, (as we show later (see pp. 117–19), remarriage is often offered and adopted as a solution to the problems of divorcees and other lone parents, even though second or subsequent partnerships are even more likely to end in divorce than first marriages. It is as if divorce is more manageable if it is treated as a temporary aberration or momentary failure within a conventional sequence of personal and family changes. Consequently, most people's views of marriage remain very traditional. An indication of this is that weddings are still an important part of popular culture and over half of those marrying for the first time do so in church. Many of the divorced people who ask for a church ceremony for their second marriage are expressing a wish for what they regard as a *real* wedding and the public recognition of their new relationship. Similarly, many of the public images of the family presented in advertising that, in turn, feed into popular consciousness are based on highly conventional stereotypes. These rarely reflect the many different household groupings to which we may belong during our lifetime. The persistence of such conventional images helps us to understand why, when high levels of divorce appear to challenge and undermine traditional family patterns, governments, policy-making and professional bodies frequently seem to sidestep serious discussion of either the trends themselves or how they should respond to their consequences.

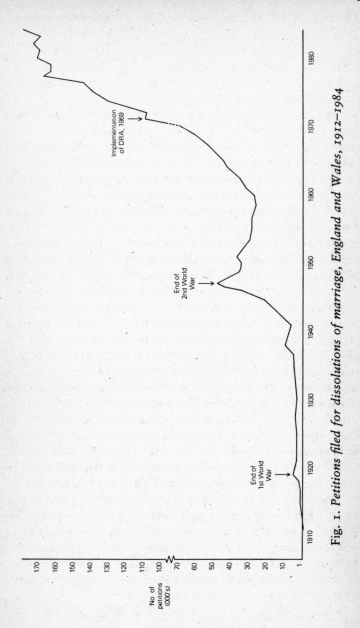

Fig. 1. *Petitions filed for dissolutions of marriage, England and Wales, 1912–1984*

'DIVORCE-CRAZY BRITAIN?' MARRIAGE BREAKDOWN IN THE 1970s

In the 1970s in Britain, as in many other industrial nations, both the number of divorces and the rate of marriage breakdown increased dramatically. During the 1970s both these measures doubled and if these trends were to continue it is calculated that one in ten couples would divorce before their sixth wedding anniversary; one in five before their twelfth anniversary; and one in four before they have been married for fifteen years.[1]

It is, however, important to set what has happened in this recent period in a longer-term context. An increase in the number of marriages in the early years of the Second World War was followed by a marked increase in the number of divorces in the immediate postwar period as large numbers of these wartime marriages broke down when couples were reunited after the war, as well as the more general disruptive effect of war on all marriages. The rate of divorce then remained fairly stable, perhaps because of changes in attitude that had occurred while the war persisted. Then a striking increase began. Between 1960 and 1970 there was a steady 9 per cent annual growth in the divorce rate, so that by the end of the decade the number had doubled, reaching 58,000 in 1970 (see Fig. 1). By 1972 it had doubled again, partly because of the backlog of long-dead marriages which received their official burial as a result of the new provisions of the 1969 Act (see chapter 2). Although the number of divorces continued to rise steeply until 1978, the most recent period has been one of relative stability.[2] Since 1980, decrees absolute granted in England and Wales have remained in the region of 145,000 a year.[3] While it is very difficult to predict how the current divorce rate is likely to be affected by the increasing proportion of marriages which involve at least one remarried partner (see pp. 37–9), changing patterns of women's employment (pp. 89–90) and the present economic recession (pp. 156–7), we have reached an apparently stable point where governments, relevant state institutions and policy-making bodies, as well as the churches, legal, medical and welfare professions, should perhaps review their response to this major social trend.

There are highly contradictory elements in the political and public responses to these changes. As in earlier generations, the prophets of doom are never far from view and, in often unconscious repetition of earlier moral commentators, hail current divorce rates as portents of the entire decline of Western civilization.[4] Others, from a more pragmatic standpoint generated by working in the frontline of those occupations which now constitute a growing 'divorce industry', have tried hard although largely unsuccessfully to draw attention to the scale of the problem and the largely hidden social and economic costs of high rates of marriage breakdown. For example, the Report of an interdepartmental working party on marriage guidance entitled *Marriage Matters*, published in 1979, argued that the state should accept a responsibility – shared with caring individuals and independent initiatives – for relieving private misery and exercising social concern by the provision of services through statutory and other public agencies to help with marital problems.

An important part of the working party's argument rested on the 'massive drain on the public purse, affecting many local and central government departments'.[5] This point has been made more recently by the Director of the Marriage Research Centre, psychiatrist Dr Jack Dominian, who has drawn attention not only to the costs generated by legal aid, benefits to one-parent families and the numbers of children taken into care, but also the psychiatric illness and emotional distress which sometimes accompany marriage breakdown.[6] The latter are a significant cause of absence from work – through which, it is suggested, more days are lost than through industrial disputes. Because the consequences of divorce are so pervasive, the social and economic consequences of contemporary divorce rates can never be appreciated fully by any single government department or, for that matter, any one of the specialized agencies, professions and 'expert' disciplines that now take a professional interest in divorce. However, despite considerable public debate, some reform and occasional shortlived moral panics generated in the popular press, divorce for most people is still something to be ignored unless they are directly affected by it.

While attempts to heighten public consciousness about divorce may, at least in the eyes of their initiators, have been largely unsuccessful, the increase in the number of adults in the population who at any one time are contemplating, in the process of, or recovering from divorce, has inevitably altered social perceptions about patterns of marriage breakdown. In a recent survey of public attitudes to marriage and divorce, almost 80 per cent of those interviewed knew personally one or two people who were separated or divorced.[7] The speed of change itself is significant. Whereas many of those who divorced in the early 1970s were likely to describe themselves as 'the black sheep' of their families because they were the first members of their family to divorce, a decade later divorced people frequently portray themselves as part of a growing social trend.[8] Social class differences in the divorce rate (see pp. 34–6) also affect our awareness of current trends, for levels of divorce vary considerably in different occupations, neighbourhoods and social circles. Older council-house estates and tenements, traditional dumping grounds for so-called problem families, have long generated a community way of life in which short-term, unregistered partnerships are the norm[9] and for them little has changed. Until the end of the nineteenth century, divorce was almost exclusively a pursuit of aristocrats as they were the only members of society who could afford it (see chapter 3). Perusal of recent volumes of *Who's Who* suggests that, despite its wider availability and loss of élite cachet, members of the aristocracy have not lost their proclivity for divorce. Between these extremes, the effects of change are uneven. Such differences within our society may help us to understand why divorce and its aftermath evoke such contradictory responses. The lack of public awareness of divorce until very recently may also stem from the attempt by those who did divorce to hide the fact because of the stigma and loss of respectability involved. It is only within the last decade that the cumulative increase in the number of those who have ever been divorced has meant that, despite class-based variations, we have all become more conscious of divorced people at work, in our neighbourhood and among our kin. Clearly this makes us more aware of divorce as a fact of contemporary social life.

By way of illustration it might be instructive to consider the example on divorce matters set by the British Royal Family, for, as Bagehot commented of Queen Victoria, they act as the embodiment of conventional, respectable *middle-class* values.[10] The pace of change is reflected in their own family history. In 1955 Princess Margaret was persuaded of the unsuitability of a marriage to Group

Captain Peter Townsend because he was divorced, but some twenty years later when her own marriage to Lord Snowdon ended she used the provisions of the Divorce Reform Act 1969, to divorce after two years' separation. He has subsequently remarried, and, according to popular journalistic accounts – obtained with permission of the Royal press office and thus indicative of the official image of family relationships they wish to portray – his contacts with his children and ex in-laws, including the Queen, are the very embodiment of 'civilized' post-divorce relationships. More recently when the Prince of Wales chose a bride whose parents were divorced, complicated seating arrangements at the wedding ceremony symbolized *both* parents' continuing role as parents even though they had been divorced for some time. However, if the Royal Family are to be offered as role models of the acceptable 'civilized' post-divorce re-lationships and behaviour advocated among middle-class profes-sionals, we also need to remind ourselves of the continuing effects of those deep and persistent social divisions in our society which make conformity to class-related norms of divorce behaviour difficult and, on occasion, entirely at variance with the interests and needs of individuals. Ironically, as we indicate below, divorce is much more common among working-class couples than among those who transmit and, in various ways, enforce conventional middle-class values.

One of the underlying themes of this book is the way in which interested professions, public agencies and relevant government departments have responded to the rising divorce rate of the 1970s, and we are concerned here not only with the procedures and services they provide, but also with the values and 'expert' orthodoxies they transmit. These may be communicated quite explicitly when they form part of the professional advice and guidance offered to indi-viduals or to a more general audience. Or they are transmitted tacitly, as assumptions about marriage and divorce that underly services and other professional activities.

The middle-class interest in divorce is now both theoretical and practical. The professional response to the rising divorce rate among clients, patients and customers is now matched by a greater degree of personal involvement because divorce has begun to lose its stigma – even within those professional circles in which the scandal of a

divorce formerly blighted promising careers and undermined respectability. As a result increasing numbers of those working in our
growing 'divorce industry' – judges, solicitors, barristers, counsellors, social workers, researchers and medical practitioners of various
disciplines – as well as politicians and policy-makers, are themselves
divorced. Recently, for example, when the debates on the Matrimonial and Family Proceedings Bill took place in both Houses of
Parliament they were almost as frequently punctuated by references
to the speakers' own marital status and experiences of divorce as by
the usual anecdotes from their constituents. The increase in divorce
among interested professionals has meant that much of the most
vocal and effective special pleading and the most authoritative expert
advice and comment on divorce is based upon the experience, and
supports the interests, of a necessarily limited, restricted and pre-
dominantly male cross-section of society. Although this was especially evident in the way the Matrimonial and Family Proceedings
Bill was presented as a remedy for the kind of 'hard cases' which
were brought to the attention of the Lord Chancellor, the point
holds true more generally. So, for instance, the connection between
poverty, especially for mothers, and divorce is widely ignored. As we
shall show in later chapters, much of the private law of maintenance
after divorce has little to do with the experience of the majority of
divorcees with no property beyond the former matrimonial home,
few assets and an inadequate and increasingly insecure income except
at a symbolic level. By the same token, contemporary orthodoxies of
'civilized' post-divorce relationships, difficult enough to achieve in
any event, have more to do with the *Guardian* readers of Hampstead,
or even Harrogate, than tabloid readers in Hackney or Heck-
mondwike for whom divorce is most often portrayed in terms of
Coronation Street or reports of the unusual and sensational contested
divorce cases still occasionally reported in popular newspapers.

CONFLICT AND CONFUSION: CHANGING FASHIONS IN THE EXPLANATION OF MARRIAGE BREAKDOWN

While divorce was still a relatively uncommon experience, affecting
only a very small proportion of the adult population, the breakdown
of a marriage was generally accounted for in highly individualistic

terms. Marriage was deemed to fail because one – or both – of the partners possessed certain emotional, psychological or moral defects or had simply behaved badly. The language of guilt and innocence, blame and vindication coloured both the public and personal accounts of individuals, shaped as they were by the explanatory frameworks of the time.

By the 1950s, psychological explanations following the orthodoxies of psychiatrists and counsellors had begun to overshadow the pronouncements of the Church but such explanations were still highly individualistic, laying the blame on faulty decision making (e.g. choosing the 'wrong' partner, immaturity or poor adjustment within marriage). It is only as divorce has become more *visible*, as its aftermath has affected the lives of an increasing number of families, adults and children, colleagues, friends, neighbours and kin, that we have begun to appreciate it as a social phenomenon, arising out of, and in its turn affecting, the fabric and structure of other Western industrial societies as well as our own. This realization has also permeated popular consciousness so that, for example, the participants in the Sheffield remarriage study who described themselves as being part of a modern social trend, had developed their own folk-sociology of divorce, especially when their work or earlier life-experiences had brought them into contact with relatively large numbers of other divorced people.[11] Two significant and often related elements in such explanations are, firstly, the changing role and status of women in society and, secondly, a belief that social expectations of marriage and, indeed, family life itself have risen in the post-Second-World-War period. These explanations are frequently linked, in turn, to observations about the availability of more reliable contraception and the growth of the so-called permissive society.[12] However, although such views are becoming more widely known through public discussion in the media, individual 'guilt' and 'innocence', failure and inadequacy still centre in conversations and discussions about the marital difficulties of known individuals.[13] This tension between seeing each marriage ending in divorce as a personal matter, the result of individual inadequacy or moral failure but also as part of much broader patterns and trends, lies at the heart of an adequate understanding of contemporary divorce and helps us to understand why divorce *matters*, to individuals as well as to the society of which they are members. As we show in subsequent chapters, marriage breakdown – despite its frequency – still evokes a profound sense of guilt and shame, which undermines personal identity: the individual feels called to account for failure in one of the most significant areas of their life and needs to try to make sense of what has happened against the backcloth of their own biography and personality. At the same time, the end of a marriage can never be an entirely private matter and the participants in this drama – including children who have not volunteered for their parts – often find that to a varying degree their lives are shaped by public institutions and structures, by law and its procedures, by social policy and its administrators, by various expert orthodoxies and their advocates. If, as we suggest, the high but relatively stable divorce rate of the 1980s provides a good opportunity to take stock of what is happening, we need to consider and to hold in tension both the personal and public, individual and social dimensions of contemporary patterns of divorce.

Although most academic commentators still bemoan the inadequacy of official registration data on divorce as well as the relative dearth of social research in this area, the rising divorce rate has at least generated a wider data base against which observations and explanations may be tested. The remainder of this chapter is concerned with the available evidence about contemporary patterns of divorce in Britain.

THE INCREASE OF DIVORCE: SHORT-TERM PEAKS AND UNDERLYING TRENDS

Although we are principally concerned with trends since the 1960s, it is important to consider evidence about the frequency of divorce in its longer-term historical context. For example, when we compare the effects of nineteenth-century death rates and current divorce trends on patterns of family life, it is somewhat surprising to discover that the same proportion of marriages was ended by death within a fifteen-year time-span in 1820 as those that ended in divorce in the 1980s.[14]

It is also important to recognize that it is only since the 1950s, when divorce began to be more widely available (see chapter 3), that the divorce rate can be regarded as indicative of actual levels of marriage breakdown.

Most commentators on divorce trends emphasize two factors which help explain the peaks which punctuate the overall upward trend. Firstly, the number of divorces rose markedly after both world wars and in each case, although the rate of increase diminished in the post-war period, it never returned to pre-war levels.[15] In the second place, there has been considerable discussion about the ways in which levels of divorce are affected by legal reforms or procedural changes which have made divorce easier to obtain. Such changes are generally followed by an immediate increase as many people whose marriages had already ended – often many years earlier – take advantage of the opportunity to obtain the legal termination which will enable them to remarry or simply tidy up their domestic status. However, these rises cannot of themselves be used as proof that easier procedures necessarily generate higher rates of marriage breakdown. By the same token, the arguments of those who seek to explain rises in divorce *merely* as a result of the gradual reduction in the costs and complexity of the divorce process itself are undermined by the clear upward trend in divorce which lies beneath the peaks which have followed specific reforms.[16] However the detailed evidence is interpreted, it is clear that the divorce rate should not be used as direct evidence of changes in levels of marital unhappiness or dissatisfaction with the married state. The extent of serious, disabling personal distress directly resulting from being married is still largely unknown. Although it is likely that as divorces have become more easily obtainable a steadily rising proportion of the unhappily married will choose to divorce, this does not necessarily mean that all earlier deterrents have been eliminated. This is an important issue because pundits and moralists often try to suggest that present divorce rates provide sufficient evidence to conclude that divorce is now 'too easy' and that many couples resort to divorce without real consideration of the alternatives. It is unfortunate for protagonists on both sides that the evidence needed to prove or refute such contention does not exist. As we hope to show in chapter 3, most of the available material on the experience of divorce is either anecdotal or comes from small-scale studies which cannot justifiably be used to make general statements about the divorcing population as a whole. Although it is clear that the increases in divorce in the 1970s represent a change which cannot be explained simply in terms of a backlog of potential divorces awaiting the means of dissolution, it is another matter to argue that the effect of making divorce more widely available has been to encourage individuals to seek divorce lightly and without serious consideration of its consequences. It should be recognized that such arguments could never, in any event, be settled by reference to divorce statistics alone. However, greater understanding of the circumstances in which divorce is used as a solution to problems within a marriage may be achieved by examining what is already known from registration statistics about divorcing couples. In this respect those who argue for greater public consideration and concern about marriage as a social institution make an important point. Any appreciation of the conflicts and distress within a marriage which may eventually result in its dissolution is inextricably linked to a parallel appreciation of contemporary marriage and in particular why some partnerships, stages of married life, and biographical events appear to increase the likelihood of divorce.

YOUTHFUL PARTNERSHIPS: WOULD ROMEO AND JULIET HAVE STAYED THE COURSE?

There is a well-documented association between getting married early and an increased chance that the marriage will end in divorce which holds true for most industrialized countries. The link between these factors is complex because youthful marriage is also class related and more likely to involve an already pregnant bride. These two variables are both associated with higher rates of divorce.

Several studies illustrate the 'vortex of disadvantage' experienced by some young couples of working-class origin.[17] The stresses associated with poverty – insecure employment, financial hardship and unsatisfactory housing – exacerbate the inevitable tensions of early married life as partners learn to adjust to one another and to their new circumstances. If their decision to marry is a direct result of the wife's pregnancy and this has itself caused conflict within their own families, their problems are compounded even before their baby arrives.

The results of a study by Thornes and Collard which compared a large group of divorced couples with their still-married counterparts[18] also shows that many of the very young couples who eventually split up had not benefited from the kind of parental interest and support so vividly documented in Leonard's study of young working-class couples in Swansea.[19] Thornes and Collard found that those teenage brides who described themselves as having had a close relationship with their mother in childhood and who retained supportive links with parents after marriage enjoyed some protection from divorce. The reverse was also true: those in their sample who were divorced were more likely to have experienced parental opposition to their marriage, especially where the bride was still a teenager and already pregnant. In such circumstances, reconciliation was rare so that this particularly vulnerable group of brides embarked on marriage without the customary support – which may be both emotional and material – of their own families. This means that some very young couples face the early days of partnership and impending parenthood with little sense of continuity with their own earlier lives and isolated from their families. They may also find themselves without access to the economic exchanges that frequently help to sustain relationships between parents and their adult children. Such gifts are widely regarded as symbols and tokens of the love and goodwill parents generally feel towards their newly married children. Leonard's study provides a picture – easily recognized by those who live or work in such areas – of a working-class community in which parents, and mothers particularly, spoil their children during their courtship and period of engagement and make considerable financial sacrifices to give them a 'proper' wedding. They also help them to set up their new home by offering financial gifts, loans and other economic services or, if an independent home is impossible at first, by sheltering them within their own household. By contrast, Thornes' and Collard's divorced sample included a significant minority of couples married in their teens, who had experienced many or all the deprivations strongly associated with eventual divorce: a premarital pregnancy which generated family disapproval; a very short courtship unmarked by a formal engagement period before marriage or a honeymoon afterwards;[20] accommodation difficulties in the first months of marriage; and isolation from one or both sets of parents.

The vulnerability of such youthful marriages prompts questions about the reasons for early marriage and the ways in which, if at all, such patterns are changing. For example, since the early 1970s the average age at first marriage has risen slightly, and there has been a decrease in the proportion of pregnant brides which may have contributed indirectly to the levelling-off in the divorce rate from the late 1970s onwards.

Not only is the age of marriage class related but there are also significant class differences in women's beliefs about the best, or ideal age to marry. Dunnell found that while only 3.1 per cent of women in Class I favoured teenage marriage, 12 per cent of women in Class V thought the teenage years the best time to marry.[21] As the criteria used to designate social class position are based on occupation, we need to consider how young women's expectations and experience of paid employment affect their decision to marry. These issues were explored in a recent government survey of a representative sample of women of different working ages and social backgrounds.[22] Although there was evidence – especially among the younger age groups – of a shift in attitudes so that few women now hold traditional views about a woman's place being in the home, the writers found a great deal of evidence that the majority of women still put home and family first. Thus they tend to regard paid work, and to make decisions about it, as something which must be accommodated to domestic demands and responsibilities.

As long as most women still regard marriage and motherhood as their main career, it is not surprising that young women trapped in unskilled, dead-end jobs or, increasingly, without jobs at all, look to marriage, or more particularly motherhood, as a means of escape from the tedium of their working lives. Despite dramatic changes in the working lives of the small minority of women in high-status professional occupations, most women still regard family and domestic roles and responsibilities as their chief source of personal worth and fulfilment. Several recent studies of groups of working-class teenage girls demonstrate how their spare time and leisure are organized around the pursuit of a potential partner,[23] and are supported by romantic hopes and dreams which also retain a measure of pragmatic realism about available alter-natives.[24]

For working-class young men, the association between paid work and marriage as the foundation of their own household and family is rather different as prevalent beliefs, buttressed by the economic realities of the labour market, dictate that they will assume the role of primary breadwinner.[25] In this context, the fact that working-class couples marry earlier than their middle-class counterparts makes good sense as the earnings curve of manual workers is quite different from those in the professions or white-collar occupations. Most manual workers reach their maximum earnings relatively young, which – with good fortune – remain stable until they begin to lose their place as 'prime' workers in their forties and fifties, while most non-manual workers enjoy a salary scale which may begin lower but increases throughout their working life. As a result, they are most likely to postpone marriage until their career and standard of living are more established. Also, if they have lived away from home as students, they may have had the opportunity to enter into cohabiting relationships away from watchful parents and are thus even less likely to marry young.[26] Although students are by no means the only people to live together in unregistered relationships, it is significant that the recent increased popularity of cohabitation as a prelude to marriage has followed the expansion of opportunities in further and higher education which took place in the 1960s and 1970s. Although it is impossible to provide evidence from the available data, it seems likely that the slight increase in the median ages of men and women marrying for the first time in the early 1970s is associated with the greater acceptability of cohabitation.[27] Overall, there may be little change in the age at which first partnerships are formed as courtship is now increasingly likely to include a period of joint residence before the marriage takes place.

As yet there is little evidence of how changing patterns of em-ployment, and especially high rates of unemployment among the young, are affecting the marriage behaviour of today's teenagers. There are likely to be significant gender differences as the lack of paid employment is a much more significant deterrent for young men than their brides. Without what Willis has described recently as the 'golden key' of a wage packet, which gives access to the privacy and independence of living separately from parents, it is difficult for workless young men to lay the foundation for courtship, marriage and parenthood.[28]

Before leaving the matter of age and divorce we should note that those who marry at more advanced ages are, like the young, more prone to divorce. While this older group probably does not suffer the material disadvantages of the young, there may be a common factor in that both groups will tend to be out of step with their contemporaries and so may find it harder to get support and companionship from others at the same point in their life cycle. Thus, just as the young teenage bride may lose touch with her (unmarried) peer group when she has a child, those marrying late may find themselves isolated with a young child when their contemporaries' children are leaving home.

DIVORCE AND THE PRESENCE OF CHILDREN: DO CHILDREN REALLY 'MAKE A MARRIAGE'?

In popular belief marriage and having children are so closely associated that a married couple without children may not be regarded as a real family until they begin to produce children of their own. The assumption that having children automatically follows marriage cannot be understood simply as a relic of an earlier period before accessible and reliable contraception could be taken for granted, an item in a series of tacit beliefs and assumptions that merely legitimated the inevitability of conception. Such beliefs have persisted, helping us to understand, for example, why childless couples are so often regarded with pity or disapproval.

It is somewhat ironic that the Church of England has only recently abandoned a version of the wedding service in which the primary purpose of marriage was declared as 'the procreation of children'[29] at a time when the increased acceptability of unmarried domestic partnerships means that marriage itself may be more closely associated with the decision to have children than ever before. The results of a recent public-opinion survey show that although there is fairly widespread public approval of cohabitation as a preliminary to marriage, among both women and men, old as well as young, the proportion of the sample who indicated their approval for cohabitation as an alternative to marriage dropped significantly. The disadvantages for any children involved was the second most commonly cited reason for disapproval after religious and moral considerations.[30]

These findings are confirmed in a recent study of unmarried, cohabiting couples. Almost all of the sample saw the decision to marry as being linked in some way to having children and only a very small minority consciously intended to remain unmarried after they became parents.[31] Given the underlying strength of such beliefs, it is not surprising that there is strong public support for the idea that children set the seal on marriage as a social institution. Childless marriages are in a sense regarded as more of a personal matter between individuals and thus conditional upon their continuing compatibility. In the public opinion survey, the sample was also asked: 'Do you think, as is often said, that children cement a married relationship?' Sixty-two per cent agreed, 24 per cent disagreed and 14 per cent of the sample said it depended on the circumstances. However, the next question in the survey was: 'Would you advise a young married couple who were not getting on well to have a child?' Only 14 per cent answered 'yes' to this question; 74 per cent said 'no'; 12 per cent said that it depended on the circumstances. Thus, while the sample saw having children as a way of setting a seal on a satisfactory, even adequate, marriage, there was little support for the idea of childbearing as a form of Elastoplast to bind estranged partners together more closely and more permanently.

Associated trends in divorce and fertility have been the subject of a good deal of investigation and even greater speculation, while the apparent association between childlessness and instability in marriage has become part of popular mythology.[32] In a recent investigation using official registration data Haskey concluded that 'Patterns and trends in the family sizes of divorcing couples generally resemble those of married couples.'[33] If divorced couples produce fewer children overall, or have smaller families than their still-married counterparts, this is partly the result of their relative lack of opportunity as their marriages have not lasted as long, though there is evidence that suggests that divorce rates may be slightly higher among those who either have a very large number of children or no children at all.

The material from Thornes and Collard's study, though of a

rather different character, sheds further light on this issue. When they examined those divorced couples whose marriage problems had, by their own report, begun very early in their partnership, they found that such couples had either had their first child very early on and others had followed, or they remained childless, even if the marriage itself went on for some considerable time after the onset of problems. Both patterns help us to understand something about the way children, in reality or simply in prospect, can affect a marriage. It is very clear that the arrival of children inevitably alters their parents' relationship and may affect their satisfaction with marriage more generally. Many clinicians would argue that this transition to parenthood is much more difficult in a very new and undeveloped partnership.[34] In addition, where there is an early recognition of serious problems, including sexual difficulties which might affect the likelihood of conception, a decision may be made, consciously or unconsciously, to defer parenthood until such difficulties are resolved.

Although children may not necessarily cement a marriage, they certainly do change it. Not only is everyday domestic life entirely transformed by the arrival of a first baby,[35] but becoming a parent often affects adults in other more subtle ways. Many new parents, of whatever age, find that as they learn to deal with the new challenges and responsibilities of parenthood, they find themselves face to face with conflicts and hidden anxieties about their own childhood experiences and their relationship with their own parents.[36] Although there is still relatively little evidence about the way men are affected by fatherhood, it is clear that among mothers stressful periods of one kind or another in the childbearing years are an almost universal experience. Depression is common, particularly among mothers of children under five,[37] and many women find that, because their lives are almost entirely circumscribed by childcare and domestic responsibilities, they seem to grow apart from their husbands. This distance cannot always be bridged as children get older and less demanding. Thus, it is clear that at least some of the difficulties in marriage that eventually lead to divorce are directly related to the presence of children. However, a comparison between the average length of marriage of childless couples and divorcing parents suggests that the presence of children delays or postpones the decision to divorce; in 1984 the median duration for childless divorcing couples was eight years, as compared with eleven years for couples who had at least one child under sixteen.[38]

The survey of public beliefs referred to earlier also includes indirect confirmation that separation and divorce are regarded as more serious matters when children are involved. Interviewees were asked to respond to a series of hypothetical personal stories involving common marriage problems (infidelity, violence, boredom, growing apart) by suggesting whether the couples should 'sort out their own difficulties'; 'seek outside help' or 'consider splitting up'. While the bored childless couple was most often advised to split up, the percentage offering this advice fell dramatically if the couple was presented as having children. By the same token, violence within a marriage was seen as a reason for splitting up by 43 per cent of our sample if the couple were childless. If they had children, nearly 60 per cent suggested that they should seek outside help and a further 10 per cent advised them to sort out their own problems.

Thus, having children clearly alters a married partnership but it is also clear that divorce is generally regarded much more seriously if they are present. Although children do not necessarily cement a marriage, their presence seems to delay its legal end.

LENGTH OF MARRIAGE BEFORE DIVORCE: DO COUPLES STILL TRY TO 'MAKE THEIR MARRIAGES WORK'?

Data on the length of marriages ending in divorce is frequently used to justify widely divergent conclusions about the nature of modern marriage. In 1984 the median duration of all marriages ending in divorce was 10.2 years, an average which has not changed significantly since 1964. However, Leete's review of the period between 1964 and 1976 also points to an increase, from 11 per cent to 18 per cent, in the proportion of all divorces granted to couples who had been married for less than five years.[39] By 1984, this had reached 28 per cent, thus giving some support to those who believe that nowadays some couples rush into divorce without giving their marriages a real chance. These figures do, however, need careful interpretation. Changes in the legal procedures have cut down the waiting period for the majority of couples (see pp. 39, 58), including in 1984 those who, before the implementation of the Matrimonial and Family Proceedings Act 1984, would normally have been unable to obtain a divorce within the first two years of marriage.[40] It is also important to recognize that the most recent figures also include a far higher proportion of *second* divorces which, as we shall see, tend to occur more quickly than first divorces (see pp. 37–9).

In any event, such official figures about the legal duration of marriage tell us very little about the actual length of the partnership. This is because they are based on information provided in the divorce petition and measure the period between a legal marriage and its official dissolution. Neither of these events now necessarily marks the real beginning or the end of the relationship from the partners' own point of view. Couples who live together before marriage often use the date they moved in together rather than their wedding as an anniversary of when their relationship began, at least between themselves. Consequently, an increasing number of couples have a longer history together than their wedding date suggests.

Sequence of events in the natural history of a marriage

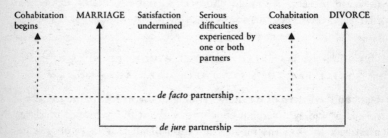

Defining the point at which a marriage *ends* is even more difficult once the date of its legal dissolution is rejected. In research carried out before the implementation of the Divorce Reform Act 1969, Chester found that the median period between separation and divorce was 2.9 years.[41] With the reforms in both divorce law and its procedures since then, we would expect this time to be considerably shorter for those who have divorced in the last few years.

There is other evidence which sheds some light on the kinds of factors influencing the length of the period between the recognition of serious difficulties and the end of cohabitation. As we have already suggested, problems often begin very early for many of the couples who do eventually divorce. More than half the divorcees in Thornes and Collard's sample believed that their difficulties had begun within two years of marriage, a finding confirmed in other survey data.[42] Thornes and Collard and the National Opinion Poll (N.O.P.) survey also demonstrate similar and significant gender differences, with women tending to report difficulties much earlier (this issue will be discussed more fully in chapter 3). While some early difficulties arise from the circumstances in which the marriage itself took place – perhaps it was the result of a hasty decision and/or premarital pregnancy – evidence also highlights expressions of frustrated expectations and considerable disappointment with marriage itself.

Although we commonly speak of the decision to split up as if it were always made with the same rational clarity we are expected to give to choosing, for example, a life insurance policy, the reality is much more complex. When divorced couples themselves describe the period between the recognition of difficulties and the end of cohabitation, it often includes temporary separations and reconciliations.[43] Although to an outsider, a third party waiting in the wings, members of their family or their professional advisers, such vacillation may appear pointless and sometimes destructive, many divorcees see such behaviour as part of an ultimately fruitless, final effort to make a marriage work. In this light, it is significant that although two-thirds of the divorcees in the N.O.P. survey felt that generally people do not try hard enough to make a marriage work these days, only one in five of them felt guilty about not having tried hard enough themselves.

This kind of evidence suggests that, although there were many expressions of disquiet both inside and outside Parliament about the removal of the discretionary ban on divorce in the first three years of marriage, and its replacement by an absolute one-year ban, the evidence we have summarized does not suggest this change will lead to any long-term change in divorce behaviour – a view that is supported by the situation in Scotland where there has never been a ban on divorce in the first years of marriage.

THE GROUNDS USED IN DIVORCE PETITIONS:
EVIDENCE OF CAUSE OR A LEGAL FICTION

Published data on divorces includes the ground or 'facts' presented to the court to demonstrate that irretrievable breakdown of the marriage has occurred. Most commentators suggest that these need to be interpreted with very great caution and that it would be unwise to use them as evidence of the cause of marital disruption either for individual couples or to draw general conclusions about trends in marriage breakdown. The interpretation of such changes is also affected by the Divorce Reform Act 1969, which borrowed some of the terminology of earlier matrimonial offences but used them rather differently.

Generally, trends in the use of the various 'facts' or grounds since 1971 do not confirm the fears voiced at the time the Act was passed that the five-year separation clause, which allowed divorce against the wishes of the other spouse, would generate a growing army of 'feckless Casanovas'. Although this ground was used by a quarter of petitioners in the years immediately following divorce reform, by 1984 it accounted for only 7 per cent of petitions.[44]

The use of this ground enables even the small proportion of spouses who cannot persuade their resistant partners to use grounds which will allow them to end their marriage immediately, to obtain a divorce in the end. This desire – at least on one spouse's part – to complete the legal dissolution of the marriage as quickly as possible helps us to understand more about the ways in which different grounds are used. It also reminds us that the choice of grounds is unlikely to tell us very much about why the marriage has ended but may indicate rather more about spouses' plans for the future. For example, in a recent survey of divorced people over a third admitted that the grounds used in the petition had been chosen for convenience.[45] Two main factors are likely to be involved here: the first is the desire to divorce as quickly as possible so that one or both partners can legalize new partnerships. Secondly, in certain circumstances partners may be unwilling to make use of their spouse's adulterous relationship as an obvious ground and may then be advised to use the ground of 'unreasonable behaviour' if they are unwilling to wait two years.

The rapid increase in the proportion of divorce petitions initiated by women in recent decades has also been the subject of considerable comment and speculation. After the removal of discriminatory divorce grounds in 1923 (see chapter 2), the proportion of women petitioners has risen, unevenly at first, but steadily since 1959.[46] In 1984 71 per cent of all petitions were initiated by wives. As chapter 3 will show, the processes involved in ending a marriage legally, economically and emotionally are complicated and it would be unjustifiable to conclude that because more women now initiate the divorce proceedings, they have necessarily taken the first steps to end the marriage. However, petitions for divorce using behaviour as grounds have risen in parallel with the increase in the proportion of wife petitioners, and there is survey evidence that divorced women have more complaints about the conduct of ex-partners than divorced men.

Though a wide variety of complaints can be used to demonstrate the 'fact' of unreasonable behaviour, evidence of physical violence is used in a very large proportion of cases. Murch and his colleagues found that seventy of the ninety-six women in their sample who used the unreasonable behaviour clause gave evidence of physical violence.[47] In another study of recently divorced people almost half reported some physical violence in their previous marriage. While 20 per cent of the women used evidence of violence in support of a petition based on unreasonable behaviour, a further 20 per cent claimed there had been violence but that they had chosen to base their petitions on some other evidence.

In 1984, a quarter of all divorces were based on two years' separation with consent. This ground was used more often by men than women. Leete also found that the ground was favoured by younger petitioners whose marriages had been relatively short, and it is possible that those whose marriage ends within three years of outset and who have to wait to initiate divorce proceedings make greater use of it. Those who have been married for over three years may make use of a 'fact' which will enable them to obtain their divorce more quickly.

Thus, while it would be unwise to draw any conclusions about the real causes of marriage breakdown from these legal facts (or fictions), changes in their relative popularity and gender differences in how they are used raise important issues about the ways in which existing legal provisions and processes shape contemporary divorce behaviour.

SOCIAL CLASS AND DIVORCE

We have already referred to the relationship between social class and patterns of marriage and divorce. Those who still prefer to regard marriage breakdown either as a random stroke of ill-fortune which visits its consequences on rich and poor alike or as the result of individual moral shortcomings or failings, may find evidence of trends or patterns in divorce which are related to other features of the economic, occupational or domestic structure of contemporary society somewhat disconcerting.

There are, however, a number of difficulties in the interpretation of such data, chiefly because of differences in the kinds of classification used as well as other problems of method. The observations which follow are offered speculatively and – hopefully for some of our readers – as a stimulus to further research.

A recent study of social class and divorce undertaken by Haskey[48] confirms the general findings of earlier research. There is evidence of a clear social-class gradient: members of Social Class I are least likely to divorce and Social Class V most at risk. Using other official sources of data about the occupational distribution of the male population he calculated the expected number of divorces in each

Social class of husband		Standardized divorce rate
I	Professional	47
II	Intermediate	83
IIIN	Skilled, non-manual	108
IIIM	Skilled, manual	97
IV	Partly skilled	111
V	Unskilled	220
	Armed forces	270
	Unemployed	225
	All social classes	100

Source: Haskey, op. cit, Table 7.

social class and then compared this with the actual number of divorces in his sample. The standardized divorce rates listed above indicate which groups have relatively high and low rates, where the expected number for each class equals 100.

If we are to understand the relationship between divorce and social class more clearly we must first consider how belonging to a particular social class exposes or insulates partners from the stresses which might lead to marriage breakdown. By the same token, class-related factors are also likely to affect the processes determining why some stressful marriages end in divorce while others do not. Material factors, as well as other more subtle aspects of stigma and loss of respectability, are significant here.

In earlier sections, we pointed to the web of interconnected disadvantages suffered by some very young working-class couples (see pp. 23–4). Their experiences illustrate very clearly how poverty, insecure dead-end jobs, difficulties in gaining access to independent housing all exacerbate the difficulties endemic to a hastily agreed marriage, especially if it is the result of pre-marital pregnancy. In each social group above them the likelihood of young men and women experiencing this particular set of interlocking disadvantages diminishes; they will marry later, and the higher their social class the better their standard of living and the greater their job security. They are also more likely to enjoy both material and emotional support from parents at the start of their marriage.

Thus, if we focus on those marriages in which the problems that eventually lead to divorce become apparent at a very early stage, the obvious material deprivations experienced by those who grow up and start adulthood in the lowest social classes are likely to affect their marriages adversely from the start. For those whose problems only emerge later, the effects of class-related factors, which might deter them from divorce – joint ownership of property; belonging to an occupation or profession that still discourages divorce – are much more complex. In particular the broad social-class categories used by Haskey may obscure such subtle differences, as Haskey himself found when he looked at the relationship between divorce and occupation.

Those who contemplate divorce must ask themselves – not necessarily consciously – 'What do I have to lose by it?' and balance

their answer against their degree of present unhappiness and their
hopes, real or imagined, for the future. In general, it is their present
standard of living and their respectability, good name or reputation
which are at stake and, although there are exceptions, professional
middle-class women and men have more to lose than their working-
class counterparts. At one extreme, Marsden's early study of separated women included some who were actually better off on the
supplementary benefit received after their separation order was made
than they had been with their husband's housekeeping money,[49] so
that in material terms at least, the incentives to divorce in the face of
an unhappy marriage were very high. At the other extreme, considerable wealth, or even modest material comfort and security, may
deter wives, if not husbands,[50] from divorce. It can also enable
estranged partners to live such sufficiently separate lives that formal
divorce is unnecessary unless one or other of them wants to remarry.

Middle-class people also have more to lose when they contemplate
dividing their assets and domestic goods. The households of manual
workers, especially those in semi- and unskilled occupations, still
contain fewer consumer goods; apart from ownership or tenancy of
their present home, they are also less likely to own savings or assets.
Although the prospect of splitting the best dinner service or sur-
rendering valuable joint insurance policies is not usually offered as
conscious or sufficient reason for *not* divorcing in the face of obvious
distress and unhappiness, the valued household objects which contribute to their particular lifestyle as well as the savings, pension
rights and so on must certainly be considered as one of the ties that
bind middle-class couples to one another.

The value of the kind of social respectability which accrues from
the possession of an unimpeachable family and domestic life is much
harder to assess because its importance is not directly related to class
itself. Broadly speaking, it is those whose access to forms of status
based on power, wealth, or occupational prestige is limited or under
threat,[51] who rely most on domestic and family sources of respectability. Divorced members of the aristocracy have a long history
of weathering and surviving the scandal involved and members of
what has been variously called the 'rough' or 'disreputable' working
classes have little to lose. It is therefore within some sectors of the
middle class that concern about family respectability is strongest.[52]

REMARRIAGE . . . AND THE POSSIBILITY OF A SECOND DIVORCE

Since the 1960s increases in divorce and remarriage have been closely linked. Between 1970 and 1976 the percentage of all marriages that included at least one remarrying partner rose from 18 per cent to 30 per cent[53] and since has remained more or less constant. The marked increase in the number of divorcees in the marriage market has not only improved the chances of remarriage for divorcees looking for suitable partners but has also increased the likelihood that previously single people will marry a divorced partner.

Although, as the table indicates, those who remarry after divorce are most likely to marry another divorced person, marriages between divorced and single people are also increasingly common. When considering the particular pressures on second marriages, it is necessary to remember that in contrast to first partnerships, remarried pairings are much more diverse when all the possible combinations of age, previous marital and parental status are all taken into account.[54] Although the trends in divorce outlined above mean that large numbers of relatively young divorcees re-enter the marriage market after an early and relatively short first partnership, remarriage can take place at many different ages and stages in people's working and personal lives.

Marriage and Remarriage – England and Wales 1984

Combinations of previous marital statuses, brides and grooms. Percentages.

Grooms	Brides		
	Single	Divorced	Widowed
Single	64.2	8.4	0.6
Divorced	9.8	12.3	1.2
Widowed	0.6	1.3	1.7

Source: OPCS Monitor, *Marriages 1984,* FM 85/2, Table 2.

Although the average age difference between remarrying partners is only a little greater than for first partnerships (three years instead of two), this general picture obscures an increasing number of partnerships between divorced and single people where the gap is much wider or where the conventional pattern of older man–younger woman is reversed.

Given the wider range of potential pairings accepted by those who remarry after divorce and thus the size of the pool of potentially eligible partners (in demographic terms at least), it is not surprising that second partnerships are now so common. Indeed, as the Sheffield remarriage study indicated very clearly, there is now strong institutional support for remarriage as a means of re-creating normal family life for divorced parents and their children. Many of the couples in this study described how their attempts to find greater fulfilment in a second partnership were encouraged informally by friends and family and, more formally, by professional advisors. For mothers and the minority of fathers with custody of children, a second partnership was often proposed as a solution to both the emotional and financial problems of single parenthood.[55]

Two main factors affect a divorced individual's likelihood of remarriage: opportunity, as determined by the availability of potential partners, and the inclination, need or desire to do so. Haskey concludes that likelihood of young divorcees remarrying is greater and that a larger proportion of men than women eventually remarry.[56] Both of these groups, young divorcees and divorced men of all ages, enjoy advantages in the marriage market because their field of eligibles may more easily include single people. Although the number of divorced women marrying single men younger than themselves has increased recently, such partnerships do not enjoy the same social approval as, for example, a divorced man in his late thirties marrying a much younger single woman. Younger divorcees are also much more likely to want to remarry because, like their single and newly wed peers, they still look forward to a conventional family career – setting up home and having children. For reasons we shall consider in chapter 3, men of all ages show their greater need of marriage by remarrying more quickly and in greater numbers, something which, as Haskey observes, has a long history.

Despite popular beliefs that remarried partners will get it right the second time round, the number of second divorces has increased in parallel with rising remarriage rates: the relative contribution to the total number of divorces made by those divorcing for a second or subsequent time doubled between 1970 and 1981. Although the total number of divorcees has now levelled off, the proportion of second divorces continues to increase.

In general, second marriages which are dissolved end more quickly than first marriages; the median length of second marriages is seven years (as compared with ten for first marriages). Among this group older partners tend to end a second marriage even more quickly. Haskey has also estimated the probability of second marriages breaking down, if present trends continue, as over half of those who divorce and remarry in their early twenties will divorce again. Among this group men are more at risk than women.[57]

More detailed consideration of the particular pressures upon second marriages is beyond the scope of this book, but current trends in patterns of marriage, divorce, remarriage and second divorce seem to support our view that in the 1980s divorce does matter, not least because despite popular beliefs remarriage does not seem to solve the problems generated by divorce at either a personal or public level.

2

DIVORCE AND THE COURTS

Divorce is the legal transition that marks the final stage in the breakdown of a marriage, its formal dissolution and a legal re-arrangement of the relationship between the spouses, particularly in relation to the children and property rights. People have come to think and speak of divorce and breakdown of marriage as synonymous, and are tempted to use the divorce rate as a measure of the stability or instability of marriage. As we have mentioned already and will discuss further below, this is extremely misleading, particularly in respect of times past.

For most of its history the law of divorce has not been so much concerned with the effects of permanent separation and the consequential readjustments, as with the licence to remarry. Its primary function was to regulate the conditions under which such licence was to be granted. The consequences, in terms of children and financial provision had, of course, to be dealt with but they were subsidiary; in fact, they were officially described as 'ancillary relief' (the 'ancillary matters' of the present system) and thus peripheral to the divorce itself.

Given this primary purpose, the concept of matrimonial offence made sense. As in ordinary contract law, a person who wanted to be free of his or her contractual obligations had to show that the other party had been 'guilty' of a major breach of the contract. All this was changed in 1969 when Parliament, in the Divorce Reform Act, formally accepted 'irretrievable breakdown' as the basis for divorce. This completely changed the emphasis of the law. The divorce itself, that is the ending of the marriage relationship and the licence to remarry, has become more and more a formality and the former ancillary matters, the children and property rights, now occupy 90 per cent of the time of the court.

This confusion between breakdown of the marriage relationship and its consequences and the licence to remarry underlies much of the discussion about divorce law reform and is at the root of many of the bitter controversies surrounding it. Two separate and largely distinct themes each carrying its own strongly emotive charge have become hopelessly entangled: the preservation of the religious concept of marriage as an indissoluble union for life, as a sacrament of the church, and the secular anxiety, the preservation of the stability of marriage as a vital social need. The interaction of these two themes can be seen in the short account of the development of divorce law which is given in this chapter.

Until the mid-nineteenth century in England, marriage was the exclusive concern of the Church of England. The only ceremony which was recognized as creating a valid marriage was a Church marriage and all matrimonial disputes were dealt with by the Church's own courts which applied their own system of law, the canon law. The ordinary courts did not deal with matrimonial matters at all. This caused difficulties for Roman Catholics and Nonconformists but the judges of the ordinary courts got round some of these (e.g. where legitimacy of children or proof of bigamy were involved) by a device often used to adapt an unduly rigid legal system to the social situation of the time: the technique of presuming that the requirements of the law have been complied with, unless the contrary is proved. Thus, if it were proved that a man and woman had cohabited for a reasonable time and the woman was known by the man's name, the ordinary courts of law would presume that they had been lawfully married somewhere at some time. Since there was no central register of marriages, it was virtually impossible to prove that they had not been validly married. This was known as a 'common law marriage'. All that was required was evidence that the parties had agreed to marry and if that was not available it was presumed, unless the contrary was proved.

Canon law regarded marriage as a sacrament of the Church, and forbade remarriage in the lifetime of the other spouse. ('Those whom God hath joined together let no man put asunder.') A licence to remarry would therefore strike at the heart of sacramental marriage; but canon law did not forbid permanent separation. In fact, it had a developed system of law to deal with it. The Church courts granted

what was called divorce *a mensa et toro* ('from table and hearth')
in cases of adultery, cruelty or desertion, which was the equivalent
of a decree of judicial separation today and made orders for custody
of the children and financial support for wives and children (called
'permanent alimony').

None of this applied in Scotland where, from the sixteenth century, marriage was a matter for the civil courts and canon law did
not apply. Divorce in the modern sense, which used to be called
divorce *a vinculo* (which enabled the divorced spouses to remarry),
was available from then onwards, a situation which from time to
time tempted desperate people in England to go to Scotland to get
a divorce and led to much subsequent litigation in England to
determine the validity, in English law, of such divorces. There is
no evidence that marriages in Scotland were more unstable than
in England and no reason to think that the canon law ban on
divorce *a vinculo* was designed primarily to preserve stability in
marriage. It was a necessary consequence of the sacramental concept.

The history of divorce law in England, like so much legal history,
is the story of gradual social change punctuated at intervals, in this
case very long intervals, by reforming legislation when social pressures reached a critical level. In the case of divorce the change is the
gradual evolution of the concept of marriage from *marriage as a
sacrament of the Church* to *marriage as a partnership*. The final
stage has not yet been reached (and may never be completely because
the concept of partnership may never quite satisfy the unique emotions which are involved in the act of getting married). We will
return to this issue in the final chapter.

Sacramental marriage was regulated by the Church, it was
indissoluble, and it created no property rights between the spouses.
('The twain shall be of one flesh.') By contrast, marriage as a partnership is a matter for the civil law; it is formed by agreement, i.e.
contract, and thus it follows logically that it should be possible to
dissolve it by agreement or order of the court if the contract becomes
unworkable or one party has broken a basic term of the agreement.
Property rights should therefore depend on the terms of the
agreement, some assets being separately owned, others jointly
owned. Each party should be responsible for all the obligations of

the partnership towards third parties (e.g. children) with a right to contribution from the other party. Although the process of evolution has gone a long way, there are still some difficulties about this approach. For example, attempts to introduce pre-marriage contract, providing for what is to happen if there is a subsequent divorce, would be frustrated because at present any agreement on marriage which contemplates divorce is contrary to public policy and so void. Even if they were not void they would not bind the discretion of the court. However, such contracts have been introduced in the U.S., and might provide an unpleasant surprise for bridegrooms if brides were able to fix their price for giving up their careers!

This evolution in marriage can be traced along different, though complementary, legal paths – formation of marriage, dissolution of marriage (i.e. the development of the licence to remarry), development of property rights between spouses, and relationships to children.

FORMATION OF MARRIAGE

The passing of the Marriage Act 1836, was a major step. This Act introduced the first form of civil marriage before a registrar in a register office and established a central register of births, deaths and marriages. Even the liberal Lord Morley described it as the 'removal of marriage to the bleak and frigid zone of civil contract'.[1] It was one of the first major measures to be passed by the newly reformed House of Commons after the Reform Act 1832, which entirely changed the character and complexion of the House of Commons by extending the vote to urban middle-class males, many of whom were elected to the new Parliament. This provided both the stimulus for and the means to carry out radical reforms in every department of the law which lasted for the next fifty years. But the Marriage Act stopped at the introduction of civil marriage, it did not go on as it might have done to provide for the dissolution of such civil marriages and for property rights arising from them. This produced an illogical situation from which the law has not yet finally shaken itself free. Civil marriage took on by default, as it were, the characteristics of sacramental marriage, that is, its indissolubility and the lack of property rights.

DISSOLUTION OF MARRIAGE

There were always social pressures against the canon law's ban on remarriage and the Church had to fight many battles to retain it. After Henry VIII's break with the Church of Rome, the Church of England set out to redraft canon law for England, and, not surprisingly, introduced a form of divorce which permitted remarriage. So, in the sixteenth century, England, like Scotland, acquired a system of divorce. But in England it did not last long: the sacramental concept soon reasserted itself. In 1601, the Court of Star Chamber declared that the reformed canon law had never been properly promulgated and was invalid.[2]

Remarriage was again forbidden. But the social pressures did not abate; they became concentrated instead in an issue which, though few were directly affected by it, had a strong emotive appeal to male legislators. This was the rigid rule of common law that any child born to a married woman was conclusively presumed to be the child of her husband, unless he could prove that he was 'beyond the four seas' at the time of conception. The object of the rule was to protect children from being wrongly bastardized. Its terms were so rigid because of the extreme difficulty the courts had in deciding the issue of paternity before the days of blood tests. This is one of the explanations for the different attitude held for so long by the courts and society generally towards adultery by husbands and that by wives. As a result of this rule husbands were vulnerable to having other men's children 'foisted' on them by adulterous wives, a particularly serious matter where they had no legitimate heir. The only way for men to avoid this danger was to find some way of breaking the marriage tie. At the end of the seventeenth century, Lord Roos and a Mr Lakener were enterprising enough to petition Parliament to pass private Acts of Parliament dissolving their marriages, permitting them to marry again and declaring that the adulterine children of their wives were bastards. They were successful and the way was opened for other husbands who were at risk of 'foisting', but it was an exceedingly cumbersome and expensive procedure. However, between 1700 and 1857, 317 of these private Acts were passed by Parliament, enough to establish a set of recognized principles and practice. The element of 'foisting' became increasingly hypothetical and eventually a few wives, in very exceptional circumstances, succeeded in obtaining private Acts dissolving their marriages and permitting them to marry again. However, since they were not at risk of having other women's children foisted on them, they had to show that their husbands' behaviour had been exceptionally outrageous.[3]

Reform of this extraordinary and highly 'élitist' procedure did not attract the immediate interest of the new House of Commons after the Reform Act, perhaps because there was then little pressure for divorce from urban middle-class husbands. But pressure of a different kind eventually made itself felt: the gross inequity of a law that enabled the rich to get divorced but denied it to the rest of the population attracted increasing criticism. Even some judges were openly critical. In 1845, Mr Justice Maule, in sentencing a poor man convicted of bigamy to one day's imprisonment told him, with biting irony, exactly what he should have done to obtain a private Act dissolving his marriage and how much it would have cost him. He concluded with the words, 'As an English judge it is my duty to tell you that this is not a country in which there is one law for the rich and another for the poor.'[4] In 1850 the first of many royal commissions on marriage and divorce was appointed. It recommended that a court of law should be established with power to grant decrees of divorce and to take over all matrimonial disputes and matters from the Church courts. It was a period of great political instability with governments being defeated and reformed and defeated again, so progress in divorce reform was slow. The opposition was powerful and several attempts to legislate failed, but in 1857 the government eventually introduced a Bill in the House of Lords on the lines recommended by the Royal Commission, providing for a 'Court for Divorce and Matrimonial Causes'. Its judges were to be the senior judges of the existing courts, with an additional judge to be called the Judge Ordinary, and the Bill also provided for the abolition of the jurisdiction of the Church courts. Surprisingly, it passed the House of Lords without opposition; the Archbishop of Canterbury and some of the bishops supported it, but other bishops opposed it strenuously. In the Commons, it ran into difficulties with Mr Gladstone – then out of office – who opposed it with fanatical zeal and energy. He was determined to preserve sacramental marriage at all costs but was eventually defeated. However, he had one success: the Bill provided that after a decree of divorce, either spouse might marry again 'as if the prior marriage had been dissolved by death'. This meant that divorced persons would have the right to be re-married in church. Gladstone secured a limited amendment providing that no clergyman of the Church of England should be compelled to solemnize the marriage of a person who had been divorced (i.e. the guilty party). It was not until 1925 that this provision was extended to both parties, and the controversy, of course, still divides the Anglican Church today.

The Act, called the Matrimonial Causes Act 1857, although generally regarded as the foundation of English divorce law, was in fact little more than a codification of the practice developed in relation to private divorce Acts and its transfer from Parliamentary private bill committees to a court of law. Even the nomenclature was carried over. Private Bills are begun by a petition; divorce proceedings still begin with a document called a 'petition'. The only ground for divorce provided by the Act was adultery and significant distinctions between the rights of husbands and wives continued. Husbands could petition on the ground of adultery alone, but wives had to prove adultery plus incest, bigamy, rape, sodomy, cruelty, or desertion for at least two years. It was not until 1923 that this – to modern eyes – monstrous piece of sex discrimination was removed. The date is significant. The movement for sex equality in the law was powerfully stimulated by the 1914–18 war, but another equally salient influence may have been the increasing availability of reasonably safe contraception. Without it, given prevailing social and cultural norms, the risk of wives becoming pregnant and foisting their adulterine children on husbands was great enough for adultery by wives to remain a more serious matter than adultery by husbands. However, the situation in practice was not as harsh on wives as it appeared. Judges, like other people, are influenced, consciously and unconsciously by prevailing social pressures and tend to adapt the law as far as they can in response to them. Thus, reported cases from about 1900 onwards show that when judges were satisfied that a husband had committed adultery they were prepared to make the necessary additional finding of cruelty or desertion on relatively weak evidence, without insisting on proof of serious misconduct on the part of the husband. In this way discrimination between the sexes was much reduced in practice.

The modelling of the 1857 Act on previous Parliamentary practice had, and still has, a profound influence on the development of English divorce law. The passing of a private divorce bill was a legislative rather than a judicial proceeding. So, the private bill committees were free to consider each petition for a private Act on its individual merits, and this they did. They were bound by no rules of law, and if they considered that the petitioning husband had behaved badly they rejected his petition even though there was no doubt as to his wife's adultery. They saw their function primarily as relieving the genuinely aggrieved spouse, not penalizing the 'guilty' spouse. The Act transferred this process to the newly constituted court and so converted it into a judicial act, but of a unique kind. To preserve the flexibility of the Parliamentary practice, it gave the court similar powers to refuse a divorce to a petitioner who had behaved badly towards the other spouse, that is, a petitioner who could not be said to be aggrieved.

In a judicial context, this meant that the judges were given discretion to refuse a divorce within the limits set by the provisions of the Act. For the judges, this was a revolutionary and unwelcome innovation. Hitherto, the law had been structured in such a way that judges had no discretion. Once the facts of a case had been found – in those days always by a jury – the judge had to apply the law to those facts regardless of the consequences. This is 'justice according to law', but under this Act judges were required to make value judgements and do justice on an individual basis for the first time. It caused considerable consternation. None the less, as divorce law in this country has developed, the discretionary element has steadily increased to the point reached in the most recent legislation where the outcome of the case now almost entirely rests with the discretion of the judges who administer it. Judges trained in other branches of the law still show – and occasionally express until they get used to it – considerable unease at the discretionary decisions they are required to make in family law.

The 1857 Act governed divorce, almost unchanged, for the next eighty years, but in response to changing social attitudes the actual practice of the law changed greatly over the years. At first, the number of divorces granted by the new court was very small and grew slowly for many years. All cases were heard in London and were dealt with by a small group of specialist lawyers. The limited powers of the court over property made divorce financially unattractive to the wives of adulterous husbands. But the disruption of family life by the 1914–18 war not only led to a considerable increase in the number of divorce petitions, but also modified the attitude of large sections of society to the idea of divorce itself. Wartime conditions greatly increased opportunities for adultery by both sexes and marital breakdown came closer to home for people in all walks of life.

The existing system came under severe stress from many quarters. Increases in the number of cases overwhelmed the court in London so that arrangements had to be made for undefended cases to be dealt with in other centres. Judges of the King's Bench division were given power to hear such cases when sitting as assize judges – an unfamiliar and unwelcome addition to their normal role of trying criminal cases and claims for damages in civil cases. Inevitably, the 'undefended divorce list' became a chore, all the more so because only one side appeared in court. Judges accustomed to presiding over contested cases had great difficulty in finding a role for themselves when faced with a list of twenty or thirty uncontested divorce cases, and tended to regard it as a pure formality of doubtful value. In consequence, divorce became easier and cheaper in relative terms and as the cases were now being heard all over the country, it was seen to be so by the public. The judges of the Divorce Court in London had a similar role problem but they saw it as maintaining standards. This meant making divorce an appropriately solemn affair, not to be achieved without difficulty, and demanding scrupulous compliance with the rules of procedure and practice.

The philosophy underlying divorce law also came under pressure. To preserve the principle that in the past Parliament only intervened by passing a private divorce Bill in order to relieve an aggrieved spouse of the tie of marriage, the 1857 Act had to codify the circumstances which had led private bill committees to reject divorce bills. This was done by introducing two kinds of bars to divorce. Connivance, collusion and condonation were absolute bars, while conduct conducing and the commission by the petitioner of adultery, cruelty or desertion were discretionary bars. Codification of the law always changes the law although it is supposed only to make it more precise. In this instance however, it completely changed the question, 'Is this a genuinely aggrieved petitioner?' into 'Has this petitioner connived at or condoned the adultery, or colluded with the other spouse in petitioning for a divorce?' As a result divorce judges, especially in uncontested cases, acquired an inquisitorial role as they looked for evidence themselves of connivance, condonation or collusion but without any machinery beyond their own suspicions to guide them. An unsupported inquisitor is easily deceived and virtually helpless unless litigants or their legal advisers make very obvious mistakes. In the conditions prevailing after the 1914–18 war people wanted to be relieved of marriages which had completely broken down in order to marry again. Often, both parties wanted the divorce and could agree between themselves on the arrangements they wished to make, but this constituted collusion and the absolute bar on collusion hung over their heads like the sword of Damocles. Collusion went underground, divorce lawyers developed techniques for collaborating without colluding and the courts gave up the distasteful and time-consuming task of looking for evidence of collusion, unless it was thrust under their noses.

Since the law itself remained unchanged, the real causes of marital breakdown and the true source of grievance in many cases – cruelty or desertion – never came before the courts at all. Licence to remarry continued to depend on proof of adultery, so proof of adultery was provided. Between the wars it became the done thing for husbands who wanted a divorce, or in some cases whose wives wanted a divorce, to supply evidence of their adultery. The convention required the husband to take a woman to a hotel for the night (experienced divorce solicitors could often put their clients in touch with a suitable woman) and, after making sure the chambermaid saw them in bed together, to send the hotel bill to the wife or her solicitors. At the hearing of the undefended case the petitioning wife identified the husband's signature in the hotel register and the chambermaid identified a photograph of the husband. Adultery was proved and a divorce was granted. The alternative, if no co-operation could be obtained, was for the petitioner to employ a private enquiry agent to follow his or her husband or wife until evidence of adultery was obtained. Private enquiry agents became a growth industry. In this way, most people who wanted a divorce and could afford it were eventually able to obtain one.

The numbers of cases steadily increased and the whole process eventually became scandalous. A. P. Herbert, the well-known writer and satirist, published *Holy Deadlock* which exposed and mocked the whole process. Later, he became one of the members of Parliament for Oxford University (in those days the older universities elected members to Parliament) and in 1937 he introduced a private member's Bill which was to be the first major reform of divorce law since 1857. After a long struggle, he got his Bill through Parliament and it became the Matrimonial Causes Act 1937. The principal reform was an enlargement of the grounds for divorce to include desertion for three years, cruelty, and incurable insanity. The Act also contained a provision that no petition for divorce could be presented until three years had passed since the marriage, with the proviso that a judge could give leave for the presentation of a petition within this time limit if the case were one of 'exceptional hardship' or 'exceptional depravity'.

In view of the recent controversy in Parliament and in the media about the Matrimonial and Family Proceedings Act 1984, it is interesting to trace the origins of this three-year bar. There was no time bar in the 1857 Act, so a divorce petition could be presented at any time after the marriage. The opposition to that Act had not been based on concern for stability of marriage, but on the attack on the sacramental nature of marriage. A. P. Herbert's original Bill provided for a three-year ban, unqualified by exceptional hardship or depravity. This was intended as a tactical concession to opponents of the Bill who argued that it would make divorce 'easy' and so undermine the stability of marriage. It was a restrictive provision in a Bill otherwise intended to liberalize divorce, but without it he thought that the chances of the Bill passing the House of Commons were poor. The reaction in the House of Lords was surprising. Perhaps because in the past the aristocracy had had more experience of divorce than the middle classes, the peers objected strongly to this clause as an unjustifiable interference with the existing freedom to petition for divorce at any stage in a marriage! Lord Atkin and some of the other law lords condemned it in strong language and were prepared to move an amendment deleting it altogether. The sponsors of the Bill were very alarmed, fearing that if it were passed the Commons would reject the whole Bill, so an alternative amendment, giving the court discretion to permit the start of divorce proceedings within the three years in cases of exceptional hardship or exceptional depravity, was hastily drafted and passed. The introduction and repetition of the word 'exceptional' was presumably intended to appease the Bill's opponents in the Commons, but it produced extra-ordinary difficulties for the judges who had to apply it. Hardship may be 'exceptional' but is depravity ever anything but 'exceptional', and what is 'depravity' anyway?

Nearly fifty years later and after much criticism from judges and others, the government proposed to repeal it in the 1984 Bill but were unwilling to remove the time bar altogether, thus bringing English law into line with Scots law. They, like their predecessors, feared that it might not get past the House of Commons. So the limit was reduced to one year and there are no exceptions. In practice, this limitation is probably of little importance. Very few marriages break down completely within a year and probably little hardship is caused in those that do by waiting a year.

The 1937 Act tapped a large reservoir of cases in which, for one reason or another, the parties had not been able or willing to use the subterfuges which had been devised to evade the rigidity of the old law. The introduction of incurable insanity as a ground for divorce provided much-needed relief to a considerable number of spouses, although the requirements were stringent. The insanity had to be proved to be incurable and the patient had to have been detained under order for at least five years. In 1937, and for another twenty years or more, serious mental illness was virtually incurable: there was no effective drug treatment and comparatively few patients went into mental hospitals voluntarily. These were true cases of marriages which had broken down irretrievably, although that con-cept had not yet become generally acceptable.

The extension of the grounds for divorce to include cruelty and desertion enabled many petitioners to rely on the real cause of their matrimonial difficulties. Both had been grounds for separation (divorce *a mensa et toro*) in the Church courts and for judicial separation in the Divorce Court from 1857 onwards, though they were rarely used. However, despite a body of reported cases upon both, judges in 1937 did not have much experience of either cruelty or desertion. The reported cases established that to prove cruelty there must be evidence of injury to health and to prove desertion evidence of actual separation. It was not difficult to prove cruelty if there had been actual violence, or desertion if the parties had actually separated, but continuing social pressure for divorce and judicial experience of the distress in many unhappy marriages led to the gradual relaxation of these criteria. Judges ceased to insist on such stringent tests. The need to prove injury to health could be satisfied by evidence of insomnia, palpitations and other symptoms of anxiety or depression. The concept of what constituted cruel conduct was also broadened, gradually becoming more sophisticated, though for a long time judges were very cautious about mental cruelty.

At this period, mental cruelty was a popular ground for divorce in the United States of America, and newspaper reports gave the impression that almost any complaint about behaviour, however apparently trivial, was enough to obtain a divorce. The divorce statistics in the United States seemed to confirm this, and made the courts anxious to avoid the same thing happening in England. Judges in the Church courts, however, had always recognized that mental cruelty was a very real thing and potentially more destructive of marriage than occasional violence.

A similar process took place on desertion, the concept of which was extended as experience revealed that in some cases, particularly in relatively poor families, neither spouse could actually leave the matrimonial home because no alternative accommodation could be found or afforded. 'Desertion under the same roof', where the spouses were occupying separate parts of the house and living as separately as possible, came to be recognized. This raised questions of degree – for example, how separately were they living, and was it sufficiently separate? This kind of problem directed attention away from the facts of the separation and towards the state of the marital relationship.

These developments subtly changed the role of judges administering the new law, a change which has never been noticed, much less studied. Deciding whether or not two people have committed adultery when they deny it is much the same as trying any other issue of fact: the evidence is confined in its scope both in time and place, and the decision does not depend, except as to credibility, on the character or personalities of the persons concerned. But defended cruelty cases and disputes about desertion were different. The complaints often covered most of the period of the marriage and were set out in the pleadings at great length. Hearings lasted for many days. Both spouses spent hours in the witness box being examined and cross-examined. Many separate issues had to be decided, and the impact of the behaviour on each spouse had to be assessed. All this involved careful study of the personalities and temperaments of the people involved, and demanded a great deal of human understanding. In other words, judges had to make very difficult value judgements in these cases. It was a long-standing tradition that judges did not make value judgements, they made findings of fact, so they had to learn a new role and new techniques. Looking back now that this phase is over, it is astonishing that so many judges and barristers had the patience to endure these long-drawn-out struggles, and the humanity to deal with them sensitively and percipiently. In fact, they provided a unique learning experience for the generation of judges and barristers who dealt with them in the 1950s and 1960s. They listened to stories of hundreds of married lives in which the idiosyncrasies, sexual and otherwise, of apparently normal members of society were described and, moreover, tested by cross-examination, revealing all sorts of aspects of the personalities involved – demonstrations, in effect, of dynamic psychology in almost a laboratory setting. They discovered that violence was not uncommon in respectable middle-class houses, and they learned a great deal about the cultural differences between one class and another, and between one part of the country and another. They learned to appreciate the wide differences in acceptable behaviour between spouses. When a wife at Leeds or Sheffield Assizes who was prepared for some violence on Friday nights complained that her husband had 'braid' her, the judge had to understand that she had been treated with violence of a kind that no woman was expected to tolerate, and that the marriage was finished. Few people can have acquired so comprehensive an insight into the range of behaviour of 'ordinary' people. It certainly made them revise their norms of behaviour and realize how fine a line divides the criminal in the dock from the rest of society, and how elusive is the concept of 'conduct' in married life.

The cumulative effect of this experience led most judges to the conclusion that such marriages must somehow be dissolved to avoid manifest injustice and even absurdity. For many years, two things stood in the way: the absolute ban on collusion meant that the parties or their lawyers could not discuss their differences or make any arrangements for divorce; and the grave handicap of being the 'guilty party' when it came to financial arrangements and custody of the children.

Sophisticated divorce lawyers and experienced divorce judges evaded the collusion trap in various ways. The favoured method was a form of plea bargaining: the barristers on each side would negotiate together outside the court, explaining what their respective clients wanted and were prepared to give and, when an understanding (the word 'agreement' was never used) had been reached, they saw the judge in his private room and began with the words, 'I have told my learned friend what my client, win or lose [the vital words!], is prepared to do.' The other barrister would then say that there didn't seem much point in wasting money going on fighting the case. So a 'settlement' was reached which was obviously sensible and no one mentioned the word collusion. Eventually in 1968, Parliament amended the law to permit, subject to safeguards, this kind of 're-spectable' collusion. It was a much bigger step than it seemed at the time along the road to the acceptance of marriage as a partnership which could be dissolved by agreement.

The difficulty about being the 'guilty' spouse was also solved not by a change of approach in the financial proceedings but by a simple stratagem which occurred to some judge (probably Lord Denning), who asked if there was any reason why each party should not be given a decree of divorce. There was nothing in rules of court against it, though the logic was dubious, so 'joint decrees' became the key which unlocked many doors. Both parties were 'innocent' and both 'guilty'.

By the 1960s, it had become obvious, at least to the more recently appointed judges, that innocence and guilt were inappropriate terms in most divorces and largely irrelevant. What mattered to them was the state of the marital relationship and the arrangements for the wife and children after divorce, so they used their influence as far as they legitimately could to get hopeless marriages dissolved, and proper arrangements made for the future.

At this stage, something quite unexpected occurred. There had been renewed controversy in the Church of England over the re-marriage of divorced persons in church, and increasing anxiety among both clergy and laity at the rising divorce rate and the apparently increasing instability of marriages. The Archbishop of Canterbury set up a commission consisting of clergy and Anglican lay men and women experienced in divorce work, including a divorce judge (Mr Justice Phillimore) and a solicitor (Miss Joan Rubinstein) to enquire into all aspects of divorce. The commission's report was published in 1966, under the title *Putting Asunder*. It criticized the basis of the existing law and the whole concept of divorce for 'matrimonial offences', particularly the fact that a person could be divorced for a single act of adultery, which might have been an impulsive encounter. It disapproved of the prevailing practice of referring to the 'innocent' and 'guilty' spouse, and recognized that both parties are, to some extent, responsible in unhappy marriages.

Its main recommendation was that the Anglican Church should accept that divorce was permissible but only where the marriage had 'irretrievably broken down'. This would mean finally abandoning the sacramental concept of marriage, but there were two corollaries to this recommendation: the law should require proof that the breakdown was 'irretrievable' and the court should hold an 'inquisition – the Report's word – for this purpose into the state of the marriage, and that reconciliation should have been attempted. Coming from such a body as the Church of England, the primary recommendation was a radical one, probably well in advance of public opinion, but in accordance with developing judicial thinking. The two corollaries on the other hand were very conservative, designed to make divorce difficult to obtain and thus to slow down the rate in the hope of promoting stability of marriages generally.

The Law Commission then undertook a comprehensive review of matrimonial law in all its aspects. From this it was clear that even if it was desirable in theory, a judicial inquisition into the marriage in every divorce case was completely impracticable in terms of time and judge-power, and, more important, the issue, 'Has this marriage irretrievably broken down?' could not be decided by the judicial process, if there was a dispute about it. Thus, if one party maintained that the breakdown was irretrievable, and the other contended that reconciliation was possible, the court, while it might guess that reconciliation was most unlikely, could not make a definite finding of future fact. Some couples actually became reconciled during or after a bitterly fought case, not many it is true, but enough to create a doubt. But 'irretrievable breakdown' is one of those felicitous and influential literary expressions which pass into the language and sometimes into the law.

The Law Commission's review resulted in two draft Bills which were introduced in Parliament and passed into law with very few changes, as the Divorce Reform Act 1969, and the Matrimonial Property and Proceedings Act 1970, later consolidated together as the Matrimonial Causes Act 1973. So, after another long interval, this time just over thirty years, divorce law was reformed again.

'Irretrievable breakdown' was accepted as the sole ground for divorce (Section 1), but there was to be no judicial inquisition and no compulsory attempt at reconciliation. The difficulty of proving irretrievable breakdown was avoided by an ingenious and novel legislative device. Section 2 of the 1969 Act provided that, for the purposes of a divorce, irretrievable breakdown could only be established by proving one of five 'facts'. They were:

1. adultery coupled with a finding that the petitioner finds it 'intolerable' to live with the respondent;
2. behaviour such that the petitioner could not reasonably be expected to live with the respondent;
3. desertion for two years;
4. living apart for two years, the respondent consenting to a divorce; and
5. living apart for five years, the respondent not consenting to a divorce.

Parliament, in other words, created a legal presumption that if any one of these 'facts' was proved, the marriage had irretrievably broken down so no further enquiry by the court was required. A very small gesture towards reconciliation was included in Section 3, which required the petitioner's solicitor to file a certificate with the court stating whether he had discussed the possibility of reconciliation with the petitioner and provided the names and addresses of persons qualified to help in reconciliation. He was under no obligation to do either of these things, only to file a certificate as to what he had or had not done! The old bars of connivance, condonation, collusion and conduct conducing were swept away.

With the latest reform of the divorce law, the concept of marriage as a partnership has almost been reached. It can be dissolved by the court when it has become unworkable, as shown by one of the five specified facts, but it cannot yet be dissolved by the parties themselves.

After the Act, the number of divorces continued to rise, in fact much more steeply than before, though it seems now to have levelled out at about 150,000 divorces per year. *Putting Asunder*, through no fault of its authors only half of whose recommendations have been implemented, has had the paradoxical effect of making divorce easier.

In addition, the 'law in action' has developed in ways which were not foreseen by the supporters of the new Act. The qualification to adultery that the petitioner should find it intolerable to live with the respondent adds nothing. He or she would not be petitioning if they did not find it intolerable but now it must be stated specifically. The second fact is invariably, and misleadingly, referred to as 'unreasonable behaviour' which implies an objective standard, whereas the Act specifies a subjective one, i.e. 'unreasonable to expect the petitioner to live with the respondent'. Some respondents resent being said to have behaved unreasonably but might be able to accept that it is not reasonable to expect their spouses to live with them. Others seemingly do not mind.

The two-year waiting period for desertion, or mutual separation, has proved to be too long, with the consequence that a great many petitions are filed on 'behaviour' to avoid delay, sometimes with the understanding acquiescence of the respondent who wants a divorce as much as the petitioner. So, a practice has developed of making the complaints of behaviour as inoffensive as possible to avoid a fight and not mentioning more serious matters which may have been the real cause of the breakdown. Petitions, therefore, are tending to get 'weaker' and the task of the court in undefended cases more and more invidious. In the very few defended cases the court is put in a paradoxical situation. The more determined the defence, the more obvious it becomes that the marriage has irretrievably broken down. Often, the conduct of the defence itself is the best evidence of behaviour that the petitioner cannot reasonably be expected to put up with. The result is that practically no undefended cases are rejected, and very few defences succeed.

This has highlighted the anomalous role of the court at the dissolution stage in undefended cases which was implicit in the earlier law. The rubber stamp is a painfully apt analogy. It became irresistible in cases of two years' separation with consent of the respondent. The parties had agreed on a divorce: all that remained for the judge was to find the two years' separation proved which required no more than a sentence or two from the petitioner in the witness box. Judges felt that they were in a ludicrous position and the costs of a court hearing seemed unjustifiable. Thus, in 1977 a new procedure, called the Special Procedure, was introduced by the Matrimonial Causes Rules. Under this procedure the case was dealt with by a registrar entirely on paper. He was required to consider the petition and an affidavit sworn by the petitioner verifying the facts alleged and, if satisfied that two years' separation and the respondent's consent had been proved, to certify his finding on a standard form. The case was then placed in a list with many others before a judge who formally pronounced a decree of divorce for all the cases in the list, without himself seeing or hearing any of them.

The convenience and cheapness of this procedure and the increasing pressure on the system as the number of cases rose soon led to its extension to all cases which were not defended. The present position is that all undefended cases are now dealt with simply as paper transactions, reducing the role of the court to a formality. The standard required to establish unreasonable behaviour has inevitably become almost a formality too. Registrars, sitting in an office filling in forms as a routine, are not in a position to reject any case unless the complaints are absolutely trivial. All this has been done by administrative orders without reference to Parliament. The one thing that could not be done without legislation was to give the registrar actual power to dissolve marriages, so the cases must still be put before a judge with the registrar's certificate that the facts alleged have been sufficiently proved for the judge formally to pronounce that the marriage is dissolved. In practice, the result is that in the space of ten years divorce has become obtainable by the unilateral act of one party, with only the purely formal intervention of the courts. The next step will be to permit the parties to file a declaration in writing with the court that their marriage has been dissolved from a stated date.

MATRIMONIAL PROPERTY LAW

Matrimonial property law has evolved more slowly and in response to different kinds of social pressure. Common Law, the body of rules, practices and traditions built up over the centuries by judges before the days of legislation by Parliament, adopted one doctrine from canon law: the principle that in marriage 'the twain shall be of one flesh' and applied it literally, adding, in effect, that the flesh was the husband's. All property belonging to a married woman on marriage and anything coming to her after marriage, immediately became the property of her husband and she had no right or control over it. Some vestigial remains of this rule still persist: a husband cannot rape his wife; neither husband nor wife can generally be compelled to give evidence in court against each other, though there are exceptions to this rule; and for tax purposes, the property of husband and wife is still aggregated together and the husband is liable for the tax on both.

Wives were powerless to protest, but not their fathers. They objected strongly to the idea that gifts to a married daughter went straight to the son-in-law, and they were in a position to employ lawyers to prevent it. Judges, of course, also had daughters and so were sympathetic to attempts to evade the common law rule. So the marriage settlement was devised, under which, in its simplest form, property intended for the benefit of a married woman was conveyed to trustees, in trust for the married woman during her life and then for the children. The husband had no interest in or control of such property, though there was usually a trust to pay the income to him for his life, if he survived his wife. Such settlements often contained elaborate provisions to prevent husbands from getting hold of the income during the wife's lifetime. It was customary also for the husband, or his family, to settle funds on the husband for life and then to the widow and children. The object was to provide security for the wife against the risk of the husband losing all his money, or being made bankrupt. These settlements were strictly enforced by judges. In this way an elaborate body of judge-made matrimonial property law was built up, but only for wives whose families had the necessary resources. In such cases, a marriage settlement was almost always made. But it did not apply to a wife's earnings which still became the husband's property.

For a long time there was no pressure to reform the common law rule. Those with money were protected by their marriage settlements and others had nothing to protect until married women began earning. In the nineteenth century, it became possible for women to earn considerable incomes as writers, actresses, teachers and so on. But reform in this branch of the law was a low priority even for Liberal Members of Parliament. However, articulate women induced Parliament to act, albeit grudgingly at first. The Married Women's Property Act 1870 gave a married woman full control over her earnings, but little more, a reform which hardly touched Members of Parliament and their friends. However, in the course of the next ten years opinion changed abruptly and dramatically. In 1882, Parliament passed another Married Women's Property Act, this time a long and complex piece of legislation, the effect of which was to give a married woman complete control over her own property, whether she had a marriage settlement or not. It was complex because Parliament did not take the simple course of providing that, for property purposes, a married woman should be treated as a single woman; instead it devised a kind of universal marriage settlement for all married women. This probably reflected accurately the politically effective pressure of the time. The 1880s was one of the periods (the 1920s was another) in which influential political opinion became concerned about the extent to which the law discriminated against women and particularly married women, but sex equality, carried too far, had alarming implications. On the other hand, no politician could openly oppose the principle that there should not be one law for the rich and another for the poor, so it was much more acceptable to extend the advantages of a marriage settlement to all married women than to give them the same property rights as a man or an unmarried woman.

The 1882 Act, in its complicated way, gave married women with resources of their own everything they could ask for, so far as their own property was concerned, but it did nothing at all for the great majority who were entirely dependent on their husbands. It did not give them – or their richer sisters – any rights to family assets built up during a marriage by the joint efforts of husband and wife. In contrast to the various systems of community of property in force in continental countries, under which family assets are held in common, the 1882 Act established a system of separate property under which husband and wife are treated in law, in relation to property rights, as if they were strangers. Subject to some minor amendments, this is still the law.

In the 1950s and 1960s, Lord Denning nearly succeeded in changing it. Basing his reasoning on a provision in the 1882 Act (Section 17) which in disputes between husband and wife about the ownership or possession of property appeared to give the judge discretion to make such order 'as he thinks fit', he developed two principles in a series of judgments in the Court of Appeal. The first was that a deserted wife could not be turned out of the matrimonial home without the leave of the court, either by the husband or by anyone to whom he had sold or mortgaged it. This became known as the 'deserted wife's equity'. The other was that the court, in deciding whether a wife had a right to a share in the family assets, could take into account her contribution to the welfare of the family in bringing up the children and making the home. This was in the long-established tradition by which judges used to mould the law – and still do – by small stages, on a case-to-case basis, to do justice to the parties in a changing social environment. Both attempts, however, foundered completely when challenged in the House of Lords. The Lords reasserted the principle that property rights between husband and wife were governed by the strict rules which apply between strangers. Parliament, however, intervened to re-establish Lord Denning's first principle by legislation and provided that neither spouse could evict the other from the matrimonial home without an order of the court (Matrimonial Homes Act 1967). It stopped short, however, of giving each spouse a share in the matrimonial home. The non-owning spouse now has a right of occupation, subject to the order of the court. The Act contains provisions which are intended to protect this right of occupation against third parties to whom the property has been sold or mortgaged by the other spouse, but they have proved of limited value because this right is effective against third parties only if it is registered as a charge under the Land Charges Act 1972. Spouses who are living together amicably do not register charges against one another and when the relationship deteriorates, it is usually too late.

There is an unmistakable echo in this Act of the same old piecemeal, reluctant, and complicated approach to reform of this part of the law. It reflects the continuing conflict between property law and family law. Property lawyers fight tenaciously to preserve the strict property rights of legal owners only making minimal concessions to family rights when forced to do so by pressure of public opinion, and then surrounding them with elaborate rules which greatly reduce their efficacy in practice. Until quite recently it was the almost invariable practice of solicitors to put the matrimonial home into the husband's name, unless specifically instructed to put it into joint names, and they generally included when drafting wills for husbands a provision that the widow's interest in his estate should cease on remarriage.

A remarkable illustration of the persistence of this attitude was revealed, as recently as 1980, in the case of *Williams and Glyn's Bank Ltd* v. *Boland*.[5] Up to that time, all property lawyers had assumed without question that a wife who was living with her husband in a house which was in his name was not in 'actual occupation' of it, at least not for the purpose of the provisions of the Land Registration Act 1925. This was designed to protect the interests of persons who have contributed to the purchase of the property and are living in it, but have not registered that interest in it in the Land Registry, against third parties who have either bought it or taken a mortgage on it from the person who is the registered owner. A wife's presence in the property was assumed to be just a facet of her husband's occupation so that a wife who had provided part of the purchase money but had not registered her interest could be made homeless by her husband selling or mortgaging it without her knowledge.

Times, however, have changed. In 1980, judges in the Court of Appeal and the House of Lords unanimously rejected this idea, and said that 'actual occupation' meant what it said. The judgments show a quite different attitude to the position of the married woman so in that case the bank lost to the wife – amid cries of despair from the banking world that they would now have to ask their male customers awkward questions about the state of their marriages before lending them money on the security of their homes!

Social attitudes to matrimonial property are also changing, sometimes ahead of the law. Most couples who have married in the last twenty years regard their home as their joint property and it is now more likely to be in joint names than only in the husband's. This process has been stimulated by the building societies who wish to enhance their security by having two incomes to pay the instalments, and is another step on the road to marriage as a partnership.

In practice, however, matrimonial property law only becomes significant to individuals when their marriage is breaking up and divorce is imminent. The powers of the court to make orders about financial and property matters after divorce are, therefore, of crucial importance. The evolution of these powers was a very slow process until 1970. Then, in an enormous leap forward, the court was given complete control over the capital and property of both spouses. This has entirely altered the relative positions of husbands and wives.

Matrimonial property law after divorce

In cases of separation, the Church courts usually ordered the husband to pay permanent alimony, as it was called, to the wife. Their normal practice was to fix the amount at about one-third of the husband's income. This is the origin of the 'one-third rule' which the Divorce Court adopted as its guideline, and which is still often referred to by advocates and judges in spite of fundamental changes in the economic and social climate in which these decisions have to be made. In its private divorce Acts, Parliament usually required the husband to make some arrangements for the support of his adulterous wife, which was not unreasonable since he had acquired all her property on marriage. It also varied the terms of marriage settlements to fit into the new situation, but rarely deprived the wife of her income from the funds provided by her family.

The 1857 Act gave the court the same powers, converting the

absolute power of Parliament to do what it thought just in each
private Act into a judicial discretion to do what the court thought
reasonable in each case. But this only applied to income. The court
could order permanent maintenance for the wife and children and it
could vary the terms of marriage settlements, but the sanctity of
capital and property rights was jealously preserved so the court
could do nothing to provide a home for the wife and children. This
position was maintained throughout the period 1857–1963. Only
one small breach was made in the defences. The word 'settlement',
when used in legislation, has always been given a remarkably elastic
meaning by judges. Thus, it was possible to say that the purchase of
a house in the joint names of husband and wife was a post-nuptial
marriage settlement and therefore subject to the court's power to
vary marriage settlements. In this way, the court could extinguish
the rights of either husband or wife in the property in the settlement
to do justice between them. Then in 1963, the court was given power
to order the payment of a lump sum of money by one spouse to the
other (or to the children). This sometimes made it possible to provide
a home for the wife and children but, speaking generally, the courts
adopted a very conservative approach to lump-sum orders.

Over the years 1857 to 1970, the difficulties of deciding what was
a reasonable amount to order an ex-husband to pay his ex-wife led
to the development of more or less stereotyped solutions. Whenever
a court or any other body is required to decide what is just or
reasonable in case after case, stereotypes inevitably emerge and in
this case, a ready-made stereotype was available in the 'one-third
rule' which was modified. It became the amount required to bring
the wife's income up to one-third of the combined incomes. Under
modern conditions, income tax and social benefits of one kind or
another have distorted the original stereotype out of recognition,
and led to long and confusing arguments about what should be
included in the calculation as income and what should be excluded.
Even so, it is still used to provide a starting point from which to
work upwards or downwards. Some hypothetical figure is probably
necessary to guide the mind in this exceptionally unstructured exercise of discretion and the one-third rule is no more arbitrary than
any other starting point.

Each successive Matrimonial Causes Act has directed the court to 'have regard to' the conduct of the parties, in assessing the amount to be ordered, but each Act has scrupulously avoided giving any indication of what Parliament considered relevant conduct, or how it should be reflected in the amount of the order. Here, too, stereotypes were developed, but these can be more conveniently discussed later in relation to the 1984 Act.

In 1970 fundamental changes were made by the Matrimonial Proceedings and Property Act to take account of the no-less-fundamental change in the conceptual basis for divorce which was made by the Divorce Reform Act passed in the preceding year. Divorce for irretrievable breakdown has quite different implications for post-divorce financial matters than divorce for a matrimonial offence. The most important of these changes gave a new power to the court to make what are called 'property adjustment orders', an apt name, and one which signified the intention underlying this Act. It enables the court to transfer any property from one spouse to the other as it thinks just. Together with the power to order payment of a lump sum, which was continued from the 1963 Act, these two powers give the court complete control over all the assets owned by the spouses at the time of the divorce, and enables it to reallocate them between the spouses, regardless of pre-existing property rights. This has transformed the position of wives. Under the previous legislation, however innocent, they were essentially in the position of supplicants for support and could only get what was, in effect, a cash allowance subject to variation upwards or more often downwards as the respective incomes and liabilities changed. The new legislation enables the court to adjust the available resources, both capital and income, between the parties as the new post-divorce situation demands. This is the logical consequence of basing divorce on irretrievable breakdown of the marital relationship instead of on the so-called matrimonial offence.

When exercising these far-reaching powers, the court was directed to take into account the contributions made by each party to the welfare of the family 'including any contribution made by looking after the home or caring for the family', so the second of the principles for which Lord Denning strove, only to be defeated in the House of Lords, has been, to a large extent, revived by Parliament. The importance of this provision is that for the first time in the context of property, it recognizes the value of the wife's work in the home and treats husband and wife as equal partners in the marriage. It is ironic that the law still only acknowledges this after the partnership has broken down but, pragmatically, this is the time when it really matters. This change has made some of the old controversies over the ownership of property largely academic: it no longer matters so much who owned what during the marriage. The court, after divorce, is free to 'adjust' property rights as it thinks just, and is able to deal with the most important asset, the home, as it thinks best for the partners themselves as well as for the children.

These are extremely wide powers to give to the court. They are a major invasion of the hitherto sacred area of capital and property rights and at first shocked lawyers and owners of property. It took some years before judges and registrars got over their professional inhibitions about interfering with these rights. They spoke anxiously of 'depriving' a man (it was almost always a man!) of his property. 'His' and 'hers' was in the forefront of their minds. But gradually the notion of 'theirs' has taken root, not only on the Bench, but in society itself. The phrase 'family assets', though it does not appear in the Act, is coming more and more into use.

The decision of Parliament to entrust these powers to the discretion of the court is a tribute to the confidence which is placed in the judiciary, but it has been criticized, largely on theoretical grounds, as giving too much power to judges and for producing uncertainty. The alternative would have been to attempt to define the shares of each party in the total resources available. This would have required a most elaborate code of rules and regulations, all of which would have had to be interpreted by the court and applied rigidly, with all the potential injustices which are inherent in any legislation which has to be applied rigidly to anything as infinitely variable as family life. Experience of other legislative exercises, such as taxation statutes and social security Acts, does not support the view that legislation can satisfactorily regulate matters which require individual attention and flexibility. It is either red tape or discretion.

Parliament recognized that it was putting a great responsibility on the court with this Act and for the first time incorporated a section (now Section 25 of the 1973 Act) giving guidelines as to how these problems should be approached, a technique which has since been used in a number of later Acts. It begins by directing the court '. . . to have regard to all the circumstances of the case including . . .' It then lists some specific factors. These are, in summary, the financial resources of each party, now and in the future, including earning capacity; their respective financial needs and obligations now and in the future; the standard of living of the family before divorce; the ages of the parties and duration of the marriage; the health of both parties; and the contributions of each to the welfare of the family. All but the last of these factors had been identified by the judges themselves as relevant and important in the exercise of their powers under the earlier legislation, but they have now been institutionalized by the Act.

The court was then required to exercise its powers 'so as to place the parties, so far as it is practicable, and, having regard to their conduct, just to do so, in the financial position in which they would have been if the marriage had not broken down . . .'

Both these requirements gave rise to considerable trouble in practice, and have since been revised by the 1984 Act. The first was so impracticable as to be virtually meaningless; the differences between living together and living apart are so great that realistic comparison is impossible. The second was extremely difficult to apply. In a supposedly no-fault divorce situation the opportunities for investigating conduct, in the ordinary case, are minimal. Both became virtually dead letters.

The directions in the 1984 Act now require the court to give first consideration to the welfare of children up to the age of eighteen years and to have regard to the conduct of each party 'if that conduct is such that it would in the opinion of the Court be inequitable to disregard it'. It remains to be seen whether these new directions will make any actual difference to the exercise of the court's discretion. The interests of any children have always been a primary consideration. It is not easy to discover any material difference between the original and the rephrased direction about conduct.

Having had to abandon the aim of putting the parties so far as is practicable into the financial position they would have enjoyed if the marriage had continued, the courts have used their discretion pragmatically to produce as fair and as practical a result as possible in each case. The Court of Appeal has not attempted to lay down 'principles' that inevitably result in restricting the discretion of the lower courts and producing unforeseen and undesirable consequences in later cases. Instead, it has repeatedly said that its judgments are not to be treated strictly as precedents but as specimen solutions to the individual problems with which it is faced which may be helpful to the lower courts in similar cases.

From this empirical approach some broad conclusions or propositions have emerged. In the majority of cases the element of 'needs' outweighs the element of resources, so the problem becomes one of balancing the inevitable hardship of each party. Usually the most pressing need is housing, priority being given (before and since the 1984 Act) to providing a home for the children. In most cases the only substantial capital asset is the former matrimonial home, almost always subject to a mortgage. The market value usually exceeds considerably the amount of the mortgage, which creates the illusion that some money can be made available for division if the house is sold, but the increase is only a reflection of the inflation of house prices generally. There is rarely enough to provide a home for the children and the custodial parent, which in practice is usually the wife, and leave something for the husband. Moving to a smaller house or a flat is generally a myth. There is little room for manoeuvre at the lower end of the property market. These cases, therefore, resolve themselves into housing problems.

The courts have evolved various permutations to balance the interests of husband, wife, and children, in differing circumstances. The contribution element, especially the contribution made by looking after the children and the home, means in most cases that the starting point is that husband and wife have an equal share in the matrimonial home, whoever is the legal owner. Sometimes it is practicable to order the house to be sold and the proceeds divided, not necessarily in equal shares; sometimes the wife can buy the husband's interest, at a reduced figure, reflecting his share of responsibility for providing a home for the children; sometimes the house is transferred to the wife altogether, the husband being compensated by the wife agreeing not to ask for maintenance – periodical payments as it is now called, although the former term is still more widely used – and taking over the mortgage liability. In other cases the house is put in trust for the wife for life or until remarriage (which it is assumed will improve her financial position) and then sold and all the proceeds divided in specified shares; occasionally the wife may be ordered to pay the husband the equivalent of rent, with a restriction on sale of the house without her consent. Some of these solutions depend on the wife's earning capacity; others rely on the benefits which the wife can claim under social security legislation, e.g. payment of mortgage interest. Another permutation, which became popular for some years, was known as a 'Mesher v. Mesher' order. Under it, the wife was given the right to occupy the former home until the youngest child was eighteen or ceased full-time education, and then the house was to be sold and the proceeds of sale equally divided with the husband. Experience, however, showed that what seemed a panacea had serious disadvantages. The wife's half-share was too little to enable her to buy a flat. As a single woman without dependents her priority for council housing was very low. Her earning capacity, eroded by years of responsibility for the children, was not enough to rent accommodation in the private sector or to qualify for a sufficient mortgage. The result for her was a serious risk of homelessness at a most difficult age, while for the husband, who would by then have re-established himself in a home, it meant a cash bonus useful for reducing his current mortgage commitment but not essential. Orders of this type have therefore become much less frequent.

Other examples of the working of these discretionary powers illustrate the problems of assessing and dealing with the resource element. Valuations, especially of small businesses, have many pitfalls as well as being expensive; difficulty in realizing a part of such valuations without destroying the husband's livelihood is often a limiting factor. Others illustrate the effect of the age and duration of the marriage element. In short marriages the primary consideration is the actual effect of the marriage on the wife's earning capacity or financial position. If there are no children and the parties are young, it may be minimal and only minor adjustments to the property rights necessary; in others, the marriage itself may have terminated the wife's periodical payments from a former husband which is a serious detriment to her if the second marriage breaks down quickly. Others again illustrate the influence of the contribution factor. A wife who has worked actively in the husband's business as well as looking after the family is likely to get a larger share of the available resources.

There is another factor which greatly influences the result in many cases. Most wives are legally aided under the Legal Aid Act 1974. Under the terms of the Act, any property or capital (but not periodical payments) 'recovered' in the proceedings is subject to a charge in favour of the Law Society for the costs incurred by the wife (or the husband if he is legally aided) in the divorce proceedings as a whole, including disputes about custody. This means that the costs have to be paid out of what is ordered to be paid and it can drastically reduce the amount available for the wife (or husband as the case may be). Fortunately, as a concession the Law Society usually agrees not to enforce their charge on the matrimonial home until it is ultimately sold, but the effect of this rule is that legally aided parties who recover anything in litigation pay for it in the end as if they were not legally aided.

CONDUCT

The factor or element of conduct, in view of the recent discussion and controversy over the 1984 Act, requires more consideration. The original 1857 Act, and all its successors required the court to 'have regard to' the conduct of both parties in deciding what is 'reasonable' (1857, 1925 and 1950 Acts) or 'just' (1970 Act) or 'equitable' (1984 Act). But Parliament has still not identified the nature of the conduct, or given any indication as to the effect it should have on the financial arrangements after divorce. The persistence of reference to it, in Act after Act, must be a reflection of an equally persistent social perception that conduct should influence the financial position of the parties after divorce. But the vagueness of the language used in all the Acts suggests an equally vaguely formulated idea. In truth, the bland non-discriminatory language ('both parties') which is used conceals the real motivation. It has never been suggested that bad conduct by the husband (except perhaps persistent financial irresponsibility) should result in a higher than normal provision for the wife. Thus reference to conduct in all these Acts is a reference to misconduct by *the wife*, and the unstated intention is in effect that it should reduce, if not exclude, the wife's claim for financial provision. In practice, the courts have never been able to do the calculus of conduct of both parties because it requires a detailed investigation of the whole marriage, a task so time-consuming and expensive as to be impracticable. Stereotyping was inevitable and the stereotype became the 'guilty wife' which, up to 1937, could only mean the adulterous wife. The law in the books required consideration of both parties' conduct: the law in action meant that a divorced wife got little or no financial provision, a result which appealed to the male population, and, formerly to much of the female population (the non-divorced). It became the practice to talk of a 'compassionate allowance' for guilty wives who were in extreme difficulties and, in spite of rebukes by the Court of Appeal who repeatedly called attention to the words of the statute, it persisted.

The result was that no wife could afford to be divorced – i.e. to be the guilty party – if she could possibly prevent it. This led to many acrimonious and bitterly contested cases between spouses, both of whom wanted a divorce. In this process, the issue of conduct as it affected the financial arrangements was submerged. What mattered was who got the divorce decree. When cruelty and desertion became grounds for divorce in 1937 the wife's position was strengthened. If she had committed adultery she herself might now petition or cross-petition for divorce on either of these new grounds which really did expose the issue of conduct to judicial investigation. If she proved either ground she usually got the decree; it was assumed that she was the more or less innocent party and her financial claims were not appreciably prejudiced.

When the matrimonial offence was abolished by the 1969 Act and replaced by 'irretrievable breakdown' the judges were free to give effect to their perception that in all but the clearest cases assessments about the conduct of married people to one another were inherently unreliable. The first case to come before the Court of Appeal on the new powers to adjust the financial position and property rights of the spouses after divorce was the well-known case of *Watchel* v. *Watchel*.[6] The Court took this opportunity of giving general guidance to the lower courts on the administration of these powers. On conduct, the Court said that, generally speaking, conduct was irrelevant unless it was 'both obvious and gross'. The phrase was taken from the judgment in the court below, where it was used descriptively to explain the situation which had actually been reached before the new legislation, namely, that experience had shown that unless conduct was obvious (i.e. easily proved) and gross (really serious), it made little difference to the result of the financial proceedings after divorce. The judgment of the Court of Appeal was, perhaps, unfortunately phrased in that it was read as a directive to ignore conduct unless it was obvious and gross. This aroused resentment in some quarters against what was seen as a piece of pseudo-legislation by the Court of Appeal and was very unpopular with husbands and their solicitors. It was, however, followed faithfully and gratefully by judges who had no desire to preside over long recriminatory hearings about conduct. Very few cases got over this hurdle, but resentment increased until vigorous lobbying by interested pressure groups induced the government to act. It proved very difficult to formulate a different approach, particularly in the face of opposition from other pressure groups and, more important, for reasons of expenditure. If conduct were to become a live issue on financial matters in many cases, it would greatly increase the number of contested cases which would overload the lists, require an increase in judge-power and, no less importantly, greatly increase the costs of providing legal aid. The result was the modification described above: conduct was to be taken into account if 'in the opinion of the court it would be inequitable to disregard it'.

Whether this modification will make much difference in practice remains to be seen. The removal of the 'gross and obvious' hurdle will mean that it will be easier to get a hearing on conduct, but what the courts will make of 'inequitable' and what effect it will have on the financial outcome remains to be seen. The one point that is clear is that it will not be possible to conclude that it would be inequitable to disregard conduct (the double negative is interesting) without investigating the conduct of both parties in some depth. Very few people in real life decide to break up their marriages without reasons which they at least find both serious and convincing.

The best way of describing the role which the courts have assumed under the current legislation is to say that they try to act as wise and conscientious trustees with unrestricted powers over the family resources for all three parties concerned, husband, wife and children.

The most worrying of these discretionary powers is assessing how much the husband should pay, weekly or monthly, for the support of the wife and children in maintenance. The task is usually carried out by a registrar and only comes to the judges on appeal. It involves determining the incomes of each party; salaries and wages are relatively easy but, in other cases, it is often difficult to extract the whole truth from reluctant individuals who have everything to gain from concealment. There is a legal duty to make a full and frank disclosure of the financial position in advance of the hearing before the registrar, but it may be necessary to examine and cross-examine the parties to get at the full facts. This leads to a great deal of ill-feeling.

The registrar must then consider the needs of both husband and wife and their obligations. Few men can afford to support two families. It is therefore difficult, if not impossible, to provide adequately for the first wife and children. Some registrars use the one-third rule as a guideline but it is notoriously unreliable. In cases of high and low incomes, it tends to produce unrealistic figures. Income tax and social security benefits add further complications.

Payments under these orders are deductible from the husband's gross income before his tax is assessed. The court is supposed to ignore any social security benefits other than child allowance which the wife receives, but it knows that social security will be available, if necessary, to bring the wife's income up to the current level of benefits. The result is that the tax-payer subsidizes both the high- and low-income groups. A husband who is in the 60 per cent tax bracket is relieved of income tax at that rate on the whole sum paid to the wife and children. At the other end of the scale the husband may be relieved of most or all of the cost of supporting his former wife and children who may be better off on social security benefits which are received regularly and reliably. From the court's point of view these cases are relatively easy; it is the middle-income cases which cause the problems. The only safe way to decide the amount to be ordered is to take a hypothetical figure and work out the tax implications for both parties and calculate how much each will have left to live on (the net incomes) and compare these figures with the needs of each party. If the results are unsatisfactory, the hypothetical figure is adjusted and the net figures recalculated. Hitherto, it has been the invariable practice to allocate the greater part of the sum to the wife and the rest to the children which produces unrealistically low figures for the children. The purpose of this is to avoid later applications – which are always contentious – to increase the wife's order when the children grow up. Orders for wives continue until remarriage or the death of husband or wife, though they can be varied by the court or by agreement from time to time as circumstances change. Orders for children last until they are eighteen or until further order.

The 1984 Act has made a number of important changes. Provision for the children is now the first priority so it seems likely that the courts will make higher orders for them and reduce wives' orders proportionately. New powers are given to the court to put a time limit on wives' orders with a view to ensuring that they start to earn when they are in a position to do so, and to dismiss a wife's claim to maintenance if she can support herself. Hitherto, this could only be done with her consent. These changes were made in response to pressure groups which claimed that hardship is caused to the second family when husbands have to continue to support their first families and particularly first wives. Much play was also made about 'alimony widows' – former wives – allegedly living in idleness and luxury at the expense of former husbands. It remains to be seen whether these powers will make much difference in practice. Most divorced women who can get employment already do so if their commitments to the children permit, and alimony widows are, one suspects, a pretty rare species.[7] The power to dismiss claims was given to encourage the so-called principle of the 'clean break'. This attractive phrase means that all financial ties between former husbands and wives should be severed by the court whenever possible. It is an excellent principle in theory, but in practice it is only possible where there is enough capital available to provide an adequate annuity for the wife or the wife has a sufficiently high earning capacity to keep herself. Where there are dependent children, it is an unrealistic concept.

CHILDREN

There is relatively little law in the statute book about children and their natural parents; most of it is judge-made. It has evolved along lines which are broadly parallel to divorce and matrimonial property.

At common law, the father was the sole guardian of his children;

the mother's position was entirely secondary. In theory, the king was the father of the whole community (*parens patriae*) and all children were his wards and under his ultimate protection. This role was delegated to the Lord Chancellor and through him to the judges of the Court of Equity who dealt with disputes about the custody of children and their financial affairs. This is the origin of the expression 'ward of court'. Anyone could (and still can) take the formal steps required to make a child a ward of court and thereafter, the judge had (and still has) all the powers of a guardian over the child. This, the Wardship Jurisdiction, still survives intact and is now exercised by the judges of the Family Division of the High Court. Parliament has never legislated about it, nor attempted to control it, and it is often used in cases which cannot be dealt with satisfactorily under any of the other codes of law.

From its early days it was accepted that the judge, as guardian, should always act in the best interests of the child, and was free to proceed as he thought fit, subject to minimal procedural constraints. For a very long time judges shared the prevailing view in society that the father was the essential figure in children's lives, supporting them and directing their upbringing and development. So in disputes between parents the father was entrusted with the care of the child, unless he had behaved in such a way as to make him unfit to act as a parent. The mother had, in law, no rights or power in relation to her children.

This discrimination against mothers had at least some rational basis in the nineteenth century. For those who could afford a divorce, nannies, housekeepers and domestic servants were readily available so that fathers had no difficulty in maintaining a home for the children. Some mothers did not play a crucial part in the care of their children even during the marriage. Separated mothers, moreover, were under such severe financial and economic handicaps that they were usually unable to make a home for their children.

This view of the welfare of children eventually began to be seriously challenged especially after one or two widely publicized cases in which obviously unsatisfactory fathers had been given custody of their children. As a result, at about the same time as the Married Women's Property Act 1882 was passed, and under the same liberal influences, Parliament passed the first Guardianship of

Infants Act in 1887. It was a modest effort to redress the balance but did little to strengthen the position of mothers.

The 1857 Act gave the Divorce Court power to make orders about the custody, maintenance and education of children in divorce proceedings, leaving decisions to the discretion of the court. This was an additional power so it was no longer obligatory to use the wardship procedure but divorce judges adopted similar principles. As a result, divorced wives very rarely received custody of their children and access was severely restricted.

The position changed considerably after the 1914–18 war. In 1925, in the second phase of Parliamentary reform to remove or reduce the legal disabilities of women, especially married women, the second Guardianship of Infants Act was passed. This went much further. Having failed to make much impression on conventional attitudes in the first Guardianship Act of 1887, Parliament this time was explicit. First, it declared that in any proceedings involving custody or upbringing of a child the 'first and paramount consideration' was the welfare of the child, and, secondly, that the court should treat the father and mother on equal terms.

It took a long time before the implications of this Act were fully appreciated and accepted by judges. They did not think that the best interests of a child were likely to be met by being placed in the custody of an adulterous mother, nor could they wholly accept the concept of the paramountcy of the welfare of the child. It was argued that the interests of the child, though paramount, were not the sole consideration. The interests of a so-called 'unimpeachable' parent (usually the father) could not be ignored even though the evidence pointed to the mother as the parent who could best look after the children.

'Guilty wives' were still rarely granted custody of their children, although as time went on a practice grew up of giving 'custody' to the father and 'care and control' to the mother. This was – and still is – a purely pragmatic distinction, the effect of which has never been clearly defined. Originally, it was introduced to solve a dilemma which arose more and more frequently as social conditions changed. On the one hand, it was felt, and felt strongly, by judges that the father, particularly an 'innocent' father, had a special role in his children's lives, and that it was wrong to 'deprive' him of his children.

This was an echo of the old common law doctrine, persisting in spite of Parliament's effort to eliminate it, combined with the perception that the role of the father was actually very important in the development of children, especially boys. On the other hand, the practical problems which more and more fathers faced due to the increasing difficulty of obtaining domestic service, made the court reluctant to put children into their day-to-day care. The mother was in a better position to make a home for them. Giving 'custody' to the father seemed to preserve his position as the parent with ultimate authority to make the important decisions, while giving 'care and control' to the mother enabled her to provide the home for them. The distinction proved largely illusory in practice; there was actually very little difference between a mother with custody and a mother with only care and control. If a dispute arose between the parents, it would have to be referred to the court and the court would have to apply the test of the best interests of the child to sort it out. This division of responsibility for a child has come to be used mostly for its psychological effect, sometimes to preserve and foster a father's interest in his children, sometimes to soften the blow to an apparently ill-used father, sometimes for reasons of prestige. 'I have custody' may mean a lot to a man even if the mother is actually bringing up the children. This type of order is gradually being replaced by that of 'joint custody' which is intended to emphasize the court's view, or the parents' view, that they should stand on an equal footing with regard to their children. This is sometimes significant for the children themselves and helps to preserve their ties with both parents (see also chapter 4). It is sometimes said an order for 'joint custody' should only be made when the parents are on reasonably amicable terms and can co-operate, but there are also cases where a sole custody order in favour of one parent can make matters even worse between them. There are other instances, though rare, where a joint custody order is used to prevent one parent from dominating the other by brandishing the custody order. If parents with joint custody cannot agree the dispute can always be referred to the court to settle.

The net result of these developments has been to eliminate the former dominant position of fathers and to put mothers into an almost equally dominant position in relation to children after divorce. This complete change of attitude by the courts, due in part to an appreciation of the severe practical difficulties of fathers in modern society, almost certainly also reflects psychological theories about the development of children and the importance of maternal care.

The maternal deprivation theories of Bowlby and others received much publicity in the 1950s and were widely accepted by psychologists and welfare officers who were then beginning to play an important role in custody cases in the courts. They transmitted these views to the courts, usually indirectly, through their written reports and recommendations which fell on increasingly receptive ears. As one generation of judges succeeds another, the younger, recently appointed judges bring to the courts different prepossessions or perceptions derived from their own experience which differ from those of older generations. The increasing divorce rate also led to a less censorious attitude to adultery generally and particularly by women, so the objections to giving custody to 'guilty' wives lost much of their force. In this way the 'law in action' gradually changes before the 'law in the books', i.e. statute law, is reformed by Parliament.

In 1969 a remarkable thing happened. In a case called *J.* v. *C.*[8] the House of Lords was faced with making an inescapable choice between awarding care of a child to foreign natural parents, or to the foster parents who had been looking after the child for many years by arrangement with the natural parents who had been working in England. The natural parents had recently established a new home in their own country. The case, which was a wardship case, was decided in favour of the foster parents. The importance of the decision lay in the attitude of the House to the provision in successive Guardianship Acts that the courts were to regard the welfare of the child as the 'first and paramount consideration'. It was declared, unequivocally, that these words meant exactly what they said, and were not subject to any glosses such as the blood tie or the interests of 'unimpeachable parents'. This ruling, of course, applied also to divorce cases, and powerfully reinforced the growing tendency to ignore questions of 'guilt' and further diminished what was left of the role of the father. The result is that the court must now examine the evidence in each case individually and decide what will be the best solution for the welfare of the child or children.

This is obviously a difficult task. Questions of welfare are concerned with the future both of the parents and the child and the answers are, inevitably, uncertain. Welfare itself is a very imprecise concept about which opinions vary. Faced with problems of this kind the court tends to start from the baseline of known facts – the present situation in which the children are living. Any decision maker instinctively approaches his decision by asking himself, 'Has the case for a change been made out?' and is inclined to prefer the known to the unknown, unless the known situation is clearly unsatisfactory. He will also think that the welfare of the child will probably be better served by the parent who can provide relatively simple and stable arrangements than by the other whose proposals are more complicated and liable to change. The case for change, however, may be clear even if it involves a considerable upheaval for all concerned and much emotional stress. But it must clearly be in the interests of the child. This approach has been encouraged and fortified by current theories which emphasize the importance of continuity of care and preservation of existing bonds – 'bonding' is becoming a familiar word in court – and is reinforced by a reluctance to speculate about the allegedly beneficial psychological effects on the child of a change from one parent to the other.

The effect of all this in practice is again that mothers have considerable advantages over fathers. At the time of separation it is usually the father who leaves the family; it is therefore usually the mother who is keeping the home for the children from which they still go to the same school and have the same friends. The continuity of care principle works in her favour. But if the mother leaves the family the picture is different. It is often very difficult for her to find accommodation for herself and the children and it takes a long time. Continuity of care now favours the father, but continuity offered by him is more or less illusory. His difficulties as a single parent often mean that another woman or women are providing the care on a temporary basis. If so, the mother's ability to offer greater stability may outweigh the continuity consideration. However, the courts are becoming familiar with the much more domesticated fathers of today and if their arrangements are working well will generally not disturb them.

To enable decisions to be made in these cases, the court has before it written evidence in the form of affidavits from both parents and often neighbours, friends or relatives, and a long report by the court welfare officer, based on interviews with the parents, grandparents and other close relatives, school teachers, and sometimes the doctor. The welfare officer nearly always sees the children alone as well as with each parent, if that can be arranged, and makes reports on the children's attitude and what they have said. At the hearing both parents give oral evidence and are cross-examined, and the welfare officer, who is usually in court, may assist with a further oral report or by answering questions. In practice, most of the important facts are not in dispute though the written evidence tends to contain highly contentious points which reflect past quarrels between the parents.

Friends and neighbours have very limited opportunities to judge capacity for parenting, so it is the oral evidence of the parents and the welfare report that are important. Experienced judges know what to look for in the evidence, and rely much on the welfare officer for a dispassionate version of the facts. For them the contentious recriminations of the past carry very little weight.

Sometimes in exceptional circumstances, the judge sees the children himself if they are old enough. This can be illuminating: the picture they present is often much less dramatic than their parents' versions and usually very practical. It is often alleged that they have been 'brain-washed' by one of the parents and are unreliable. Attempts at brain-washing are certainly made by some parents, but whether they succeed when the children have a chance to speak privately to the welfare officer or judge is another matter altogether.

All orders about children can be varied at any time if things change, or seem to be going wrong, but this happens infrequently. It is possible to experiment by making short-term orders to be reviewed in six months or a year, but this is rarely necessary. In the majority of contested custody cases, the facts before the court point decisively in one direction or another.

In a small minority of cases, the question of access by the non-custodial parent can be extremely difficult. The courts attach much importance to access which is regarded as the right of the children to keep in contact with the other parent, rather than the right of that parent. If it is asked for, the courts almost always include in the order a provision for access, often in the form 'reasonable access', at the request of the parents who prefer to make their own arrangements. Sometimes access is specified in detail, e.g. one weekend in four, staying access, or on every alternate Saturday or Sunday between stated hours. This may be done to contain disputes or to regularize the child's life. In fixing access the court is primarily concerned to balance the desirability of maintaining contact against the repeated disturbance of the child's normal life. If access means missing football it does not help to maintain contact on a friendly basis, so the courts tend to favour longer periods of access at longer intervals.

In a few cases, access becomes a war of attrition. Mothers are sometimes accused of deliberately frustrating access by one stratagem or another. Fathers sometimes refuse to accept the fact that they are divorced, or that the court is ultimately in control, and try to insist on access when they choose to demand it. Sometimes this leads to court proceedings to enforce the order for access, occasionally even to proceedings to commit the mother to prison for disobedience to the order. In such circumstances, the judge tries to mediate between the parties, to adjust the terms of access or to get undertakings as to the behaviour of the parents towards one another and often asks the welfare officer to act as a mediator. When all else fails access is stopped, usually for a fixed period. Attempts to commit mothers to prison are self-defeating. It cannot be in the children's best interests to send their mother to prison, and it is fatal to the father because nothing is so destructive of his relationship with the children. There is, unfortunately, a hard core of cases, albeit a very small proportion of the total, in which the mother is adamant in her refusal to permit access. In such cases the court may ultimately have to accept that access cannot be insisted on because the conflict is seriously upsetting the children, and it is not in their interests to persist. Although it may not be possible to discover the root cause of the conflict in these cases, it is unwise to assume that there is no underlying reason for it, obscure though it seems to be.

It is often said that the methods and setting of the courts are ill-suited to dealing with problems of the future of children. The adversary system, with lawyers on each side acting as champions for their respective clients, putting forward their cases in a hostile and contentious way, often arguing over past grievances and making debating points, does not seem to be the right way to settle these disputes. But in some cases, and they are a relatively small proportion, this system reflects the underlying reality. There is intense hostility between the parents and there has been a great deal of misrepresentation and even lying and scheming or oppressive behaviour by one parent towards the other. For this minority of cases the adversary system is the only way of getting at the truth, painful, but necessary, though it is. Most cases, fortunately, do not develop in this way. Differences of opinion can mostly be adjusted by the mediation of a welfare officer or other independent person, or by efficient and experienced solicitors and barristers, or by the judge. But it is not as easy as it sounds. Mediation requires experience and knowledge of what is actually happening to 'see through' what the parents are saying. It also demands a degree of impartiality and restraint in the mediator who is in a very powerful position *vis-à-vis* the parties, either of whom may feel unable to withstand pressure from the mediator, thus acquiescing to a solution which he or she does not really accept and which may not be in the best interests of the child. It is better that mediation should fail than that it should impose a solution – that is the function of the court.

The emphasis on the welfare of the child as the paramount consideration is encouraging the idea that the child should be separately represented by an advocate of his or her own to put the child's point of view before the court. In theory, this seems a reasonable proposition but it has considerable practical difficulties. An advocate acts on instructions from his client. He will, of course, give advice to his client but in the end he says what he is instructed to say. Who is to instruct the child's advocate and where is he going to get his information from? Older children can express their feelings and wishes to him, but he must be more than their mouthpiece. He can ask questions of the parents to test their proposals or their intentions. But in most cases, he has no alternative but to put forward a solution which he personally thinks is the best for his child-client. This requires a degree of judgement and sensitivity and is apt to encroach on the role of the judge who may be embarrassed by it. At present a very limited – but very valuable – service of this kind is provided by the Official Solicitor, a civil servant with a small department who acts in litigation for persons who are unable to instruct solicitors themselves. His services are called upon in very difficult children's cases and are invaluable to the judge. He carries out his own investigations and reports to the judge, making recommendations which are backed by great experience and are always extremely helpful. But his value to the court and the child reflect his own knowledge and experience of these problems. Without such experience, the value to the court of an advocate for the child is much diminished.

It is sometimes urged that the court should monitor some of these difficult cases and in some cases welfare officers help greatly by supervising access and smoothing difficulties, but this can only be done on a short-term basis because it is very demanding of welfare officers' limited time. Courts cannot normally monitor cases because they are neither designed nor equipped to do so. Their primary function is to settle disputes.

The widespread anxiety which is felt in Parliament and society about the damage done to children by divorce has led to various attempts to use the courts to protect them and to ensure that parents make suitable arrangements for them. Unfortunately, the capacity of the courts to perform such functions is limited and largely formal. Every divorce petition is required to set out proposed arrangements for the children, but at that stage both parents' plans are usually indefinite and heavily dependent upon decisions about future financial provision and the future of the home. No decree of divorce can be made absolute if there are dependent children until the court has certified that the proposed arrangements are satisfactory or the best that can be made in the circumstances or, occasionally, that the petitioner is not able to make any arrangements. This is much less effective in practice than it sounds. Usually only the petitioner attends before the judge. All he or she can do is to ask about the arrangements and perhaps suggest improvements. The only sanction, if the arrangements are not satisfactory, is to refuse a certificate which means that the decree absolute is held up which will very rarely help the children. It can be an opportunity for helping the parent if he or she is co-operative. But if the parent is not co-operative, or is unable to improve the arrangements, the court is, in practice, powerless. It is always very difficult for judges to act effectively if only one party is before them, whatever the subject. In the final chapter we will consider ways in which these court procedures might be modified.

To sum up: the evolution of marriage as a partnership from its origins as a sacramental relationship is almost complete. The function of the court in dissolving it is now reduced to a vestigial formality which could be dispensed with, leaving it to the individuals concerned to file a formal declaration that their partnership had been ended, though we should recognize that people may continue to prefer some ritual to mark its formal ending, as they do its beginning.

In this evolution, the legal rights of the partners have been adjusted step by step until they are now, in law, approximately equal. Joint ownership of the home and equal claims on family assets after divorce are now generally accepted. This has involved drastic changes in the legal position of the husband/father. From a position of complete dominance in law, as sole guardian of the child and sole owner of the family assets, he has been reduced to equality of rights with the wife/mother. The result, given prevailing social attitudes which see the mother as the home-maker for the children, has been to put her in a much stronger position, so much so that often she seems to be (and is) the dominant partner, not only in relation to the children but also in property matters since in many cases the needs of the children absorb most of the family assets. It is not surprising that male pressure groups have come into existence to resist these changes.

These changes have made it possible for wives to contemplate (and to undertake) divorce more easily. Whereas in the past the consequences, both economic and personal, were so powerful a deterrent that to 'grin and bear it' was usually the only practical policy, wives can now take a more balanced view of their futures when the marriage relationship deteriorates and in fact the majority of divorces are now initiated by the wife (see chapter 1).

It is, therefore, facile to argue that 'making divorce easy' undermines the stability of marriage. The 'grounds' on which a divorce can be obtained do not matter so much. The divorce rate is primarily a function of the administrative facilities for obtaining a divorce. Equalization of legal rights between the partners and social support for mothers and children have made it possible for very many more empty shells of marriages to be dissolved.

In the past, the law's contribution to stability of marriage, so-called, was limited to making it difficult to get a licence to remarry. What else it could do or have done is not obvious. In general, the law operates mainly negatively in all its branches, by prohibition or putting obstacles in the way: it rarely acts positively, because its machinery for enforcing positive orders is cumbersome and expensive, though it can be ruthless – for instance, in the imprisonment of ex-husbands who refuse to pay maintenance. In family affairs, as in most of its other aspects, its function is to adjust differences and make decisions, to limit as far as it can the adverse effects of the breakdown of the partnership for all concerned.

3

ADULTS AND DIVORCE

Most people who have been divorced find that at least some of their experiences defy description. It may be the intensity of their anger, loneliness and depression, as some continue to feed off their stories of gladiatorial legal and bureaucratic confrontations for years afterwards. Others remain puzzled and confused about what originally happened to set the whole sequence of events in train. Even those who portray themselves as winners, those who have exchanged an unhappy and destructive marriage for independence or a satisfying second partnership, frequently carry with them a legacy from the past which is difficult to explain and can never be entirely forgotten.

Our attempts to piece together a descriptive overview of the experiences of divorced people have engendered many of the same feelings of inadequacy. It is not simply that it is so very difficult to communicate the range and intensity of the personal feelings involved but rather that we have been acutely aware of the dangers of generalizing in a way which obscures differences and inequalities within the divorcing population. As we have already seen in chapter 2, the social divisions in our society which separate women and men, rich and poor, manual worker and professional, also influence how they are affected by divorce. In one sense all those who are currently going through divorce, or who have been divorced, believe that they share a common experience; feeling that they are members of an exclusive club, they exchange confidences and offer reassurances. At the same time, however, conflict within marriage and the degree of privation which follows its breakdown are both reminders of profound and continuing gender and class divisions within society.

In the past, description and analysis of the causes and consequences of marriage breakdown have been one-sided because they focused almost exclusively on the commonly experienced personal and psychological elements. Unfortunately, some of the more recent attempts to redress the balance by considering divorce within a structural perspective are just as limited: for example, the carefully orchestrated campaign about the unfair treatment of (middle-class) men in recent divorce settlements that led to the passing of the Matrimonial and Family Proceedings Act 1984, now threatens to become a major theatre of warfare in the continuing battle between the sexes. While male lobbyists defend their own interests, a much broader range of pressure groups is anxious to demonstrate the extent of the deprivation experienced by women – and dependent children – within marriage as well as after its breakdown. As we will demonstrate later in this chapter, in the face of the available and very limited evidence, our position on this matter is not neutral. However, it is important to recognize that the experience of divorce is one which generates confusion, anxiety and depression, and transcends gender and class boundaries.

What follows is constructed from a wide range of descriptive and statistical sources and there are places – which we have tried to make obvious – where the pieces do not fit together very well. There are also a number of tantalizing empty spaces where we have had to admit defeat. It is interesting to note that as the Matrimonial and Family Proceedings Bill made its way through both Houses, the frequent references to what was 'known' about contemporary patterns of divorce were outnumbered by pleas for the further research-based data needed to make an informed decision on such complex matters. We hope that many of the issues raised here may stimulate further research but we are, sadly, too world weary to do more than hope that this volume may inspire someone to unzip the public purse from which such research must, almost inevitably, be funded.

Most of the discussion in chapter 1 focused on data from public registration statistics which provide very limited information about the entire population of individuals involved. By contrast, much of this chapter is based upon a number of detailed small-scale studies of specific groups, and surveys in which sampling the divorced posed such enormous methodological problems that the findings should be treated with some caution.[1]

WHERE DOES IT ALL START?

Several pieces of research have made it possible to establish some of the significant features of the journey towards divorce which starts when one or other partner – sometimes both – first becomes aware of difficulties in their marriage. Although none of these small interview samples can be regarded as representative of the divorced population, and their recollections and observations about the past are inevitably affected by later experiences, there are certain features in their accounts which are also borne out in the experience of marriage guidance counsellors and therapists.

Although we often speak of married couples as if they were one corporate personality Jessie Bernard's observation on contemporary marriage suggests otherwise: 'There is now a very considerable body of well-authenticated research to show that there are really *two marriages* – his and hers – inside every marital union and *they do not always coincide* [our emphasis]'[2]

Thus, each partner experiences their marriage differently, consciously or unconsciously valuing different aspects of the relationship and making separate decisions about the way their needs for intimacy and autonomy are balanced with their partner's. In addition, each partner's evaluation of the marriage's past history, present state of health and future prognosis is often very different. It is not surprising therefore that the partners do not necessarily begin to experience doubts and anxieties about their marriage at the same time.

Evidence from a number of different sources suggests that women are usually aware of difficulties in their marriage at an earlier stage than comparable groups of men. For example, 80 per cent of the divorced women in the Thornes and Collard sample said their marriage problems had begun before their fifth wedding anniversary, compared with 59 per cent of the divorced men.[3] This may mean that women have higher standards and grow anxious about frustrations and difficulties which do not disturb their husbands, or it may be that they sense potential sources of disappointment and conflict more readily. This finding is confirmed in several other studies: the results of surveys of readers of *Woman* magazine illustrate the importance women attach to the quality of their marriage and family relationships generally.[4] A recent survey of unemployed couples also indicates that women are more anxious than men about the practical problems of 'making ends meet' as well as the deterioration in their partnership and the atmosphere in the home.[5]

Several influential commentators on changing patterns of marriage and family life in the post-Second-World-War period have celebrated the evolution of what has been referred to as the 'symmetrical family' – a movement towards a greater degree of equality within marriage. But men's and women's investment in marriage is still very different even if some of their images and expectations of partnership have begun to converge. Marriage continues to mean more to women. Their collective dependence upon it as an institution, or within individual partnerships, is reinforced, both emotionally and materially, in almost every aspect of their 'married lives', itself a significant phrase. A number of studies may be used to support this rather controversial contention. The first is a government survey in which over 5,000 women between the ages of sixteen and fifty-nine were interviewed about their employment histories, plans for the future and attitudes towards the relationship between paid work and women's domestic and childcare responsibilities. The results undermine many significant myths about the so-called changing role of women and the emergence of the symmetrical family – not least because the age-spread of the sample enabled the authors to examine the experiences of different age cohorts. Although there has been a marked increase in the number of married women in paid employment, most of this increase is based on the wider availability of *part-time* employment opportunities for married women. Those who argue that women no longer need to choose marriage as a career in which they exchange unpaid domestic labour and childcare for their husband's economic support do so without realistic consideration of the present employment prospects for women of all ages.[6]

It is also clear from the *Women and Employment* survey that it is not simply responsibility for the care of small children which affects women's patterns of employment. Although by the end of their working life, younger women will probably have spent more years in paid employment than their older counterparts, marriage still increases their likelihood of working part time. For the majority of women the obligations of marriage still include a wide range of domestic responsibilities – including the care of elderly kin – which compete with their commitment to a career outside the home. It is also quite clear from this survey that the majority of women – and men – in Britain still retain fairly traditional views about women's paid employment.[7] Despite the folk heroines of *Cosmopolitan* and the *Guardian* women's page such beliefs remain entirely rational given the disadvantages women continue to suffer in the labour market.

These findings are matched by evidence of the perpetuation of an equally traditional division of labour within the home. While there is some evidence from this study and others that younger married couples believe they ought to share household tasks more equally, his longer hours of work, higher pay and greater commitment to a job which may, with good fortune, last throughout their marriage, all help couples to justify an exchange based on interlocking dependencies[8] which may only be fully exposed when the marriage is in difficulties.

Thus, despite ideological changes, the majority of young women still anticipate a time when they will make marriage, home and family their main career. In this they differ from their husbands who expect their home and work lives to develop alongside one another. For most men disappointment and frustration in one sphere may be compensated for in the other. However, even the small minority of women in occupations with a real career structure still seem to find it much more difficult than their male colleagues to balance work and family responsibilities.[9]

Women are often aware earlier than their husbands of potential difficulties or conflicts in their marriages because society conditions them to place a higher value on the maintenance and development of personal relationships. Not only are women expected to work harder at sustaining contacts with kin, they are also believed to be more perceptive or intuitive about people and relationships – a belief confirmed by their participation in the 'caring' occupations generally regarded as women's work. Whatever the origins of such attributes, gender stereotyping of this kind acts as a self-fulfilling prophecy. As girls grow up they develop such skills as part of feminine identity, exercising and developing them, sometimes as a matter of survival, both within and outside the family.

Among a small sample of people who sought help with marriage problems the phrase 'something being not quite right' was often used by women to describe their earliest inklings of difficulty.[10] This is not to say that men are unaware of similar feelings but that women, despite many exceptions, are more likely to linger over such anxieties, comparing their own experiences with those of other women and perhaps discussing their fears. Brannen and Collard also found that several of the couples in their study had, either separately or together, deliberately avoided any prolonged consideration of their potential difficulties by developing new projects, interests or preoccupations which would mask unwelcome signs of strain in their partnerships. Again – although there are exceptions – it is the men who generally have the greater share of the material and emotional resources necessary to adopt this strategy. Divorced men often describe having immersed themselves in work, voluntary activities or leisure in the hope that things at home would somehow improve. Ex-wives by contrast are more likely to describe themselves as having made some effort, however misguided, to be a 'better wife' in order that their partnership might survive.

Thus it is clear from studies in which divorcees were encouraged to look back at their marriage, that many were able to recall the early signs of dissatisfaction and problems which led to the end of the marriage, even if they were unaware of their significance at the time. There is a useful distinction that can be made here between an early experiencing of, and accommodating to, such difficulties and a later, quite distinct stage when they are consciously named and seen to threaten the marriage for the first time.

KEY INCIDENTS, TRANSITIONS AND CHANGES IN CIRCUMSTANCES

The accounts of those who contemplate divorce frequently contain references to key incidents or turning points after which earlier disappointments, injuries and frustrations can no longer be ignored. Such moments of truth take many forms but are frequently described in terms indicating a sudden realization that an individual's taken-for-granted view of reality has been undermined in a way that encourages a complete reconsideration of their earlier experiences.

The event itself may not necessarily be dramatic or even directly related to the marriage: a period away from home, a temporary break from everyday routines such as a conference, company training course, period in hospital or an unaccustomed weekend alone. Others speak of changes in their working lives that engendered uncertainty – promotion or unemployment, additional caring responsibilities for a relative, a sudden crisis or stressful event, an accident, a bereavement in the family or the discovery of a life-threatening illness.

The event that calls the partnership into question may also be much closer to home, posing a direct challenge to formerly unquestioned assumptions about the state of the marriage. Perhaps most obvious is the discovery by either partner that they are in love with someone else: the marriage pales into insignificance beside the delights of this new relationship. Even if there are no obvious external pressures upon them to do so, the images, rhetoric and assumptions of romantic love encourage its victims to believe that they must eventually choose between the old and new loves, and their reappraisal of their marriage takes place in this light. Their partners, by contrast, find themselves jolted into a fundamental reconsideration of the marriage by the revelation, or the apparently accidental discovery, of their spouse's infidelity. Changes in moral values probably mean that most people do not now believe that adulterous relationships should necessarily or automatically signal the end of a marriage. None the less their existence undermines tacit, taken-for-granted rules and assumptions about the partnership. Whether the injured, 'innocent' partner employs a moral rhetoric based on blame or complains of being rejected and cast aside, much of their uncertainty and confusion is focused on the way the whole of the marriage now seems called into question. It is, of course, very hard to assess how many marriages end as a direct result of one or both partners embarking on a new relationship. Among a sample of *Woman* readers, three out of ten readers had had at least one affair since they were married, including one in five of those who rated themselves as very happily married. Those who were unhappily married were more likely to have had affairs, especially if they reported long-standing sexual difficulties in their marriage. Where wives found out about their husband's infidelity, they were more likely to say that it had affected their marriage adversely. Generally, the evidence from this survey confirms our impression that, while affairs do not always or inevitably lead to the end of a marriage, they generally cause one or, if discovered, both partners to reappraise their relationship in some way.[11]

Other much less dramatic events also precipitate this process of re-evaluation. Incidents, trivial in themselves – a forgotten anniversary, a chance sarcastic remark, excessive irritation with a partner's habits or shortcomings – suddenly seem to symbolize a lifetime of anger and frustration. As one partner begins to rehearse their dismal catalogue of injuries, slights and disappointments they frequently find themselves completely at a loss to explain why they have not 'done something about it before'. As a result, the recipient of their revelations, whether friend, lover, counsellor or advisor, finds that they too are asking the question, 'What took you so long?'

In part, at least, the answer may lie in the norms of privacy which surround contemporary married life. Although there are obviously considerable variations within and between classes, neighbourhoods, and different local and occupational communities, most people have relatively few opportunities to observe other people's marriages closely. Married couples often make careful distinctions between their behaviour in private and the image they show to the outside world. As a result it is common for partners to go on believing that their life together is quite normal and tolerable until a chance discussion casts their difficulties in a different light. This often happens when new lovers begin to exchange confidences about their marriages or earlier relationships. As a result many women, and perhaps some men, continue to tolerate even violent physical abuse, partly because there may be no alternative, but also because they believe it to be an inevitable aspect of marriage. Similarly, many couples endure the frustrations of an unsatisfactory or non-existent sexual relationship because they have no real basis for comparison. Despite the alleged openness implicit in phrases like 'the permissive society', it is still common for spouses to regard their own or each other's sexual difficulties as normal and inevitable until experience with another partner or perceptive questioning by a doctor about a related medical problem brings the issue out into the open for the first time.

BOREDOM AND GROWING APART

Infidelity, violence and sexual difficulties, even relentless nagging or studied rejection and indifference: all these are forms of marital behaviour that are generally regarded as potential threats to a partnership. There is probably much less agreement, however, about the degree to which such behaviour should be tolerated before steps are taken to end the marriage. For some, the events concerned are much less dramatic and cannot easily be equated with any of the legal 'facts' necessary to demonstrate that their marriage has broken down irretrievably. Such couples often describe a gradual realization that they have grown apart, that once the goals and preoccupations of early married life – making a home, having children – were over, they had little in common. In retrospect their reasons for getting married in the first place now seem insubstantial: their friends were all getting married, they wanted to leave home and their chosen partner was simply the person they were dating at the time.

Others, especially those from relatively long-lasting partnerships, emphasize the way changes in their working lives opened up deep divisions between them. There is as yet very little systematic evidence about the ways in which the working lives of men and women affect their marriages or *vice versa* but Haskey's recent study of the class and socio-economic status of a sample of men divorcing in 1979 pinpoints a number of particularly divorce-prone occupations (see pp. 34–6 and 156–7). In considering such occupations, it is also important to ask how the problems posed by particular occupational lifestyles and working conditions affect *both* partners. If we adopt this approach, the critical, but largely unanswered, questions include discovering how this potential source of stress affected each partner at different stages in their marriage *and* working career;[12] the framework of values used to justify the husband's (or less frequently, wife's) high level of commitment to work; the wife's access to alternative sources of support during her partner's absences; the changing effects of her own experiences of paid employment during her life and the sources and content of the beliefs and values about what constitutes a good marriage against which wives and husbands evaluate their own partnerships. There can be little doubt that wives who have learnt to accommodate to the demands of their husband's work schedule or time-consuming voluntary or leisure activities by making home and family their own particular domain often feel cheated of a satisfactory marriage judged in terms of contemporary ideals of togetherness and close companionship. Their reluctant acceptance of its inevitability is often undermined when some change in their lives alters their perceptions of their partnership and perhaps of their expectations of marriage more generally.[13]

Change of this kind is most likely to be set in motion by their own return to paid work as their children become more independent. Although married women display a wide range of patterns of employment during and after the years of child-rearing, 90 per cent of the mothers in the *Women and Employment* survey who had children then over the age of sixteen had worked either full or part time since the birth of their children. The survey also showed that the more highly qualified a woman is, the sooner she is likely to return to work after the birth of her children and that younger generations of women have tended to return more quickly than their older counterparts. Several of the women in the Sheffield remarriage study described how returning to work had made them question the durability of their own first marriages. A measure of financial independence was matched by a growth in confidence and a broadening of their horizons. Even if they did not consciously admit to looking for a potential new partner, their work often brought them into daily contact with men against whom they now began to judge their husbands in a less than favourable light. Work itself offered new challenges and enhanced their self-image. Although it is now common for husbands and others to propose 'a little job' as a potential solution to the problems of depression and social isolation that so often beset housewives, they are often ill-prepared for the transformation that follows.

It seems likely then, that some of the changes in both husbands' *and* wives' working lives (promotions, job changes, retraining, unemployment and prevailing constraints on women's job choices) may also act as 'trigger' incidents and events as we have described. Most, perhaps all, marriages are vulnerable to a potentially threatening redefinition made by one or both partners at some time or another. If this is so, the unanswered question could equally well be posed in rather less familiar terms: why do so *few* marriages end in divorce? This is a question to which we return in the final chapter.

GOING PUBLIC AND THE SEARCH FOR OUTSIDE HELP

Evidence from personal accounts suggests that even when difficulties are openly acknowledged between partners, they are not necessarily disclosed to anyone else until either one or both is ready to go public. Many different factors are involved in this decision which is often linked with the explanation to be used when the news is finally broken. For example, in some middle-class neighbourhoods and working communities, conventional divorce behaviour now entails a jointly negotiated parting by mutual consent so that regardless of the reasons articulated in private, the partners wait until their arrangements have been made and then present their agreed version of events to friends and family, including their children. Indeed, this carefully orchestrated account may be so 'civilized' that parents who have survived an era of bitterly contested divorces, often find their children's behaviour incomprehensible and are angry because their advice and support was not sought at an earlier stage.

Others who are trying to evaluate the significance of their present feelings or their partner's misdemeanours seek help and advice from others. Beliefs about the private nature of married life and the importance of loyalty to one's partner mean that this is, in itself, a highly significant step. Although some research indicates that most people prefer to seek help first from friends or family rather than professionals, Brannen and Collard found that their informants were rather more likely to turn to members of their social network *after* rather than in the midst of marriage crises and there are obvious reasons why this might be so. Potential loss of face, fears that disclosures will be passed on or that their chosen confidant might take sides mean that relative strangers or professional advisors are preferred. When the implied question is, 'Should I have to go on putting up with this?' or 'I don't think I love her/him any more: must I stay?' the advice of professionals – general practicioners (G.P.s) or *family* doctors, as they are called; lawyers with their expertise in the interpretation of divorce law or those who offer 'marriage guidance' – has obvious attractions, especially to those able to designate themselves as in the right. Unfortunately, expectations of the quality of help from professionals are not easily fulfilled. There are indications that while patients would like to discuss a range of personal and, in the narrow sense, non-medical problems with their G.P.s, few do so. The desire to talk about marriage problems is generally hidden behind questions about some specific symptom and it is often difficult for the patient to change the subject in a consultation whose content and duration are normally managed and controlled by the doctor. Although symptoms associated with sexual difficulties are more likely to lead to discussion of the patient's marriage, G.P.s do not necessarily feel either equipped or obliged to deal directly with such confidences and may see their role simply in terms of referring patients to a more specialized source of help, or, less helpfully, to send them away with a prescription for tranquillizers or antidepressants.

People who already have contact with a social-work agency and have found their support useful in the past may return for help with marriage difficulties, but they rarely request help with marital problems directly so that these only come to light during treatment for something else.

If those who seek help from their G.P.s or social workers are uncertain that they are qualified to advise on marital problems, solicitors and the marriage-counselling agencies seem better equipped as the purpose of the consultation can be shared at the outset. However, there is some evidence of potential sources of misunderstanding in the latter two groups of advisors. If 'going to a solicitor' is used as a challenge, threat or means of breaking the stalemate in a long-running period of marital conflict and uncertainty, the client may be expecting the advisor to tell them what to do in a much deeper sense than simply outlining the legal procedures involved in divorce. If this is so they are likely to be very alarmed when their solicitor simply sets in motion the formal divorce procedures.

Marriage-counselling agencies are only consulted by a relatively small proportion – perhaps less than 5 per cent – of couples with serious marital problems and some studies suggest that many of those who do are dissatisfied with the counselling they receive. It is important to recognize, however, that this does not necessarily indicate that the agencies are failing as their clients will tend to evaluate their treatment in the light of their own, often unrealistic expectations of counselling. The passive recipient of one partner's decision to end a marriage may be especially likely to consult an agency in a vain attempt to prevent the marriage from breaking up irrevocably. Similarly, there is evidence that because of the name itself some clients expect their marriage guidance counsellors to provide clear, unequivocal and highly directive advice by telling them what to do to save their marriage.[14] In both instances they are most unlikely to see their experiences in a favourable light if their marriages do eventually end in divorce.

It is significant that despite the efforts of professional advisors to act professionally and impartially, and committed as they are to non-directive counselling, divorced people often portray themselves as having acted merely on the advice of, or following instructions from their doctor, solicitor or social worker when they take steps to end their marriage. Several women in the Sheffield remarriage study who had endured prolonged physical violence at the hands of their husbands or who had suffered greatly because of their partners' continued infidelities or unpredictable behaviour appeared to have been so undermined by these experiences that even chance remarks about 'not needing to put up with this' were seen as permission and a means of escape. Each subsequent move was described in terms of what their valued confidant *told* them to do. These examples have obvious parallels with the experiences of victims of marital violence who, once they have gone public, are exposed to a range of advice from agencies of one sort or another.

There are a number of background factors affecting whether – and if so, which – available sources of professional help are used by those with marriage problems. As well as obvious gender and class differences in consulting patterns, perceptions of the nature of the problems and an individual's own role as 'guilty partner' or 'innocent victim' also affect the choice of a confidant or advisor. There are also likely to be clear differences between those who, still genuinely confused about what has happened, are seeking an opportunity to discuss their problems openly and at length with an impartial listener and those who have already come to some understanding about what is happening and are thus in need of practical support and advice.

DIVORCE AS A SEQUENCE OF INTERRELATED PERSONAL AND SOCIAL TRANSITIONS

One reason why it may be difficult to know how to respond when someone speaks of 'getting divorced' is that the phrase is used as a shorthand for the entire process which begins with the first realization of difficulty and public disclosure of crisis, only ending when the legal procedures are complete. The remainder of the chapter is concerned with divorce as a legal, economic, social and emotional transition. Paradoxically, it can be helpful to consider the parallel transitions and status passages made *into* marriage in order to understand more about what is involved in leaving it. We should remind ourselves that the divorced status is only a temporary resting-place for those already planning to remarry: although unable to do so until their divorce is finalized, in economic, social and personal terms the second partnership is an established reality. Many of our observations on specific aspects of each transitional stage shed some light, albeit obliquely, on the difficulties peculiar to those who attempt an apparently unbroken passage from one couple relationship to another.

Divorce as a legal transition

Although divorce is the change in legal status which marks the official end of a marriage partnership, its timing and significance within a much broader sequence of events varies greatly. For some, the divorce itself matters very little as the partners have already been separated for a number of years; a legal dissolution is eventually sought only because one or other partner wishes to remarry or 'tie up the loose ends' such as custody orders or maintenance. In this case the receipt of the decree absolute is unlikely to have any great emotional or social significance.

On the other hand, if formal divorce proceedings are completed within a short time of actual breakdown, their impact is likely to be greater. As we have already seen, some marriages end very suddenly, especially when there is a third party involved; in these circumstances one partner may be trying to press ahead with the legalities that will confirm decisions already made even though the other partner has not yet accepted that the marriage is about to end.

Although getting divorced encompasses many personal and social changes, most people realize that they will need legal advice and direction at an early stage. Some people are already clients of a solicitor who has acted for them before, thus having someone to turn to for general legal advice before specific strategies or details are considered, but Citizens Advice Bureaux (C.A.B.) or Legal Advice Centres are more likely to be the first point of contact for those – chiefly working-class men and women – who do not yet have their 'own' solicitor. Among Murch's sample of divorcees, the most popular means of choosing a solicitor was personal recommendation by friends. He also found that fewer than 20 per cent of the wives in his study had had any contact with a solicitor before their divorce and that they were more likely to ask C.A.B. advisors or social workers to recommend one. This study, among others, also illustrates how solicitors are used as a means of making sense of marriage problems and their legal and economic ramifications. For the individual who is considering separation or divorce as a solution to matrimonial problems, or who is the passive recipient of a partner's decision to end their marriage, the problems are experienced most directly in emotional, social and economic terms but these must be reinterpreted and restructured to fit the legal categorizations and remedies provided by the divorce procedures. As Murch suggests, solicitors often help their divorcing clients to negotiate the entire journey from initial marital problems to remarriage some years later. As a result, they become powerful figures in their clients' lives and an important source of support and continuity.[15] Thus, the divorcing client who is concerned about the grounds that will be attached to their divorce, about how long it will take and when they or their partner will be free to remarry, who will look after the children, live in the house, and how much money they will have, must rely on their solicitor's explanation and interpretation of the law and procedures of divorce. It is clear from the Sheffield remarriage study that even middle-class and professional divorcees frequently describe the legal decisions taken at the time of their divorce with uncharacteristic powerlessness and passivity.[16] In part this may be because being newly remarried they were trying to forget the events of the past, but it was clear that the legal side of divorce was portrayed as a business for experts frequently beyond the understanding and control of individuals involved. Several spoke of positive elements in such legal management, especially where solicitors were able to arrange a rapid divorce by choosing grounds of adultery or behaviour rather than separation by consent.[17]

Given the power that solicitors wield in this area both indirectly (by helping their clients to make sense of their experiences) and through direct guidance and advice, it would be helpful to know more about their own underlying assumptions about the processes of divorce. As Mnookin has suggested in a perceptive phrase, much of their behind-the-scenes negotiation with other solicitors may be aptly characterized as 'bargaining within the shadow of the law' so that their advice and eventual decisions depend on an assessment of what might happen if the dispute were heard in court. This, in turn, rests on their own, inevitably selective, perceptions of the usual assumptions made about property, maintenance, custody and access in relation to divorce. Some recent evidence from a study by Smart on solicitors' perceptions and assumptions suggests that, although most solicitors show a professional appreciation of the poverty experienced by lone mothers and the plight of divorced women, their personal sympathies more often lay with husbands who were portrayed as losing children and home but were still required to make provision for them. This was also generally true of the female solicitors interviewed.[18]

The solicitors in Smart's study also held solidly conventional views about custody and the best interests of children, even though most had acted for at least one father who was claiming custody. Their arguments were based on conventional wisdom about gender-based divisions of labour and the assumption that wives and mothers do not generally have the same earning power as husbands. By the same token it would seem unlikely that such solicitors would consider the possibility of joint custody (see chapter 5) unless this possibility was raised specifically by the clients themselves.

Although limited, most of the research-based data suggests a relatively high level of satisfaction with the way solicitors deal with divorce, although where dissatisfaction occurs it is often expressed in extreme terms. For example, a small majority of Murch's sample found their solicitors friendly and supportive and 60 per cent were satisfied with the service they had received. However, those questioned were unable to judge professional competence as a fellow lawyer would, so that their views were usually based on personal qualities and skills.

These findings are echoed in other studies, which also emphasize that divorcing clients need to feel that their solicitor is really interested in their case and is partisan on their behalf.[19] Although some of Murch's informants criticized their advisors' adversarial stance, especially if their actions went against the client's own desire to minimize potential disputes or if it led to battles in open court, Murch also suggests that the traditionally partisan stance of solicitors sometimes increases their acceptability as listeners and counsellors: 'There comes a point in emotional conflict when people feel so wounded, threatened or frightened, sometimes by the strength of their own anger, that escape and dependence on partisan support are all that are acceptable.' However, although there may be advantages in this kind of identification as a means of building a relationship between clients and advisors, such vulnerability and dependence make it difficult for the client to appraise and agree to decisions whose consequences will last long after the divorce itself has been finalized.

Thus, the personal and social significance of the legal transition that gives divorced people 'their freedom', as it is so often put, lies not so much in the divorce itself, symbolized by the decree absolute, as in the resolution of disputes about so-called 'ancillary matters', which are more closely related to the economic and social aspects of divorce.

The economic transition

Often, it is only when a marriage is under threat that the economic and material exchanges on which the partnership is based are fully exposed. From the first signs of disengagement and conflict to its final resolution, the journey towards separation and economic autonomy is punctuated by incidents and changes in behaviour, trivial in themselves but each signifying a measure of departure from the customary patterns of economic support and exchange on which the partnership was built. When, for example, a wife organizes her domestic timetable so that she rarely sits down to eat a meal with her husband; when she hoards her earnings or domestic savings in a secret running-away account; when a husband begins to reorganize his finances in a way which will minimize future maintenance obligations, or channels his surplus cash away from his family, both may be taking the first steps towards *economic* autonomy long before divorce has been consciously considered.

The clearest and most dramatic step in the process takes place when the couple stop living together under the same roof and thus sharing everyday domestic expenses. Although some, perhaps most, divorced partners can point to a particular day on which one or other partner moved out or when both moved into new accommodation, this does not necessarily coincide with establishing entirely separate, autonomous finances. In addition to obvious and continuing transfers of money through maintenance payments, usually but not always, from husband to wife, the final division of domestic and household goods may not be completed until much later. Those who have been able to divide their possessions amicably may continue to exchange and transfer objects from one household to another as their circumstances change – a woman who subsequently sets up home with a man who already owns a colour T.V. may hand 'hers' over to her ex-husband who has been making do with a black-and-white portable. By contrast, those couples who remain imprisoned by the conflicts that eventually brought their partnership to an end frequently continue to draw their respective solicitors into formal disputes about every last lampshade and curtain rail.

Potential sources of folk wisdom or 'expert' advice about the economic aspects of separation are many and varied but it is probably still true that most public images and stereotypes of the process emphasize hostility and conflict rather than compromise and co-operation. It is not surprising that separating partners, besieged by change and uncertainty at every turn, often express fears about whether they will be able to manage on their own. They fight to retain the material supports of their former life and, if possible, for the kind of financial arrangements that will enable them to start again without a drastic reduction in their accustomed standard of domestic comfort. The more there is at stake financially, the greater the use made of expert advisors, particularly lawyers and accountants.

While the dependent partner – usually but not always the wife – relies on her solicitor to ensure that she gets what she is entitled to, the solicitors in Smart's study found that they often had to explain to divorcing husbands that they would – in a telling phrase – 'be caught' for maintenance and that the solicitor's task was one of damage limitation.

As Smart's findings illustrate very well, current divorce law and procedures tend to translate continuing domestic conflicts into disputes over maintenance; the survey showed that most solicitors' letters were exchanged about maintenance arrangements and that they generated the greatest acrimony. As a result, even after the dust has settled and some have established new partnerships, most divorced people are objectively worse off than before or certainly continue to feel as if they are, thus providing a ready source for continuing conflict.

The ongoing public debate about maintenance, to which we refer again in chapter 5, is fuelled predictably by the experiences, subjective impressions and partial observations of the various participants. The fact that wives and husbands so often *both* feel that they have been the greater losers materially, as well as in other ways, illustrates an obvious truth of daily economic life: that the breadwinner(s) family wage, whether earned by one or both partners, does not go as far once it is split between two households, a reversal of the cliché that two can live as cheaply as one. This is also true of other indirect economic resources, particularly the informal, unpaid labour necessary to run a home and bring up children. Even when such work has been very unevenly distributed, and has itself been a cause of conflict within the marriage, the overworked partner – again usually but not inevitably the woman – may be surprised at how much her partner's contribution is missed when they split up. Even 'being there' as an occasional, passive childminder now becomes a service which must be paid for in cash or in kind.

As yet, we lack the kind of research-based evidence necessary to test the contradictory claims of opposing lobbies and pressure groups campaigning about the effects of maintenance. It is especially regrettable that an issue of such significance remains so woefully under-researched. However, as our discussion below of the work patterns of divorced people demonstrates, the cumulative effects of

the educational disadvantages and continuing inequalities experienced by women in a contracting labour market demonstrate all too
clearly that, despite well-publicized exceptions (the so-called hard
cases) severe economic deprivation is an inevitable result of divorce
for the majority of women with custody of dependent children. For
example, less than half of the separated and divorced women in the
Women and Employment survey included maintenance among their
current sources of income.[20] As Smart indicates, even when maintenance orders were paid regularly and in full, they were generally at
or below D.H.S.S. minimum subsistence levels and considerably
below estimates provided by the National Foster Care Association
of the real costs of caring for children. Even when realistic maintenance levels are agreed at the time of separation they do not
necessarily offer any guarantee of continuing economic security as
they may not be paid regularly because of changes in the ex-
husband's circumstances. Within a short time of separation he may
acquire a second family himself, his earnings may diminish or he
may lose his job altogether. An increasing proportion of the work
undertaken by magistrates sitting in the domestic court is now concerned with applications for variations in maintenance orders. Smart
found that many of these applications made by divorced women in
receipt of maintenance, were instigated by the D.H.S.S. in an attempt
to reduce the amount of supplementary benefit paid to such families.

The extent and degree of poverty experienced by lone parent
households, the complexity and confusion surrounding their potential sources of income and the uneasy tension between public and
private law in this area require urgent attention and reform; we
return to this subject in the final chapter.

Despite the widespread belief that remarriage will provide a solution to these and other related problems, the reality is much more
complicated. As divorce and remarriage rates have risen in the last
decade, an increasing number of household budgets is now directly
affected by transfers of income which symbolize continuing economic obligations and dependencies from earlier partnerships. Paradoxically, while solicitors, magistrates and others may encourage
wives, and especially mothers, to consider marrying again in order
to recreate a 'normal' family life for themselves and their children –
sometimes even offering advice to divorced men about ways of

enhancing their ex-wives' remarriage prospects – many middle-class divorced husbands who are paying substantial maintenance are warned against doing so themselves unless they can find a partner of independent means with no apparent desire to have children herself. Although spinsters and bachelors without children or prior economic responsibilities from earlier partnerships might seem ideal second partners from an economic stance, such pairings sometimes pose other problems (see pp. 117–20). We return also to the issues surrounding the competing obligations and needs of first and second families in the final chapter.

So far, we have discussed the economic transitions which accompany separation and divorce without direct reference to the principal source of income for most family households, i.e. the paid employment of one or both partners. Traditionally, we tend to regard 'work', in the sense of paid employment, and 'family life' as entirely separate, distinctive and autonomous areas of life so that researchers and commentators have paid little attention to the connections and overlaps between the two. However, just as some divorced people explain the failure of their marriage by referring to their own or their partner's career demands or even, conversely, their unwillingness to support the family, separation itself is likely to generate changes in job-related behaviour.

For the majority of parents, both women and men, custody of children, though treated in court as an ancillary matter, still symbolizes a transfer of a responsibility formerly *shared* to one or other *alone*: managing, with all that this phrase implies, becomes the direct daily concern of only one, the formally designated custodial parent. This sense of responsibility, underlined by dire financial necessity, frequently drives mothers back into the labour market in the months following separation. However, although roughly the same proportion of divorced mothers work in paid employment as of mothers generally, they are much more likely to be working full time than their still-married counterparts even when their children are under school age. Furthermore, as the *Women and Employment* survey indicates, they are likely to be working for different reasons, i.e. because they need money for basic essentials such as food, rent or mortgage. It is also clear from this survey that they are more likely than still-married mothers to be suffering financial stress at home and also higher levels of psychological stress at work.[21]

For lone fathers who have custody of children after divorce the problems of combining their work, domestic and childcare responsibilities are experienced somewhat differently. While lone mothers are generally expected to cope on their own despite reduced financial circumstances, custodial fathers generally receive more formal and informal help with childcare in the months immediately following separation. It is partly for this reason that they are more likely to be in full-time employment.[22] However, it is usually offered in the expectation that they will eventually employ or, even better, marry a suitable woman to look after the children so that the fathers can resume their roles and responsibilities as workers unencumbered by the distractions of childcare.

As we have seen, becoming a lone parent after divorce affects the working lives of divorced parents – whether mothers or fathers – in specific ways but the work behaviour of divorced people generally may also be affected by the economic transitions which accompany separation. Most obviously, returning to paid work, either part- or full-time, after time spent at home bringing up children may for some women mark the first step on the road to separation. Other women plan their return to work or embark on further occupational training as a way of gaining the economic independence they will need to leave their husbands. Husbands – and sometimes wives – in established careers may find themselves taking up a new job some distance away as a kind of trial separation until definite decisions are made. Many men, and also women, rely on their work and the demands of 'the office' as a temporary refuge and haven from domestic storm and stress. If this has been an effective escape mechanism in the past, it may well provide a lifeline in the first chaotic months of separation. If, on the other hand, a man sees his work simply as a means of supporting his family, his commitment to it will diminish once he loses his former place within the family circle. Many men from all walks of life leave their jobs or demote themselves by taking a less demanding post following separation, especially if they were the passive recipients of their ex-partner's decision to end their marriage. It is also likely that the loss of personal self-esteem experienced by some divorced people affects their performance at work in a way which they regard as damaging to their long-term career prospects. In this respect, changes in work behaviour and economic circumstances are closely linked with the other social and emotional transitions that are part of getting divorced.

The social transition

Many of the complexities and uncertainties engendered by becoming single again, albeit temporarily, are illuminated by comparing the experience with its obverse – getting married in the first place.

For those marrying for the first time, the process of becoming a socially recognized couple is marked by a series of informal but commonly understood stages. Although these may differ according to region, neighbourhood or class, to be known to be 'going steady', 'thinking of marriage', celebrating a formal engagement as well as the wedding itself provide partners with confirmation of the public character of their relationship, at first among friends and family and then more widely. Two significant and interrelated changes are involved: from being on your own to being part of a couple, and from being single to being legally married.

Although the cumulative effects of the rise in the divorce rate since the 1960s mean that most families, neighbourhoods and workplaces now contain many more adults who have been divorced at some time in their lives, informal social customs or even names for kin have not evolved accordingly. As a result the inevitable personal pain and loss when a marriage ends are still all too frequently compounded by embarrassment and confusion about everyday social encounters with family, friends and acquaintances. Moreover, despite prevailing mythologies about 'divorce-crazy Britain' which convey the impression that there is no longer any shame or social disapproval attached to being divorced, the experiences of those who have been directly involved suggest that, for a minority at least, the ambiguities and conflicts endemic to this change in roles and identity continue to blight their lives for many years afterwards.[23] Such difficulties have their origins in the process of becoming un-, or more accurately, demarried. Although family and friends play an important part in this process there are few social conventions and little established etiquette to guide them in their dealings with a formerly married couple who now present themselves as two separate, often hostile, individuals. Furthermore, the everyday dynamics of most established family groups or networks of friends and neighbours often provide ready sources of potential conflict so that individuals are easily led into taking sides, thus confirming many of the public stereotypes of separating partners locked in perpetual conflict. Such images are reinforced in media coverage of the separations of public figures and reports of contested divorce litigation as well as being a facet of the procedures themselves. Many of the disruptions in relationships are relatively short-lived but others cause permanent rifts or petrify into prolonged family feuds which may, for example, be the reason why one set of grandparents lose contact with their grandchildren, or why kinsfolk who were once close now cross the street to avoid one another. It is therefore not surprising that many newly separated people describe changes involving some loss of contact in their relationships with family and friends. There is some evidence that men suffer more than women in this. For example, women with custody of children are more likely to keep in contact with their in-laws because of grandparental ties, while there is less reason for continued contact between a man and his in-laws. More generally, women tend to devote more energy than their husbands to maintaining friendship and kinship ties within marriage – it is they who normally take responsibility for remembering family birthdays, arranging social engagements and so on. The husband, especially if it is he who leaves their former joint home, frequently has less experience and fewer resources with which to rebuild social networks. (Custody of the family address book, if there is one, provides a small, but significant symbol of this difference.)

Where divorced women or men withdraw from former friends, or find themselves excluded from family and social gatherings, making new friends is likely to be an important part of their attempt to build a new life for themselves. Again, it seems likely that in general men find this harder: one study suggests that it was colleagues at work who were their greatest source of advice and support at the time of separation.[24] Work is also valued as a source of friendship for women but mothers build up friendships round their domestic life and childcare. Where informal means of making new social contacts fail and they find themselves becoming increasingly isolated, divorcees of both sexes often turn to what might be termed 'victim support' groups; the local branch of Campaign for Justice in Divorce, Families Need Fathers, Gingerbread, and other one-parent-family groups, as well as to the plethora of clubs for the divorced and separated that have sprung up in most towns and cities over the last decade. Although these groups are an important source of immediate practical help and support, prolonged attachment to an organization whose name, objects and preoccupations tend to reinforce this one salient and painful element of identity may prevent some especially bruised and embittered victims of divorce from making a fresh start based on real acceptance of being on their own once more.

Those who take positive steps to end their marriage because they have met someone new do not, of course, face these problems, but the results of their attempts to make an unbroken passage from one partnership to the next suggest that this transition is not without its own complications.

Although social conventions and the public moralities which underpin them have shifted in response to the rising divorce rate of the last two decades, in most social circles those who appear to leave one partner for another still experience strong social disapproval. This may be partly because their decision offers public evidence that infidelity is more common than most of us – especially the married – care to admit, and also because it demonstrates an unwillingness or failure to make their marriage work. This feeling occurs frequently in the accounts of those who admit to marriage difficulties, and short-lived periods of reconciliation are often viewed as evidence of a formal attempt to make it work – or perhaps more realistically to demonstrate that it will not. Social encounters with family and friends may become awkward and confusing as they attempt simultaneously to delete 'Mary and John' from their consciousness and replace them with 'Mary and Alan'. These uncertainties are also shared by the individuals involved: although committed to a public face which demonstrates the wisdom of their decision and their delight and contentment in their new partnership, the private reality may be somewhat different. For the partner in transit – one or both – daily domestic life, as well as the legal and financial decisions which must be made, provides constant reminders of a past identity which undermine their attempts to become the new person – i.e. half of the Mary and Alan couple – to which their behaviour in public bears testimony. If the new partner does not share the same experience, they may be disappointed by signs of ambivalence which appear to undermine their stability as a couple. By the same token, the circumstances in which they met, fell in love and set up home together rarely allow them to affirm their commitment publicly in the same way as first-married couples. It is for this reason that so many of such couples wish to be married as soon as possible; they wait anxiously for the completion of the divorce proceedings which will provide them with an opportunity to make the formal public declaration that they hope will dispel the ambiguities surrounding their status as a couple.

This social transition also includes coming to terms with the effects of losing the status attached to being a married person. In societies such as our own, to be married is a sign of adulthood and respectability affecting women and men in rather different ways. Once a man is married he is expected to settle down in preparation for his future family responsibilities. For example, it is widely assumed by employers and personnel managers that married men are more reliable members of the workforce because of their family commitments.[25] For a man to be legally separated or divorced seems to betoken some regression from adulthood, as evidenced by the public stereotypes attached to carefree male divorcees and is confirmed by the fact that younger men often return to live with their parents for a time after their marriage ends. Another symbol of the social evaluation attached to the divorced status, also shared by women, is the lower credit rating customarily given to separated and divorced people by hire purchase companies.

As we have already suggested, most women still regard marriage as their main career and source of identity. The symbolism of the marriage service, for example, remains a powerful indication of the way women are still expected to pass from the support and control of one man to another. As a result the stereotypes attached to divorced women embody both anxiety about her wellbeing – the beleaguered lone parent – and fears about her now awoken but uncontrolled sexuality. Studies of divorced women suggest that their everyday relationships are often complicated by unwanted sexual advances from men who find it convenient to believe that divorced women are 'fair game', and the latent hostility of married female acquaintances, who fear that their husbands may be led astray. Although such incidents are of themselves unlikely to propel women into a second marriage, they illustrate some of the subtle institutional pressures placed on women to remarry after divorce in order to regain the protection and respectability conferred by being married.

The emotional transition

When individuals speak of the way their own separation, divorce and, perhaps, remarriage has affected them they draw upon events, changes and experiences which may be spread out over several years and whose consequences persist for many more.[26] It is not surprising that as a critical life event and source of physical and psychological stress divorce is second only to losing a partner through death.

The task of separating emotionally from a former partner lies at the heart of this transition and it is clear from the accounts of divorced people that the stages by which this inner journey is negotiated do not necessarily correspond to the pattern of external changes in their domestic and personal lives. Like the other transitions discussed above, the process of emotional separation is greatly affected by the circumstances in which the marriage ended and, in particular, the individual's understanding and portrayal of her/his own role as either initiator or recipient of a partner's unilateral decisions to end the partnership.[27] For the partner who takes the initiative by leaving home or by announcing their intention to do so, the period of indecision beforehand is likely to cause the greatest stress, especially if they are at the centre of a triangular relationship and wish to make an unbroken passage from one to the other. As we have already seen, it is not unusual for those who decide to leave home in pursuit of a new partnership to find that they become marooned in a kind of no-man's-land. Their journeyings between the old and new loves, from one home to another, symbolize much deeper uncertainties and ambivalence which they seem unable to resolve. Others who summon up the courage to leave violent, diminishing, or otherwise empty marriages after many years of suffering find it very hard to understand the sense of loss they experience when they finally separate. Although they have come to regard their marriages as intolerable, and find that no longer having to live together is a welcome relief, to their surprise they find themselves 'missing' their partners. They little realize that they must now peel themselves free of a relationship which has permeated their daily lives and aroused their strongest feelings of love and hate over a prolonged period, sometimes encompassing the whole of their adult life so far.

In such circumstances those who have deliberately and consciously planned to end their marriage may be unprepared for the intensity of their emotional reactions when the end finally comes. They are at a loss to understand their continuing sense of attachment to their partner. Many separating partners describe their surprise at discovering that they want and, if circumstances allow, continue to have a sexual relationship with their ex-partners for some time after separation. They are prone too to periods of anger and self-blame that they have put up with their deteriorating relationship for so long and thus, as they see it, wasted so much of their lives. Such feelings may be overlaid by a sense of failure about the end of the marriage: despite current divorce levels, lifelong marriage remains a significant ideal for many and is the standard against which people often judge their own broken partnerships.

Those who do not take the decision to end their marriage often find that its end comes swiftly and sometimes entirely unexpectedly. In such circumstances their immediate emotional response may be similar to those who lose their partner through death. The news itself and their partner's abrupt departure strike a blow rendering them temporarily unable to cope with everyday life. As the intensity of their shock and grief subsides, unlike their bereaved counterparts they must come to terms with the way their partner's continued existence provides constant reminders of the calculated rejection the departure implies. Although denial, a refusal to believe and accept what had happened, is a common immediate response to such a shock, not only may deserted spouses remain imprisoned by such feelings for considerable periods of time but their intensity may prevent them from taking any of the necessary practical steps to deal with the legal, economic or personal consequences of the events which have taken place. Once such feelings have become entrenched it is also difficult for the victims, as they often describe themselves, to work through any of the later stages of grieving, severing the bonds of attachment, making sense of the past, or affirming their own identity as a single individual.

Others who separate more slowly and with less apparent acrimony may also find it difficult to express strong feelings, including anger, guilt and a sense of loss for rather different reasons. If the consciously articulated reason for parting is that the partners have grown apart and that no love remains between them, the expression of strong feelings of loss would undermine their carefully constructed account. If they are committed to a 'civilized' parting which will give least possible pain to their friends, family and, especially, their children, they are unlikely to admit to the strong emotions the final separation may arouse. However, where such feelings persist and individuals remain marooned in the insecurities and internal conflicts generated by a broken marriage, it is often very difficult for them to move on psychologically. As a result, their attempts to make a fresh start are constantly frustrated as they hang on to past conflicts which are most easily expressed in continuing legal battles with ex-partners over access or maintenance and which also cast their shadow over new partnerships.

Despite media coverage of the amicable, civilized partings of public figures such as Princess Margaret, only a minority of couples actually describe their separation as one of mutual consent. Those who do tend to be older and are more likely to be middle class. Where the decision to part is reached slowly it is more likely to be accompanied by the kind of rows and heated arguments which, though painful at the time, allow the expression of strong feelings and provide a source of conflict resolution through reaching some sort of shared understanding and agreement about what went wrong.

The sequences of events and the accompanying emotional transitions we have described are very often characterized by sudden, apparently unpremeditated decisions and changes of plan, and great emotional volatility. It is common for couples to split up, embark on new relationships, even for one partner to set up home with someone else and then return home for a period of temporary reconciliation. When this happens their inevitable feelings of confusion are often compounded by a strong sense of powerlessness: the circumstances of their lives seem out of control, and they are driven by intense and uncontrollable feelings of anger, love and hate. Any awareness of how this may be affecting their children, far from helping them to take control once again, may initially exacerbate their sense of inadequacy and guilt.

Whenever individuals face a sudden or far-reaching change in their lives, the search for meaning is an important way of reconstructing their identity or self-image, making sense of the past, and providing a foundation for starting again. For separating couples the structure and rhetoric of the divorce procedures themselves provide an obvious framework of explanation. Although guilt and innocence no longer form part of official legal rhetoric, they are still widely used by divorced people themselves, especially when the respondent's adultery, unreasonable behaviour or desertion is used as grounds in the divorce petition itself. The rhetoric of blame is still powerful, so that all the pain, loss, insecurity and uncertainty which follow the end of marriage are crystallized either into guilt and self-blame or anger and blaming one's partner. This is one of the reasons why in chapter 5 we suggest reforms in divorce procedure. A procedure based on the dissolution of a domestic partnership would help to eliminate the aspects of procedure and terminology which perpetuate notions of legal guilt and innocence.

Most people who live through separation and divorce find that their physical or psychological health was affected at some stage between their first recognition of marriage difficulties and the time when they felt they had got over it. There are, however, important differences between those whose periods of physical illness or psychological stress are temporary, being closely linked to changes and transitions in their lives, and those for whom divorce leaves permanent scars.

Firstly there is some evidence that those who characterize themselves as the initiators of their separation experience most ill-health at the time of indecision before they take definite steps to end their marriage; for them the actual separation may bring relief from symptoms. By contrast, those who are the passive recipients of a partner's decision to leave home may 'fall apart' at the unwelcome news and then experience several months of depression and generally poor health as they struggle to pick up the pieces and make a fresh start.[28]

Most of the available research evidence indicates that more women than men consult their G.P. with related health problems at the time of separation or divorce, but this finding should be interpreted in the light of gender differences in health and consulting behaviour generally. For example, many of those women who eventually separate will have already consulted their G.P. because of periods of depression or anxiety and are much more likely to regard their G.P., or more accurately, the prescriptions for tranquillizers or antidepressants provided, as a source of support. Men are less likely to consult a G.P. unless their symptoms become particularly severe and affect their capacity to work. They are more likely to do so if persuaded by someone close to them, a new partner or other member of their family.

Marriage difficulties, separation and divorce also engender an increased dependence on alcohol in many people. It acts as a source of comfort, a means of dulling the pain or bolstering confidence. Although there is little reliable evidence, men are generally more likely to use alcohol in this way, partly because they are less likely to rely on prescriptions for tranquillizers but also because they have greater access to a drinking culture and the financial resources to buy it.

When divorced people look back over this period in their lives they often describe it as 'a nightmare', a period of 'missing time' that they would not want to live through again. For a minority, however, their sentence appears to have no end. It is clear that many years later some women and men still portray the break-up of their marriage as a completely negative, catastrophic event which has left permanent physical, emotional and psychological scars.

Regrettably, there is little reliable data which would enable us to isolate particularly vulnerable groups of divorced people. However, it is likely that those who did not wish their marriage to end, who take a long time to accept the inevitability and reality of separation, whose whole way of life, including their work roles – paid or domestic – is drastically undermined and diminished by divorce, who would like to, but do not, remarry are among those whose suffering is most prolonged. It is clear from the accounts of divorced people themselves, as well as therapeutic descriptions and analyses of the process of loss of attachment, that most people eventually complete the journey out of their marriage, even though it may be one of intense isolation and loneliness at the time. However, the distress experienced by those who, for a variety of reasons, get stuck on the way is considerable and, according to commentators like Dominian, growing.[29] In any event such human misery should at least provoke us to consider if some of this pain is avoidable and whether as a society, or as individuals we could do more to reduce or alleviate it.

NEW PARTNERSHIPS AND THE LEGACY OF DIVORCE

Several aspects of our earlier discussion of personal and social transitions that must be negotiated when a marriage ends help us to understand why, despite all that they have so recently endured, many people remarry within a very short time after divorce. It seems likely that most of those who do have new partners in prospect before they take steps to dissolve their first marriage. Women in unsatisfactory marriages with dependent children who have made marriage their main career now have little prospect of obtaining work in a diminishing labour market. Consequently, they are faced with a stark choice between staying with their present partner, subjecting themselves and their children to the long-term poverty of living on supplementary benefit, or finding a new marriage partner.

Thus women frequently endure loveless, empty or even violent marriages until they have someone else in view. For these women, there are other personal and emotional consequences. Lacking the alternative sources of personal identity and self-esteem provided, for example, by fulfilling paid employment, they are much less likely than their better-educated, work-experienced sisters to believe that they could ever manage on their own without a man to supply material and emotional support. For others, both women and men, meeting and falling in love with someone new causes them to redefine their present partnership in a way which sometimes brings about its end. It is clear that those trying to make an unbroken passage from one relationship to the next face problems not experienced by those marrying for the first time or those who complete the transitions of divorce before embarking on a second partnership.

We have already described some of the social ambiguities surrounding 'demarriage' (see pp. 108–12). Those who make an immediate transition into a new couple relationship often find it difficult to signify their commitment to one another openly or to be accepted as a couple while either or both of the earlier marriages have not yet been formally dissolved. Many of these divorcing partners are preoccupied – even obsessed – by their need to complete formal divorce proceedings as rapidly as possible because they plan to marry again at the first opportunity. They often ask their solicitors to use adultery or unreasonable behaviour as the ground and may make unwise concessions over maintenance or the arrangements for children which may surface again later as a cause for future conflict.

Those who leave one partnership for another often cherish very high expectations of the new relationship. The rhetoric of their accounts and explanations frequently contains many references to the way their new partner has 'changed my whole life', increasing their self-confidence and helping them to discover new aspects of their identity. They may also emphasize how their view of marriage itself has changed, partly from the post-mortems carried out on former partnerships which play an important part in the conversation of second courtships.[30]

For those with children, whether living with them in their new household or not, making a completely fresh start poses much more obvious difficulties. The children and the contact they necessitate between ex-partners mean that the past can never be entirely forgotten. Physical likenesses, similarities of temperament, shared memories and taken-for-granted family traditions and rituals can act as potent reminders of a past which is difficult to ignore. It pre-dates the new partnership and may undermine the sense of a new beginning on which the early stages of romantic attachment are often based.

The discovery that your second partner is not so very different from your first, that your own responses are depressingly familiar or even that, constituted of the daily trivia of domestic life, one marriage is very like another, brings its own bitter disenchantment. By contrast, those who consciously decide, or are forced by circumstances, to pause and take stock between one marriage and the next are able to deal with some elements of the emotional and material legacy of their divorce before embarking on a new partnership. By the same token, women who extend their potential roles beyond that of wife, and men who learn to control even a minimal domestic régime are likely to be much more appreciative of the comforts of partnership when they are regained. They are also much less likely to embark on a second partnership simply from the belief that they cannot cope on their own, or that their children need a second parent figure within the household in order to enjoy the benefits of ordinary family life.

Remarriages involve a wide variety of potential pairings. In recent times, the most common combination has been where both partners are divorced. However, this does not necessarily mean that the new relationship precipitated the end of both marriages: one or both could have been separated and/or divorced for some time. There are important differences in the ways couples respond to the problems of moving straight from one partnership to another. Where both partners are negotiating similar transitions, each may bring parallel emotional and material legacies with them into their new relationship. Although these may leave their mark on the atmosphere and texture of their newly constituted domestic life, they are, at least, likely to be understood and appreciated by both. By contrast, single people who have never been through a similar experience may find aspects of their new partner's behaviour hard to understand and as their life together develops, other previously unacknowledged differences may emerge.

Most remarriages between divorced and previously unmarried persons are marriages in which one partner is already a parent and the other is not. At the time the couple first meet, fall in love and decide to set up home together this difference may not seem important unless children from a former marriage are present. Bachelors who move in with divorced custodial mothers find that they have suddenly acquired many of the economic and social responsibilities of fatherhood and must compete with the children for their mother's attention. Spinsters who marry divorced men often find that their domestic standard of living is directly affected by payments to his former family, and their life together may seem to be dictated by his arrangements over access to his children. Perhaps most undermining of all is the realization that, for both economic and emotional reasons, their new partner may not share their desire to start a family of their own, as a 'natural' next step after their marriage.

Although a full analysis of the potential causes of divorce in second and subsequent marriages is beyond the scope of this book and, in any event, would require considerable further research, we have tried to draw attention to some of the special features of remarriages which help to explain why an even greater proportion of second than first marriages now end in divorce. Politicians and religious leaders, policymakers and practitioners who lend their voices to periodic public panics about the 'evils' and 'tragedy' of divorce and the paramount need to support marriage should remember that many of those now divorcing are battle-scarred victims of a second or third attempt at marriage. Before we criticize this growing minority for their failure as marriage partners, opinion setters – church leaders, media-created experts, counsellors, teachers and public figures – should give sober and realistic consideration to the tension between ideals and reality in this most significant area of people's lives. It is ironic that men and women often only appreciate the material and emotional exchanges on which a marriage is based when they are leaving it. As we suggest in the final chapter this insight, cynical and unromantic though it appears in the light of contemporary images of love and fulfilment in marriage, has much greater value at the beginning of a marriage when the foundations for partnership are laid.

4

DIVORCE AND CHILDREN

Much of the public concern about divorce is focused on children who, to quote the usual journalistic cliché, are seen as the 'innocent victims'. Accordingly, it is commonly assumed that divorces occur because parents are all too ready to pursue their own selfish pleasures at the expense of their children. Although the material presented in chapter 3 undermines glib generalizations of this kind, this particular perception of divorce does draw attention to one important feature of it – that the interests of parents and children may diverge and what may be best for children is not necessarily the same as what is best for the adults. It is true, of course, that parenthood is always some kind of compromise between the needs of adults and children but the conflicts tend to be much sharper and more obvious when divorce is contemplated and these may be much harder to reconcile.

This conflict of interest makes it more difficult for those immediately involved as well as those with a professional concern to take the children's needs fully into consideration. Even professionally trained people find the spectacle of another's divorce may arouse latent feelings about their own relationships with adults and children. We all have the experience of being children and we retain emotionally charged memories of our own childhood but we are not necessarily consciously aware of the ways experiences affect us, making it difficult to think clearly about an issue that is, quite literally, too close for comfort. It is all too easy to brush aside the problems as if they did not exist or to attempt to impose facile and dogmatic solutions which may have more to do with our own fears and defences than the needs of those who are having to face the ending of a marriage, whether adults or children.

About two-thirds of divorces in Britain are of marriages with children and about a third of these children are under five at the time. When a marriage ends the parents have to make decisions about where their children are to live, who is to look after them and a host of other practical details. As we have already suggested, these issues must be faced at a time when the parents are likely to be feeling battered and depressed by what has happened as well as very uncertain and confused about their own futures. It is thus very common for unusually difficult and demanding children, upset by what they see happening, to be seeking reassurance and support from parents just at a time when they are caught up in their own emotional turmoil and able to offer little comfort to anyone else, let alone make considered judgements about the long-term future.

Our divorce law, in theory at least, gives prominence to the welfare of children. A court can only grant a divorce if it is 'satisfied' with the plans outlined for the children or if it is felt that they are the best possible in the circumstances. If there is no dispute about the children, there is a very brief hearing – a few minutes is common – at which the judge is told what the parent(s) intend to do. Searching questions are rare and almost invariably the court is 'satisfied' by whatever is proposed – or, at least, by the often rather simplified, if not misleading, account that may be presented at these children's appointments. In the final chapter we will discuss these court procedures in more detail and the role they are intended to serve.

In a small proportion of cases, parents are still in dispute about the basic arrangements for their children when they reach the formal conclusion of the legal process of divorce so the court must then decide the issues for them and will make an order setting out who is to have custody, care and control and access. There is a good deal of legal debate about what these concepts mean exactly but, roughly speaking, custody concerns the important long-term questions about a child's education or religion, while care and control relates to day-to-day matters. Custody can be granted to one parent or it may be held jointly by both as is the formal legal situation during marriage.[1] Access is the right of children and their non-custodial parents to meet.

Although these matters are formally decided in court in only a very small number of divorces, we should not conclude that all has been easy for other parents. There may have been a great deal of discussion, arguments and dispute behind the scenes and this is likely to have involved solicitors and perhaps counsellors, as well as parents, potential new partners and other members of the family. In reaching decisions about children, as we saw in chapter 2, courts are not given any specific rules to operate but, rather, a judge has to consider the welfare of children and use his – or occasionally her – discretion about what this means in a specific case. In order to assess judicial decision-making about children or to provide any kind of help or guidance for parents, we must have a clear idea of the needs of children and how these may be best met at divorce. This is the subject of this chapter and we will begin by describing ways in which children react to the separation of their parents.

We begin by reiterating an observation and a warning we made in earlier chapters – divorces, and indeed children, vary. For some, divorce may be the culmination of years of strife and comings and goings, while for others it is relatively sudden, perhaps a genuine surprise for some of those closely concerned. Other marriages suffer a slow decay with little open quarrelling or dispute. The spouses simply grow apart to a point where they recognize there is no marriage left. Some divorces involve new partners; others don't. From the point of view of a child, the way in which the marriage ends and the attitudes of parents and others close to them are likely to be of considerable significance. For example, many, if not most, parents seem to believe that the less said to children the better – a point that is contradicted by research studies – and the children often get a very distorted idea of what is happening and have little or no opportunity to talk about their fears and fantasies. For others there is opportunity for discussion and to ask questions.

Children react differently to these events. Not only does it make an enormous difference whether they are five or fifteen, but much depends on the kind of child they are, how they deal with difficulties, the kind of relationships they have with their parents and their own expectations of family life. There is not a single set of reactions of children to divorce, but there are some common themes – both features of the situation and children's reactions – which occur very frequently and allow us to talk about divorce and children in general.

HOW CHILDREN MAY REACT TO A MARITAL SEPARATION

One of the first signs that children may be affected by an impending or actual separation, is their fear of being left alone.[2] In younger children this may take the form of clinging and perhaps insisting on having the bedroom light on at night as they used to when younger. Similarly, a child who has previously settled easily at bedtime may begin to demand endless drinks and stories or perhaps that a parent should sit with them until they are asleep. Children who have formerly gone to school or nursery quite happily may refuse to be left at the school gate or protest at the whole idea of going. They may stay in bed and defeat all attempts to get them dressed. Many parents have described being in a shop or other public place with their child. The child turns round, cannot immediately see the parent and goes into a blind panic believing that they have been abandoned.

Behaviour of this kind by the child is a clear indication that he or she is anxious that their remaining parent may disappear, an understandable fear if you consider marital separation from a child's point of view. Young children generally believe that social relationships, especially those with their parents and other family members, are everlasting. These people are the constant feature in a child's life and the base from which a child looks out to the rest of the world. Separation and divorce are deeply disturbing because they demonstrate to a child that social relationships can end, even those as fundamental as the ones they have with their own parents or the bond between their parents. When their parents' marriage breaks up, children may have experienced a parent leaving the home and have been through a profound change, if not the end, of their relationship with a parent. If one parent can leave, why not the other? As a result children hold on to what they have got, perhaps literally, by clinging or by constantly demanding reassurance. Sometimes a child will ask the direct question 'Will you go too?' but for many it is too dangerous a question to express. The only answer to these fears is continuing reassurance and, for younger children, this will mean not only verbal assurances but direct demonstration over a period of time. As the child settles into a new pattern of living and finds, hopefully, that important relationships do persist, the anxieties and fears gradually subside.

Despite what some parents might prefer to believe, it is rare for a child to welcome a separation. They may welcome the end of bickering and strife, or violence if this has occurred, but very few children want their parents to part. Children usually retain the fantasy of their parents getting back together again for years after a separation. And this may not simply remain a fantasy. Some children will go to great lengths to devise situations to bring their parents together again, perhaps by producing an emotional crisis or illness in the hope that the absent parent will visit and a reunion follow. Part of the resentment that can mark the arrival of new partners is that they may be seen by a child as a barrier to reunion or simply as a demonstration that the absent parent is unlikely to return.

It is important to remember that children do not choose a parental separation; rather, it is imposed on them. To make it worse, it is imposed by the very people on whom a child depends most and to whom they look for protection of their interests. This adds to a child's sense of abandonment and disturbing feelings of power-lessness. This can make a child angry, sad and depressed. Many of us get angry when others do things to us which we don't want and are against our interests but the feelings are likely to be especially strong when we know the other person is aware that their actions will hurt us. So it is for many children. But anger for a child is more complicated because it may be accompanied by the fear that to be angry with one or both parents may drive them away. So the anger may become a dangerous feeling which must be hidden. More simply, there may also be a conflict between feelings of love and anger for a parent. Anger may lead a child to feel guilty for having bad feelings about their parent.

If anger is too threatening to express directly, it may be transferred to a safer target. In some families, brothers and sisters become par-ticularly quarrelsome and cross with each other or the anger may be displaced on to friends at school. Observation in schools suggests that children may become aggressive and demanding with their peers. This, of course, may drive their friends away so a child may feel even more abandoned and unloved. For others, anger is turned inwards and the child becomes depressed. Thus, many children endure a phase of depressed sadness as their parents separate.

In the upheaval of divorce, children may return, or regress, to earlier patterns of behaviour that they had already given up as they got older. A child once dry at night may begin bedwetting again for a period. Young children who drink from a cup may demand a bottle or talk in baby language. These kinds of regressive behaviour are usually short lived and interpretations of their cause vary. Some see them as bids for attention while others interpret the return to an earlier phase of behaviour as an attempt by the child to evoke the calmer and more secure relationships with the parents and within the family which characterized the period before separation was considered.

It is often said that children feel guilty and responsible for their parents' divorce, believing that something they have done has driven their parents apart. While guilt is common, this is not usually its origin. In fact, there is evidence that such feelings of responsibility seem to be confined to very young children and even then appear to be quite rare. The widespread belief that children bear such feelings of responsibility despite evidence to the contrary is perhaps an indication of what adults would prefer to believe about the origins of their child's unhappiness. If a child is obviously upset by what is going on, it is perhaps easier to accept that the upset is due to a childish misunderstanding of the cause of what is happening – the inappropriate guilt – than to accept that it is directly caused by the parents making a decision that the child does not want and may continue to resent deeply for some time afterwards.

For older children there may be a tendency to cope with what is happening at home by throwing themselves into activities outside. Some may choose school for this, so teachers, instead of seeing a change towards demanding and aggressive behaviour and perhaps a lack of interest in school work, may notice that a child is suddenly investing almost all his or her energies in school activities and may be quite reluctant to go home at the end of the day. For teenagers, boyfriends and girlfriends may seem much more attractive and reassuring than warring parents or depressed parents who seem totally preoccupied with their own problems. There is some evidence to suggest that children who have experienced a parental divorce are likely to get into sexual relationships and perhaps marriage at a slightly earlier age. Where older children are unhappy at home, getting married as early as possible may be seen as a means of escape. However, as we saw in chapter 1, early marriages are more likely to end in divorce, especially if the bride is pregnant. This may help to explain, at least in part, why the children of divorced parents are more likely to divorce in later years.[3]

Immediately after a separation some parents get into a phase of brief and rather frantic sexual relationships. These are often all too apparent to the children who may find their parents' overt sexuality very hard to cope with, especially if it coincides with their own adolescence. Links between a parent's and their children's sexuality are seldom acknowledged and there is some clinical evidence that a parent's extramarital affair sometimes provokes a teenager into their first sexual relationship. Less obviously, the influence may also run in the other direction and outward displays of growing sexuality in an adolescent may lead a parent to explore new sexual relationships outside their marriage. Children may be deeply confused by a parent who has a whole series of sexual partners over a brief period. Each is a confirmation of the end of the relationship between the parents, and the alterations in domestic routines occasioned by each change of partner add to the general feelings of instability and uncertainty. A child is likely to resent the emotion and energy a parent puts into new relationships and may take this as further confirmation that their interests are being ignored. Some parents try to avoid difficulties of this kind by conducting their relationships out of sight and sound of their children. Up to a point this seems a better solution, at least until patterns become more settled. However, children almost always pick up more of what is emotionally relevant to them than adults like to imagine. An inadequately hidden parental sexual relationship may be worse for a child than an open one. The other problem about secrecy is that the parent may come to resent the restrictions it may place on what they can do and this resentment may colour their feelings for their children.

The overt distress of children when their parents separate and eventually divorce that we have described is generally short lived. It may last for a matter of months or a year and then gradually subside. The time this takes depends very much on what happens after the divorce and the quality of the children's relationship with *both* parents. Broadly speaking, the better their relationship with their parents, the less marked the distress will be and the shorter its duration.[4] However, there are other factors involved: boys for instance tend to be more disturbed than girls.[5] As most children live with their mothers after divorce, so boys are more likely to lose a close relationship with their same-sex parent. But this cannot be the whole story, as boys also seem to be the more disturbed by conflict between parents who are still living together. It is also possible that boys who are distressed are less likely than girls to receive support from peers and adults in situations like school.

For the minority of children whose disturbance persists, further problems may arise. Their emotional turmoils may spill over into learning difficulties and school work may suffer. For a few their difficulties may result in a referral to a child guidance clinic or similar agency. There is little indication from the research work how frequent these more serious problems may be. However, around 60 per cent of the children seen in child guidance clinics come from separated families. This is about twice the proportion we would expect but there are likely to be all sorts of selective factors at work. For some it may be that they are sent for help more readily because they are known to come from a 'broken' family which may be seen as reason enough for a child needing help. Indeed we have direct evidence that professional people may have very negative expectations of children who have experienced a parental divorce.[6] For other children there may be an opposite effect and quite severe difficulties may be ignored because they are thought to arise from their parents' marital problems and thus to be much less amenable to direct treatment.

Some recently divorced parents do not consider that their children are showing any signs of distress or disturbance at all. As we have already pointed out, children vary a great deal and in some circumstances their lives may not be greatly affected by their parents' separation. However, it is not unnatural that parents tend to minimize their children's problems especially if they feel that their own actions may be part of the cause. If a child does not show any obvious signs of disturbance, it may be that they are given few opportunities to express their feelings. Clinical experience suggests that in the longer term it is better that such feelings are expressed and it may be important to provide a child with a situation or a person with whom they feel safe enough to air their feelings and anxieties more freely.

Given the enormous importance of parental relationships to children, it is important to underline the fact that we should *expect* children to get upset at a marital separation and that, at least in the early phases, their distress is more likely to be shown at times when the effects of change are most apparent, for example when a child goes to visit the other parent or returns from such a visit. It is all too easy for warring parents to misinterpret the child's distress in these situations and see it as a sign that they do not want to go on the visit, or to return afterwards, rather than as evidence of a much more generalized distress at what has happened which finds open expression at particular poignant and symbolic times. Trying to understand a child's complex feelings at these times may be of great importance in providing emotional support and making appropriate practical arrangements.

We also need to consider the longer-term effects of parental divorce which may follow children into adulthood. Although this question has been the topic of much research, the answer is still not at all clear. We can say with some confidence that if there are effects that persist over many years they are only slight. If they were more marked, the answer would have been more apparent from the research studies. However, research on the long-term consequences is difficult because it has to cover a long time-scale and must include a large number of individuals in order to get a valid result. Such large-scale research usually employs rather rough-and-ready methods as there is neither time nor resources to make a detailed investigation of each case. Typically, one group of adults who experienced a parental divorce in childhood is compared with another group whose parents stayed together. Most of the studies do not get beyond these all too crude categories of 'divorced' v. 'intact'. Among those in the divorced group will be some for whom the disturbance came very early in childhood, others for whom it was much later. Some will have step-parents through parents' remarriage; others, a childhood in a single-parent household. Equally significantly, many but not all will have lost contact with their non-custodial parent. There will be as much variety in the group whose parents remained married. For some, their parents' marriages will have been marked by conflict and strife, others by calm disinterest, and others still will have enjoyed 'good' marriages.

All of these factors are likely to influence children and thus make it difficult to derive a clear answer from the research. There is also the difficulty that we are always dealing with events that happened in the past. To follow a group into adulthood means that we are talking of divorces that took place a generation ago. Divorce itself and the effects it may have on children have changed over time. A generation ago, divorce was much rarer and subject to much greater social disapproval. Perhaps that made it harder for children. Today, most school children will have several class members who have been through a parental separation. Teachers are much less likely to ignore such children's likely sensitivities when family matters are discussed in class. Changes of these kinds may make it easier for children today.

In addition to the increased likelihood of children who have experienced their parents' divorce eventually divorcing themselves, other studies suggest that juvenile delinquency, and depression and other psychological difficulties may be more common later in life. But it is important not to over-dramatize these effects. For example, the divorce rate for those who have experienced a parental divorce is at most a few percentage points above those whose parental marriages persisted. Although differences like this may be statistically significant, in the sense that the finding is unlikely to be due to chance, this is very far from saying that *all* children of divorced parents will themselves experience a divorce and where it happens the nature of the causal link itself is likely to be very complex.

SOME ISSUES OF THEORY AND PRACTICE

It would obviously be useful to know how the *age* of a child at the time when their parents' marriage ends may influence the outcome. In the longer term it does seem as if younger children – those under about five – are more likely to show effects than those of older ages. Some people find this surprising, perhaps because they assume that there may be a connection between immediate reactions such as disturbances in children's behaviour which are more obvious among older children and longer-term outcomes. Thus it is important to recognize that what is seen at the time and what happens in the longer term may not be linked at all. Indeed, sometimes the opposite may hold true; a child who gets very upset at the time of the divorce and who expresses their feelings very strongly and clearly may come to terms with things more easily than one who shows less external reaction and bottles up feelings. Adults find children who express their anger and pain very disturbing and so may come to feel that the child who expresses little is reacting well. But the opposite may be true in the longer term.

It is not clear why younger children may show more longer-term problems. It could be that these children are more vulnerable to changes in family relationships and that difficulties arise because they have less understanding of what has happened. On the other hand, the differences may be the result of what happens after the divorce and the fact that the earlier in childhood this occurs the longer the child is likely to live in a situation of social and economic disadvantage and to experience the inevitable changes in family and domestic life which follow from their custodial parent's new partnership. As we comment elsewhere in this book, divorce has profound economic consequences, especially for mothers and children and these, in turn, may influence all sorts of aspects of life. An indication of how persistent these effects may be is given in a recent study that suggests that the economic position achieved in adult life may be reduced as a direct result of a parental divorce in childhood.[7] Another way of describing this process would be to say that divorce is a major cause of downward social mobility for mothers and children. While the majority of children still grow up into the same economic and social grouping as their parents, divorce breaks this continuity, leaving children in a more disadvantaged position than would otherwise be expected. Their adult occupational and income level is likely to be lower than would be expected from reference to their pre-divorce family social position. Surprisingly, little is known about how these intergenerational processes operate when parents divorce and perhaps remarry, and attention is only now beginning to be paid to the effects of such events as well as, for example, parental illness or unemployment. It is an active and very significant area of research which, if the work continues, should shed a great deal of light on the ways in which family events and changes affect children's life chances.

In the last few years there has been a great increase in research on the effects of divorce on children in the U.S.A. and to a lesser extent in Britain and Western Europe. Rather than comparing children of divorced and non-divorced parents, the emphasis has shifted to the various aspects of the divorce process and the ways in which these may affect children. From this work there is a clear message: it is what happens *after* the separation that is of primary importance to children. As we have said, in general the children who maintain a good relationship with both parents are less disturbed and their disturbance lasts for the shortest time.

Looking back at the post-Second-World-War decades of child psychology it is clear, with hindsight of course, that we have over-emphasized the role of the mother–child relationship and tended to ignore fathers and most of the other varied relationships with relatives and friends that go to make up the social worlds of children.[8] Fathers, if mentioned at all in the influential books of twenty years ago, were seen as emotional and financial supports for mothers rather than having any important direct role in the lives of children. Maternal deprivation was seen as the central problem. Provided mother was around, the child's social needs were seen as being met.

In such a climate divorce was not seen as so much of a problem for children and this helps to explain why it was so little studied. At divorce children would stay with their mother, so preserving their 'primary attachment'. If father chose to visit occasionally, all well and good, provided that the children did not appear to get upset, but access was usually seen as a very optional extra. In fact, some psychologists went much further than this and regarded access as a rather selfish indulgence on the part of fathers which, they argued, was only likely to stir up bad memories for children. Much better, they thought, for the father to keep out of the way so that the children could settle into their new life without unwelcome interruptions. The fact that the loss of the father also often meant the loss of one set of grandparents and other relatives was not even thought to be worthy of comment.

Sometimes, despite the continuity of the attachment to the mother, children were seen to be upset by divorce. This was usually attributed not to the loss of important people from the children's lives, but to the continuing effects of having lived through the final stages of an ending marriage. For example, a number of studies had shown that children in marriages where there was a good deal of friction and quarrelling were slightly more likely to show disturbances in their behaviour than those in marriages that were rated as 'good'.[9] These so-called conflicted marriages were thought to disturb children because they led to 'distorted' attachments between mother and child. It was argued, not unreasonably, that such friction was often likely to precede divorce and so could be used as the explanation for the children's subsequent distress.[10] Some psychologists found this line of reasoning so compelling that they argued strongly for divorce on the grounds that it was obviously better for children than a 'bad' marriage, a tenet which has now become part of the popular wisdom surrounding divorce.

This position was supported by studies which compared three groups of children: those living with parents whose marriages were marked by conflict, those whose parents' marriage was rated as 'good' and a group whose parents had divorced some time in the past. The highest proportion of children with psychological problems was found in the group who were living with parents with conflicted marriages, a lower proportion among those from the divorced families and the lowest among those with parents with 'good' marriages. Apart from the point that a child's psychological problems may be a cause as well as an effect of marital conflicts, there is another flaw in the logic of this argument. The divorces themselves had happened in some cases many years before the children were evaluated, so we would expect that they might have got over the worst of their problems. On the other hand, those living with conflicted parents were experiencing that situation at the same time as their own behaviour was being assessed so their difficulties were likely to be at their height.

Another reason why we should not accept this evidence for divorce being better than a 'bad' marriage is that bad marriages sometimes improve. Thus, we cannot ignore the possibility that some children will eventually experience a much better home situation with both their parents still present. There is, therefore, no single answer to the question of which is better. Situations have to be assessed in terms of the likely consequences of the different courses of action open to the parents. Some parents stay together for their children and, indeed, for many of them this may be the best compromise for all concerned.

For others, it leads to so much bitterness and frustration that it is not a good option.

Evidence that children are likely to show more disturbances in their behaviour after the divorce of their parents than a death is also used to support this argument, by suggesting that only in the former situation had children experienced parental conflict. While we are not trying to dismiss the idea that children, at least for a time, may become upset if their parents are getting on very badly, it is an inadequate explanation for these findings and fails to see the situation from the children's point of view.

As we have already described, children, in general, do not want their parents to part and become angry and upset when they do so. The children are hurt because the parents have chosen to do something that the children find deeply upsetting. The death of a parent engenders quite different feelings, a great sense of loss and sadness but not the same kind of anger that is so frequent at divorce. There is, however, one instructive exception where there is an element of choice: when a parent commits suicide. Significantly, clinical studies of children who have had to face this situation show that they react very similarly to children in the midst of divorce. Worst of all is the situation, sadly not uncommon, when a parent commits suicide in the aftermath of divorce.

There is one further challenge to the parental conflict theory that we should consider. We have already referred to recent studies indicating that post-divorce contact with both parents is important. This seems to be true even when there is continuing conflict between the parents.[11] Children in such situations seem better off than those who have completely lost contact with the non-custodial parent – usually, of course, the father. While conflict is upsetting for children, its effects are partially separable from those arising from the loss of a parent.

Opinions on remarriage also tend to be rather different today than they were when the views of the maternal-deprivation school prevailed. The greater the emphasis that is placed on the mother–child relationship, the more desirable remarriage will often seem for children. The mother–child relationship remains intact and she gains the support of a new parent whilst the child has a new family. In custody disputes the parent able to produce a new partner often won the day and much social work policy was based on the same assumptions. But even then some psychological evidence, which was largely ignored, showed that matters were not quite so simple and that children with step-parents might face more difficulties than those with single parents.[12] It has been suggested that children may be particularly resentful of a step-parent if he or she is presented as a replacement for the 'real' parent. Moreover, as was mentioned earlier in this book, the dynamics of a second marriage often involves a rewriting of the history of the earlier marriage (or marriages) so that it is seen as a sort of bad dream. Expectations of second marriages are often higher than of the first. All of this leaves little space for the children of the first marriage, who may find it very difficult to adjust to a parent's reinterpretation of the past. In addition, the custodial parent and new partner may try to discourage children from seeing their other parent now that they are a 'proper' family once more. Thus, remarriage, like divorce, may tend to bring out the conflict of interests between parents and children. But on the positive side we should note that remarriage usually brings a substantial improvement in the economic position of the custodial single parent and the children. Indeed, for single-parent families in lower income groups, it may be the only way out of the poverty trap in which they are so often caught.

As well as changes in social relationships, there are other factors at divorce which may be very important in the lives of children. Divorce often leads to a move to a new neighbourhood, another school and loss of friends. While many children have to cope with moves and all the changes in their lives that these may bring, it is likely to be much harder at the time of a divorce because security and continuity are especially important to them. Once again, adults' and children's needs may be pulling in different directions. Adults may feel a strong need to start again somewhere new or to get out of the neighbourhood where they are likely to encounter their ex-spouse. For the children, this may mean more upheaval in their lives and a reduced chance of maintaining a good relationship with their other parent.

The fall in the standard of living which almost always accompanies divorce can affect children's lives in many ways. For example, the opportunity for new experiences may be reduced if there is no money to pay for holidays or school trips. Indeed, studies of children in single-parent families show that many of the disadvantages the children may suffer are directly related to the income level of the households.[13] Some of the very poorest households in Britain are those of divorced mothers and their children. Not surprisingly, male-headed single-parent households tend to be rather better off than those headed by women, and the men are more likely to be employed outside the home.

COPING WITH THE NEEDS OF CHILDREN

Given what we now understand of the needs of children at divorce, how well does the system that exists to cope with divorce serve to meet those needs? A short answer must be, not very well. It is in this area that as a society we demonstrate most clearly our own inability to come to terms with our current levels of divorce.

Let us begin this discussion by summarizing the main needs of children who experience a marital separation. Over the period of separation, children will be upset and distressed but in the longer term they are most likely to settle down satisfactorily if they are able to retain a good relationship with both parents. The traditional view of a child living with one parent and the other becoming, at best, an occasional visitor is increasingly challenged by studies that show for most children a more equal division of time between two parents is desirable. It is clear that a realistic and satisfactory relationship is unlikely to persist and grow unless a child spends enough time with the other parent to do everyday things. The idea of an access visit being a couple of hours on a Saturday afternoon is clearly inadequate. This often provokes the 'Saturday parent' or 'Father Christmas' syndrome where men are forced into a desperate attempt to hold the relationship together by the constant provision of gifts and treats because they do not have sufficient time with their children. As research has confirmed, it is the duration of each visit not the frequency that is most important.[14] Child and parent need time to settle into a more natural relationship and this will mean overnight stays. As a visiting father once explained, a good landmark for a reasonable relationship is when the parent is able to express their feelings to their child when they are angry with them about something with the knowledge that they will be together long enough to 'make it up'. The Saturday parent seldom feels safe enough to do this and may be afraid that their anger might sever the very thin strand which links them to their child.

It is also important to look beyond parents to the wider family and other friends. Relatives are frequently of great significance in childhood and the loss of one parent at divorce often entails loss of one whole side of a child's family. Childhood friends, too, can be lost through a marital separation, especially if both parents move from the neighbourhood of their original home and there is a change of school. When ex-spouses choose to live at some distance from each other this may impose many practical difficulties for the child who is trying to continue to have a relationship with both.

From a child's point of view, it is not enough to have a parent physically present: a parent must have time and a reasonable amount of emotional energy available for their children. Marital separation often brings with it depression, anxiety and ill-health for the spouses. These may be exacerbated by practical difficulties about such things as housing and, above all, lack of money, leading to a situation where parents may be physically present and psychologically absent. If the needs of children are to be met, it is vital that as much emotional and material support as possible is available for adults so that they can function effectively as parents.

Children need accurate information about what is happening to their parents' marriage and its implications for their own lives. This must be given to them in an appropriate way so that they can understand in their own terms what is happening. Frequently, they only learn after the event but not before their fears have been aroused. This adds to their sense of powerlessness and allows fantasies to grow which may be much worse than reality. They also need op-portunities for talking about their experiences and fears and for comparing them with those of others. Perhaps the single most common concern of children is that they feel as if they are in a unique situation facing problems no other child has ever suffered. It may be very difficult for a child to find a context in which they feel confident and safe enough to talk about more disturbing aspects of their life. Too often members of the wider family will take the side of one or other parent – something that usually adds to a child's distress and makes them feel very unwilling to express their real feelings.

Let us turn to institutional supports for those facing divorce, to consider whether the system tends to increase or decrease the likelihood of children's needs being met. In the strict sense, divorce is a legal matter so we will begin with the courts.

Custody

At divorce, the courts will make an order which sets out the arrangements for the care of the children. Most often this is by consent; the parents have made some agreement and the courts endorse it. When there is no agreement the judge in court will make the decision.

In about 80 per cent of cases, custody is given to the mother, and in the remainder it is either given to the father, held jointly by the two parents or by a third party such as a local authority.[15] It is widely believed that the proportion of joint custody and sole custody to father orders have increased in recent years. They may have done: the figures we have given are the best available but they are derived from surveys that are nearly a decade old. Incredibly, statistics on many aspects of the legal system are not routinely published so we are forced back on informed guesswork. Our feeling is that changes in the proportions of different kinds of orders are much less marked than many people seem to believe.

The fact that most custody orders are given to mothers reflects the assumptions that are held in our society about child care. Women provide by far the largest proportion of child care within marriage and the same continues after divorce. But while the court system is not responsible for the great disparity between the number of orders given to women and men, it appears to encourage the trend. It is still possible to find in the judgements of the Court of Appeal cases where judges are saying, in effect, if all else is equal and as a general principle, custody should be given to the mother rather than the father.

The question of the relative merits of mothers or fathers as the preferred post-divorce single parent is usually seen as the basic issue in discussions of custody after divorce. Historically, as we saw in chapter 2, we have moved from a situation of more or less total father domination in the last century to more or less automatic custody to the mother in the post-Second-World-War years, partly as a result of the prevalence of the doctrine of maternal deprivation. In the last couple of decades, a few fathers have begun to argue their cases more strongly. They pointed out that the ability to care for children is not inevitably confined to women and that men can and do make entirely satisfactory parents. In fact, nearly one in seven of all single-parent households is headed by a man and the research studies show that there is little difference in the outcomes for the children from those headed by women.[16]

Others have based their arguments on the psychological work on parent–child relations which has tried to correct the biases of the maternal-attachment theories of the post-Second-World-War era and on the growing research on father–child relations.[17] Some women have tried to counter arguments of this kind by suggesting that these challenges to more or less automatic maternal custody represent a totally unwelcome extension of male power into almost the only area of life where women more or less retain control. Other women have taken a rather different view and have supported attempts to move towards a more equal parental role for men and women.

Arguments about these matters have spread far beyond the court room and are reflected in public debate and, increasingly, in fiction and film. *Kramer v. Kramer*, *Paris, Texas* and *Table for Five* are examples of films where the rival claims of mothers and fathers over their children form the central theme.

It is not our intention to pursue any of these arguments about the relative merits of women and men as single parents. Indeed, we would suggest that the continued emphasis on the struggles of mothers versus fathers only emphasizes the extent to which decisions about children at divorce continue to be dominated by the needs of adults rather than children. The central question is not whether custody should go to father or mother but how best a court can encourage and foster the continued relationships of the child with *both* parents. The awarding of sole custody at divorce suggests that, henceforth, only one parent is to play a significant part in the child's life, an impression reinforced by the lack of emphasis on access. Even when non-custodial parents continue to visit after the divorce, they often feel that their 'loss' of custody matched by the 'victory' of the other parent has diminished their identity as a real parent.

Within marriage, custody is held jointly and equally by both parents and it is necessary to question whether that situation should be changed by divorce. Indeed, this could be put more positively; at the end of a marriage it might be desirable to reaffirm the role of both parents and so make it clear that although the divorce is the end of the parents' marital relationship, their parental rights – to use an old-fashioned term – and duties persist. One way to symbolize the two partners' continuing roles is to have a joint custody order or, as some have suggested, to make no order at all about custody so that the situation that obtained in the marriage persists. Though the percentage of joint custody orders given in English courts is still probably very small, support for them is growing. Indeed, as we shall discuss further in the final chapter, the Report of the Booth Committee, a committee set up by the Lord Chancellor's Department to look into the working of divorce law, suggests that joint custody will often be the desirable arrangement.[18] In other countries such as the U.S.A., New Zealand or Australia where there has been much longer experience with joint custody – or its equivalent – there is growing evidence that the usual British fear that 'when it works it is unnecessary and when it is necessary it is unworkable' is ill founded. Californian research, for instance, has shown that even when joint custody is imposed by the courts against the wishes of one or both parents, parents are less likely to return to the court with future disagreements than when they are originally given a sole custody order.[19]

Joint custody itself says nothing about the actual living arrangements for the children and it should not be confused with what is perhaps best called shared custody but is often described as joint or split custody. These are arrangements where children divide their time more or less equally between the two homes. Again, such arrangements are becoming increasingly common, especially in North America and the old Commonwealth. Though professional people have often been very critical of such arrangements, claiming that they serve the interests of adults more than the child, this is not the picture that emerges from the research.[20] Several American studies suggest that, within limits, the more equally children divide their time between the two parents, the better their post-divorce adjustment. However, it might be answered that these studies all look at arrangements that parents chose to set up for themselves. Consequently, the most favourable outcomes in the shared-custody groups may occur because the kind of parents who choose these sorts of arrangements also do other things which account for the difference. Certainly, these studies do not provide evidence that shared custody would necessarily be the best solution to impose on all parents. However, they do indicate that it is the preferred arrangement when parents want to do it.

ACCESS

Where custody is given to one parent, and probably in many joint-custody situations too, the child has a main home with one parent who has care and control, and visits the other. In between one-third and one-half of cases, an access order is made. This may simply say 'reasonable' access with no indication as to what 'reasonable' might be, or occasionally the access is specified with particular times and places.

Though the data is now nearly a decade old and things may have changed a little, the indications are that within a couple of years of a separation only about half of all non-custodial parents see their children on a regular basis.[21] Courts do little to encourage access. The fact that access orders are not made in so many cases hardly suggests that much emphasis is put on the relationship with the non-custodial parent. In cases where there is a direct conflict between the interests of the custodial parent and that of the child's relationships with the non-custodial parent, the custodial parent invariably wins. This is illustrated in cases where custodial parents wish to take their children abroad so effectively cutting off the child from the other parent. Courts always appear to sanction such arrangements.[22]

That courts give so little encouragement to non-custodial parents to remain in touch with their children, is not a sufficient explanation of why so many choose to disappear. We are, of course, talking almost entirely about men. The very sparse evidence we have does not suggest that non-custodial mothers behave very differently from fathers though their feelings and the social pressures they may experience are probably dissimilar.

Recent research findings offer a number of reasons for men disappearing. These include:

1.   Some men believe that it is in their children's interests for them to disappear. They may feel that their visits will upset the children or that their continued presence makes it less likely that their ex-spouses will settle down with a new partner. Often, and especially in the early days after separation, a child's distress at what has happened is most likely to be apparent before and after a visit from the father. This may lead either parent to try to reduce or stop the visiting. As we have already commented, it would be odd if any child accepted such a radical change in their lives without distress and in the long term it is probably much better that these feelings are expressed at the time. The real issue here is the capacity of the parents to understand and accept the expression of such feelings at a time when they are likely to be feeling very vulnerable themselves.

2.   It is often said, not least by mothers with custody, that some fathers have no real interest in their children. Doubtless this is sometimes true, but we suspect that this reason is sometimes used to cover others.

3.   Some men believe, incorrectly of course, that if they do not see their children they will not be required to pay maintenance. More realistically, others assume that if they have no contact with their old families it will be hard for them to be traced and forced to pay maintenance. Others connect maintenance and access in another way so that they see the money they pay as an entitlement to visit. Custodial parents who want to discourage access visits may, if their circumstances permit, offer to forgo maintenance if the children's father agrees not to visit.

4.   Some men are prevented from seeing their children by their ex-spouse. Preventing contact with children is the most obvious weapon available to a custodial parent and some use it in continuing battles with their ex-partner. After a long journey the father arrives to find the house empty, or that, as usual, a child turns out to be 'ill' on access days. More bluntly, a father may simply be told on the doorstep that he cannot see his children. There are few sanctions in such cases and without persistence and the ability to find the right kind of help the situation may seem hopeless to the men concerned.

5. Some men feel that they want to move away and start again after a separation especially if their spouse has a new partner. The distance may create too many problems eventually for the visiting arrangements to survive.

6. A new partner may be very resentful of the contact with the children of the first marriage and bring pressure to try to end it. Conversely, the custodial parent may attempt to argue for an access order which tries to prevent the children having contact with the ex-spouse's new partner. Although it is not hard to understand the feelings that give rise to such attempts, they are unrealistic and unreasonable from the point of view of both the adults and children and, in general, courts have not sanctioned them. But pressures from both the new and old spouse may effectively reduce access.

7. Access visits may be so painful and upsetting that a father cannot bear to continue with them. This may be because the visits make it necessary for him to go on meeting the ex-spouse and even her new partner, or because the father himself finds it very difficult to readjust to a new and more limited kind of relationship with his children. The latter is particularly likely if access visits are brief.

Occasionally, the conditions in an access order are closely specified so it seems impossible for any parent to continue to conform to them, e.g. a few hours a month in the old matrimonial home in the presence of the ex-spouse. Similarly, if access is brief and the father's home is far away there is the problem of where to take the children. As one might expect, the problems of access are most acute at the beginning and are usually resolved over time provided, of course, that some pattern of visiting continues.

8. Last among the reasons we shall mention, but certainly not least, is the point made by many men we have interviewed – that all too often continued contact is not supported or encouraged by anyone. Few men had received any sensible advice or help – if they had, it was usually from a court welfare officer, one of the few solicitors who specialize in family law, or from another parent who had experienced a divorce.

As we have already indicated on several occasions, court decisions have a much wider relevance than for the small number of cases that are formally decided there. They are a most important way in which society indicates what it expects of parents. Divorce has been described as a passage without a rite because there are few well-known procedures, rules and ceremonies to fall back on. Many parents feel unsure of themselves and uncertain of what is best for them or their children. Often they will turn to solicitors for advice. 'How often is "reasonable" access?' 'Is it bad for one child to live with one parent and the other child with the other parent?' Usually the solicitor will try first to answer such questions in the legal sense of what judges have said in past cases, so, for example, if a solicitor is asked about the relevance of a parent's homosexuality to the upbringing of children, their concern will be with how this might affect the issue in a custody dispute in the courtroom. This may mean they would give a rather different answer than the one a parent might get from a psychologist or social worker. Thus, until very recently English courts almost always denied a mother custody if she was thought to be a lesbian, while homosexual fathers were not given access. However, there has never been any good psychological evidence that the gender-role identity or other aspects of development in children have any relation to a parent's sexual orientation.[23]

When solicitors open discussions with their opposite number while dealing with a divorce case they begin to 'bargain in the shadow of the law': they argue the issues in the knowledge of what they think a judge might say if the matter came to court. Solicitors are bound to work for their clients' interests. This means that they, encouraged by their clients, may be tempted to pull out every available argument to further their client's case. Affidavits are written which cast the worst possible light on the other spouse's behaviour which, of course, will upset that spouse a great deal when they come to read it. It is not uncommon for couples to be near to an agreement when each of them goes to a solicitor to try and finalize matters. This results in a sudden increase in the general level of aggression and anger between them, which all too often focuses on arrangements for the children. It is one of the dangers of the adversarial system under which our divorce courts operate. Of course, it need not be like this. More experienced solicitors, especially those who specialize in family matters, and who belong to the Solicitors' Family Law Association, will do all they can to counsel moderation and make sure that nothing that is unnecessarily offensive to the other party appears in any of the court papers. Those with experience also know that the traditional kind of 'no holds barred' affidavit is likely to be counter-productive, not only because of its effect on the other spouse, but also because a judge may see it as evidence of the unreasonable nature of its author. In fact, the judge is unlikely to be concerned about the details of the past marital disputes and will be much more influenced by what is said in the courtroom. In the final chapter, we will discuss some of the suggestions that have been made for altering court procedures in order to blunt some effects of the adversarial system. As we shall see in the next chapter, some of the proposals of the Booth Committee are designed to reduce the possibilities for spouses to introduce inflammatory material in court proceedings. Increasingly, the traditional system of courts and solicitors is being extended, and even altered fundamentally by the growing number and range of conciliation and mediation services. These too are discussed in the final chapter.

Before ending this chapter on children we will take a brief look at schools and the health service – two other social institutions with a particular concern for children – which like the court system itself are only slowly coming to terms with the social consequences of current levels of divorce.

Children of school age spend more of their waking lives at school than at home. Therefore, what happens at school may affect very significantly how they weather the storms of marital separation and divorce. We have already described how a child's distress may spill over into their relationships with schoolfriends and teachers.

Among the signs that may lead a teacher to suspect that things are not all well at home is a sudden increase in absence rates. It is not simply that children under stress are more likely to become ill, but parents whose lives are going through great difficulty and upheaval may find it almost impossible to create enough order in the home to ensure that a child gets to school regularly and on time. There may be severe practical difficulties – the father who drove his children to school on the way to work may have left home and taken the car with him, or in the immediate aftermath of a separation there may not be enough money for the children's bus fares. It may be some time before the school is told 'officially' what is going on by one of the parents and at this stage children may not find it easy to talk to their teachers about what is happening. By the same token, teachers may rightly feel reluctant to ask directly unless the children have demonstrated a desire to talk.

Broadly speaking, a school has three roles in relation to marital separation. The first is to encourage parents to keep them informed about a child's domestic arrangements so that the school knows, for example, whom to call in cases of emergency, whom to invite to open days or whom to send school reports to. The latter is a frequent source of friction as schools have, in general, been very slow to recognize the need, if not duty, to keep *both* parents informed if they do not live together. It is clear that even where there is a sole-custody order, the non-custodial parent has the right – unless this has been specifically denied by the court – to be kept informed by a school of their children's progress and to meet teachers to discuss school matters. Clearly, providing two reports and seeing the parents separately may demand more of a teacher's time. However, it can be very upsetting for a child – as well as a parent – to feel that a mother or father has been excluded from such an important part of that child's life.

The second role of a school is to provide the context for those children in difficulty to be recognized and given appropriate help and support. Great tact is necessary here but it is important to remember that, apart from the parent(s), the only other adults a child may see regularly are at school. If a child is clearly upset and distressed, school may be the one place where they can get comfort and help.

The other role is a much broader one, giving children some knowledge of the diversity of family life, its stresses and strains as well as its strengths, and providing a place where, in a neutral atmosphere, they can talk about their experiences of their own families. Children often find such discussions enormously reassuring and a great relief when, for example, they discover that other children share their feelings about step-parents, access visits and so on.

In this secular age, many people turn to their doctors at times of personal troubles. Studies of couples who have recently separated suggest that a majority of women and a rather smaller number of men consult their general practitioner at this time. People often go with rather vague complaints like 'nerves', 'tiredness' and an inability to sleep and they may not mention their marital problems directly; the usual outcome of these encounters is a prescription for tranquillizers. In the conditions of a busy surgery, it is hardly surprising that the patient may be reluctant to mention their marital situation and doctors are not always very keen to enquire because the discussion of marital problems tends to be very time-consuming.[24] Some G.P.s also feel that it is an area beyond their role or competence.

Without suggesting that all G.P.s should become amateur marriage-guidance counsellors, much better use could be made of these surgery visits. A G.P. who is well informed about the services available in the locality can provide the referrals to other people and agencies that may be required. Parents can be asked about their children and if there are concerns about their behaviour it may be useful for them to see a child psychologist. If the difficulties relate to custody and access, a local conciliation service may be more appropriate. In many areas the court welfare service will see parents to give advice without the necessity of a formal referral from a court. Indeed, the Probation Service, which provides the court welfare service has long had the responsibility to provide advice and support for those with marital problems though in recent years these functions, at least as far as adult problems are concerned, have largely been transferred to the marriage-counselling agencies.

As we have already seen, financial problems may be very pressing at the time of a separation. If this is the case, a visit to a Citizens Advice Bureau may be very helpful. They will be able to provide information about such things as the additional child benefit available to single parents. The take-up of this benefit is relatively low and it is often some time after a separation before a parent realizes that they are eligible to receive it. As the G.P.'s surgery is often the first port of call after a marital separation, there is an obvious need for the doctor and ancillary staff to be well informed about what the likely needs are and how they may be met. If difficulties arise with children – either disturbed behaviour or matters of custody and access – it seems clear that the earlier help is obtained the more valuable it is, as later things may become fixed into patterns which are much harder to change. Therefore, the provision of appropriate information and referrals to other agencies early in the separation process is an important form of preventive work. This, of course, is not simply the task of G.P.s and should be undertaken by anyone who has contact with parents and children, e.g. health visitors, school teachers, solicitors, clergy, social workers, among others.

Apart from the requirements for specific information, what many adults need at a separation is the opportunity to talk through what is happening to them and what they are feeling. At first, people will usually seek confirmation and reassurance that whatever they are doing is the right course to take. If there is a lot of hostility between the spouses, they may well want to explain to others how badly they think they have been treated and how awful their ex-partner is. At this stage it is often difficult for a third party to present other points of view or to suggest, as is usually the case, that the truth lies somewhere between the conflicting stories of the two warring spouses. People only want to hear what supports their own position and they may feel too vulnerable to accept any challenges to this. But gradually, things change and people become open to other suggestions. Before this phase is reached, it may be particularly difficult for a parent to make sensible plans, or even to think clearly about what is best for their children, as they will extend their own vulnerability to their children and thus see them as extensions of themselves. Later, as they acquire a little detachment, discussion becomes possible. Whenever anyone professional or otherwise talks to a recently separated and upset spouse they need to try and help them move from the first to the second phase. When this has been achieved, they can support them by encouraging them to consider all the possibilities, and to see how best the conflicting needs of those involved may be met. Above all, this is a process which takes time.

There has been much debate about how far this support and counselling role should be carried out by professionals or how far friends and relatives may be able to help. It is clear that many divorced people found their most effective helpers were not necessarily professionally trained. Indeed, many of the helping professions do not as yet have much training in the kinds of skills that may be most valuable in this situation. A friend who has been through it all may be more useful – especially as they are more likely to have the necessary time available unlike the overstretched professionals.

Although in the first instance it is, quite rightly, parents who will talk to their children about what is happening and the children's reactions to it, we should not forget that some children, as well as adults, are greatly helped by having someone they can trust and can talk to who is outside the situation. This may be another child who has had a similar experience or a trusted adult. It is usually very difficult to arrange such situations and it may well be that contrived attempts to do so are counter-productive because it is important for the child that the encounter happens independently of the parents. Perhaps all that parents can do is to be aware of their children's needs and to allow them to have the space, and perhaps privacy, to talk to people of their own choice. In particular, a parent who tries to influence a child's view of the other parent in negative ways will, of course, inhibit the child's necessary attempts to come to terms with the situation.

To summarize this chapter: while acknowledging the variety of divorces and reactions to them, we have tried to point to those general factors in the process of separation and divorce which affect children. Our conclusion is that, as at other times, children do best when they have supportive relationships with their parents and others close to them. While this may seem obvious, it is not always reflected in practice. For example, it is still often assumed that one parent will of necessity disappear at divorce. This is because we still tend to think of a child's needs as encompassed by their need for a 'family' by which we mean a household with one or both parents. It is more helpful to separate out some of the different requirements. Parents are important because they *are* parents not merely because of their domestic or child-care rules and responsibilities. This is not an argument for the importance of blood ties but rather for the way in which parenthood is socially constructed within our society. Children grow up assuming their parents to be important to them, not least because that is the assumption that everyone around them makes. From the child's point of view this does not change at divorce; the ties of parenthood can stretch across distance and are maintained even if meetings are brief and infrequent. The fact that a child has moved into a new household, perhaps with a potential step-parent, does not mean that their need to remain in some kind of contact with the absent parent ceases. On the contrary, the indications are that step-parents are more easily accepted if a child feels reasonably secure about their relationship with the original parents. We also have to remember the wider kinship network of grandparents, aunts and uncles and try to ensure that these people are not lost to a child at divorce. For the child, three things must be considered at divorce: the two parental relationships, the household of residence (or the two if there is a shared custody arrangement) and the wider network of kin. These are the basic requirements for a satisfactory childhood in society where serial monogamy has become a common marriage pattern. In the next chapter we will discuss some of the practicalities of how this may be achieved.

5

WAYS FORWARD:
THE PURSUIT OF PARTNERSHIP

Although this book is mainly concerned with divorce, we have found like others, especially those directly involved, that our discussions have frequently led us back to the many confusions and contradictions that surround marriage. In this final chapter, we make a number of specific and inevitably controversial suggestions about divorce procedure and practice and some more general observations about ways of fostering the kind of social climate in which *both* parents are encouraged to continue to act as real parents to their children after divorce. However, as we began to map out our somewhat Utopian vision of how unsatisfactory marriages might be ended with greater equity and dignity, we realized that we knew very little about the kind of conventional wisdom which surrounds marriage in an era of high and widely publicized divorce rates. What are the ideals, hopes and assumptions that women and men bring to marriage partnerships in the first place? How closely are the promises they make in private reflected in public in marriage services, whether civil or religious? How clearly, if at all, do they appreciate the eventual consequences for both partners of a traditional exchange – he as breadwinner, she as housekeeper/child-rearer? Put rather differently, using a jurisprudential framework, we need to understand more about the kind of contracts implied by contemporary marriage before we consider how to resolve the disputes which arise when their terms are broken and a dissolution of the partnership is required. There is, as yet, very little published evidence which provides us with answers to such questions although, as chapter 3 indicates, while economic dependence within marriage still remains the norm for most women, its exploitive consequences are only fully revealed when a marriage breaks down. It is for this reason that many feminist commentators denounce marriage, arguing that women are inevitably exploited and diminished within its confines. Whether openly acknowledged or not, it is clear that a very wide range of women's interest and pressure groups of all shades of opinion, from the Women's Institute and Mothers' Union to Women's Aid refuges, are concerned with specific measures to defend or enhance women's position within and after marriage and, through improvements in educational and employment opportunities, to liberate them from the necessity and inevitability of marriage as a main career. Such campaigns are frequently brushed aside in public debate with the justification that women's equality is already a reality in both the public and domestic spheres. A number of influential studies of aspects of British family life are frequently used as evidence of the trend towards greater 'equality' in marriage and 'symmetry' within the family more generally. However the available evidence, including the *Women and Employment* survey[1] tends to challenge this view. Even for middle-class couples, who might be expected to adhere most strongly to ideals of equality within marriage and in which the wives had often followed an independent career *before* marriage, parity is rarely achieved in practice. Although most women and many men may now expect more from their marriage, viewing it as a key source of self-expression, sharing and mutual emotional support, in reality continuing gender divisions both within and outside the home mean that women and men still seem to inhabit different worlds. As a result some of their assumptions about marriage and their experience of domestic life are divergent and, at times, potentially incompatible.

SOURCES OF STABILITY IN MARRIAGE

In chapter 3 we suggested that almost all marriages are vulnerable to potentially threatening reassessment and redefinition by one or other partner in the course of a lifetime. If we consider some of the factors which help to prevent such redefinitions leading to actual breakdown, it may enable us to understand more about the durability of contemporary partnerships.

There is a significant degree of convergence between the views of social researchers, marital therapists and, not least, married people themselves about the value of being able to talk and share difficulties as a means of negotiating the inevitable crises, changes and transitions of married life.

It is, however, necessary to recognize that the style and content of such conversation and the sharing of emotional tensions which lie beneath the surface differ greatly from class to class and within and between particular local, social and occupational communities. Furthermore, even within close-knit groups sharing similar values, individuals may hold very divergent views about what constitutes a 'normal' or 'desirable' level of intimacy because of their own family upbringing and earlier experiences of close, confiding relationships. Indeed, such differences are themselves an important source of conflict and misunderstanding in many marriages. Generally, though not always, it is women who express disappointment that their husbands do not seem to want to develop and extend the closeness and intimacy which characterized their courtship and the early stages of being 'in love'. Their sense of regret helps us to understand more about the kind of 'good communication' that enables couples to negotiate their way through the personal and family changes which inevitably punctuate the lifetime of a marriage. If we remember that it is not simply the quantity of conversation but its quality, it will help us to guard against believing that verbally fluent sections of the middle class have some kind of monopoly on good communication. Although some recollections of courtship and early married life may owe more to idealized representations of how they hoped their relationship might develop, partners who complain that they no longer talk as they used to are often referring, albeit obliquely, to other ways in which the emotional base of their partnership has been undermined. Complaints about the absence of customary small gestures of love and concern and the daily kindnesses which characterized an earlier period of married life may seem trivial but are often indicative of a more general erosion of the couple's channels of close, confiding and secure communication.

Our review of the available data on contemporary patterns of divorce in chapter 1 highlighted a particularly vulnerable group of first marriages undertaken between very young couples from lower working-class backgrounds. It is evident that for some, their obvious disadvantages in the labour and housing markets and the early arrival of children are compounded by their social isolation. Several studies of early married life highlight the importance of the closely entwined web of emotional and material support offered to young couples who marry and set up home within a close-knit network of family and friends. By contrast, in other studies of 'troubled' marriages some couples portrayed themselves as particularly isolated and lacking in social supports.[2]

Changing patterns of kinship and the effects of geographical and occupational mobility have generated a good deal of debate among sociologists of the family in the post-Second-World-War period. However, their observations and conclusions must be modified in the light of recent and profound change in patterns of employment as well, of course, as trends in divorce, remarriage and subsequent family formation. It is, however, possible to make some *very tentative* observations about the kind of class groupings, occupational communities and social environments that provide *most* and *least* potential for the development of networks of contact and support for young couples, based on family, friends or neighbours. For example, within the aristocracy and upper classes, ties of kinship still underpin many economic and business relationships and are a focus for both formal and informal leisure activities. To a lesser extent this is also likely to be true of young adults who are born into, and who may themselves form part of, the professional middle classes, although individuals 'drop out' or are 'cast off' by their family for one reason or another. Even though different generations of such families may not necessarily live in close geographical proximity to each other, access to cars, lengthy telephone calls and holidays enable them to keep in contact, and economic transfers, both direct and indirect, from parents to their adult children are common. Where professional couples set up home in a new area, local occupational communities also provide them with a parallel source of potential friends of similar backgrounds and values.

Until recently it was also possible to identify many so-called 'stable' working-class communities and neighbourhoods in which young couples courted, married and set up home within a closeknit network of family and friends. The industrial recession has already decimated many of these communities but there is, as yet, little research-based evidence of its effects upon patterns of marriage and family building. It should be noted that recent government employment policies aimed at encouraging young adults to 'get on their bikes' and travel in search of paid work can only exacerbate such isolation, as do the supplementary benefit regulations, which affect single people generally. Where mobility takes place without access to the material resources necessary to sustain real and continuing contacts with kin, or to build new friendships within their new locality, young couples, particularly mothers with young children, are likely to endure considerable and damaging social isolation.

The potential effects of post-Second-World-War trends in geographical and occupational mobility on marriage are highlighted by the relatively high levels of divorce experienced by members of Social Class IIIN. Since the 1950s, this stratum of society has expanded rapidly because of the growth in new intermediate service-type occupations as well as an overall increase in the numbers engaged in this kind of work, especially, but not exclusively, in the affluent south-east. Increasingly, posts of this type have been filled by those whose origins or first employment was on the other side of the still significant manual/non-manual divide. As a result this class contains a higher proportion of people who have experienced significant social mobility and who have also moved away from the area in which they grew up.

Haskey[3] also analysed his data on the association between class and divorce in a way that allows us to consider broad occupational differences in divorce rates. Among a sample of those divorcing in 1979 he found high levels of divorce in the following occupational groups: personal service, 'literary, artistic and sports', security and protective service, including the armed forces, and selling. By contrast, the professions, managers and clerks had relatively low levels of divorce. Although Haskey himself tries to account for such variations by referring to significant differences in how the occupations themselves are structured, this evidence may also be used to demonstrate the ways in which following certain occupations or the experience of geographical and social mobility undermine both partners' patterns of contact with family and established friends in the early years of marriage. For example, several of these divorce-prone occupations are relatively new and have expanded rapidly so that they are likely to contain a high proportion of socially mobile workers. Others entail irregular working hours and/or a great deal of travel so that workers may find it difficult to sustain relationships with family and friends who have more 'typical' patterns of work and leisure. In other occupations, frequent geographical moves or postings are the norm and these affect the whole household; for example, not only do Service wives have to endure their husbands' frequent and unforeseen absences, but they are also likely to be living a long distance away from their own families and former close friends.

In this discussion we have highlighted two factors, continuing communication between partners and access to a supportive network of family and/or friends, that often help couples to negotiate the changes endemic to any lasting partnership. We would not wish to suggest that their absence always or inevitably leads to marriage breakdown, nor that they are the only significant factors involved. Throughout the book we have been at pains to draw attention to the persistent and entrenched inequalities within and between households which are so often obscured in contemporary mythologies of 'typical' patterns of family life. Haskey's findings also provide a powerful reminder of the long-established link between poverty and marriage breakdown. Not only is the divorce rate highest for households headed by unskilled manual workers but even in 1979 the effects of rising levels of unemployment were becoming apparent. While unemployed husbands in their twenties were four times as likely to divorce as husbands from Social Class 1, older unemployed men fared even worse. For example, Haskey found that unemployed husbands in their fifties were twice as likely to divorce as unskilled manual workers of a similar age. Statistical evidence of this kind provides a limited but timely reminder of the broader family and personal consequences of unemployment and suggests questions to which, as yet, we have no reliable answers.[4] If the experience of unemployment appears to undermine many established families and households in this way, how will widespread unemployment among teenagers and young adults affect their own patterns of partnership and family building in the future? In the circumstances there seems something bitterly unjust and ironic about the present government's recent attempts to introduce courses on 'Education for Marriage and Parenthood' for school leavers just at a time when an increasing proportion are being denied access to the basic building blocks of a lasting domestic partnership – an adequate and relatively secure income and a home of their own.

Although it is obviously impossible to predict how changing patterns of employment are likely to affect future trends in divorce, the material we summarized in chapter 1 indicates that the steady increase in the number of divorces has levelled off at least temporarily so that, as a society, we have the opportunity to pause, take stock and consider whether the divorce procedures themselves or other social, fiscal or economic policies affecting divorced people cause unnecessary pain or distress.

IS DIVORCE BECOMING 'TOO EASY'?

We have shown in chapter 2 that until quite recently divorce law was concerned almost exclusively with regulating the conditions under which remarriage was legally possible during the lifetime of the other partner. It was not until 1969 that the irretrievable breakdown of marriage was recognized as the basis for divorce and an attempt made to provide a legal framework for the financial and other adjustments which ought to be made when a marriage comes to its end. It follows that, until then, divorce statistics could tell us little about the prevalence of marriage breakdown itself and thus the stability of marriage at any given period in the past. The current figures, based as they are on the legal basis of irretrievable break-down, are a better, but by no means accurate, measure of the stability or instability of marriage today. The slow process of divorce law reform has gradually made it easier for some of those whose mar-riages have broken down to obtain a divorce but there is little reason to think that it has stimulated more breakdowns. The rise in the divorce rate has been influenced more by measures which have in-creased its availability than by enlarging the grounds on which divorce could be obtained. The development of the legal-aid system has removed most of the financial barriers to divorce and the increase in employment opportunities for women and the extension of social security benefits have made it possible for very many more women to survive after divorce.

At a more general level, we need to consider the relationship between the legal system and the behaviour of individuals. Divorce is often talked of as if it were the primary regulator of marriage itself – when, for example, it is suggested that 'easy' divorce is destroying the whole basis of family life. The implicit suggestion here is that many people only remain in a marriage because they cannot get out of it. Taking the argument to its extreme, it would imply that were divorce banned, all couples would remain together. In some European countries, such as Ireland, divorce is indeed banned. However, there is no good evidence to suggest a higher quality of family life in such countries or indeed that marriage itself is particularly stable. When people do not have recourse to divorce they find other, and not necessarily better, ways of reordering their domestic life. We should remember that at the turn of the century in Britain when divorce was effectively unavailable to all but the very rich, there was a conservative argument for the extension of divorce to poorer sections of society in order to prevent people living 'in sin' and thus to uphold the sanctity of marriage.

At the other extreme, the legal system is sometimes portrayed as simply responding to social change. Thus, changes in divorce procedures are seen simply as a reflection and product of marital behaviour; so that when there is a high rate of marital breakdown the system will adjust and provide a means of formalizing the situation. In chapter 2 we saw that the law does adjust to changing circumstances. In the 1960s as divorce rates rose, court procedures were simplified so that the greater numbers could be accommodated. But neither of the extreme views of the role of the legal system can account for all the facts. The law reflects the values and behaviour of the society that creates it (or at least that part of the society that has political control) but in turn the legal system influences individuals. It is undoubtedly true that as more married people have contact with the divorced and as divorce becomes a feature of everyday life, in both fact and fiction, more people will see it as a solution to their own marital problems. But we must recognize that familiarity with divorce also brings knowledge of its emotional and financial hardships so that the encouragement is by no means all in one direction. Rather than regarding divorce as a contagious disease we should perhaps see it as a social institution which for some allows the reordering of unsatisfactory social relations.

SETTLING DISPUTES

It is now widely accepted, both by those directly involved and contributors to public debates about divorce, that divorce is a much more serious matter if it involves children. It is, therefore, vitally important to develop a system of divorce law and procedure that gives much greater attention to children's needs. Not only is this important for the thousands of children whose parents divorce each year, but it would also give substance to the diffuse desire, consciously expressed by many separating parents, to make things as easy as possible for the children. It is possible that many of their feelings of anger, guilt or shame about the breakdown of their marriage might be alleviated if they knew that they were doing everything possible to spare their children unnecessary uncertainty and conflict.

Much professional and political discussion has focused on two related issues: the introduction of family courts as first advocated in the Finer Report in 1974[5] and the recent development of a variety of conciliation services. We will discuss each of these in turn as well as other suggested changes. But before doing this, it may be useful to discuss a general theme that underlies much of what we have to say in the next section: the extent to which a formal legal system should play a part in the regulation and ordering of domestic life. Most of the recent developments in the law related to divorce and many of the proposals for further change involve a movement from public to private ordering; fewer decisions are being made by the courts and more by the individuals concerned.

One of the clearest examples of this is in the decision to divorce itself. Under the pre-1969 system a court had to decide whether or not to grant a divorce. Sometimes, individuals who wanted a divorce were refused one. However, since the concept of irretrievable breakdown was introduced this function of the court has all but disappeared. Today, if any married person wishes to divorce they can do so. In practice, if not in theory, the decision has become theirs not the court's. The court's function is to endorse and make public a private decision.

A second example of the movement towards private ordering is given by the growth of conciliation services, to be discussed in more detail below. In the traditional court system a dispute between parents about the custody of their children is settled by the decision of a judge. Each parent, or their representatives, puts forward their case and these, together with such evidence as a report from a court welfare officer, form a basis on which the judge makes a decision. With conciliation the parents separately, or together, bargain and discuss until some kind of agreement is reached. The conciliator's role is not to judge between conflicting views, but to suggest areas of common ground and compromises that may be acceptable, and to provide a forum in which discussion can take place. If an agreement is produced during conciliation, this goes to the court for what is, in effect, a rubber stamp approval. Once again, the arena of decision making has changed from the court to private negotiation.

Under our present system the court plays a role in the arrangements for children even where there is no dispute. As we have seen, the law provides that the petitioner parent shall outline arrangements for the children to the court and that a divorce shall be granted only if the court is satisfied that these are the best that can be made in the circumstances. While these children's hearings may provide a very superficial system of control, it is a *public* control. There are those who have argued that when there are no disputes between parents about children the court should have no role at all. This is the view of Goldstein, Solnit and Freud in their influential book, *Beyond the Best Interests of the Child*.[6] Even where parents are not in agreement, these authors suggest that the court's role should be restricted to determining who should have custody. All matters concerning such things as access would be for the custodial parent to decide. Clearly, if such a position were adopted it would represent a considerable change towards a private ordering system.

Those who favour a movement towards private ordering often argue that the legal system is a blunt instrument to use to intervene in social relationships and that agreements that people make for themselves are more likely to be kept than those imposed on them by a judge in court. Some commentators also suggest that public ordering encourages a further and unnecessary extension of professional intrusion into the private sphere of domestic life, which they regard as highly undesirable. Conveniently for those who wish to reduce public expenditure, arguments about a professional retreat from those areas would seem to be consistent with moves to reduce social and welfare services. On the other side, it is suggested that private ordering tends to favour the more powerful and that public intervention may be essential to protect the weak. Some feminists, for instance, have argued against the growth of conciliation on the ground that it is likely to favour men while others have suggested that in order to protect the interests of children it is necessary to have some surveillance of arrangements for children at divorce.[7] It has also been pointed out that public ceremonies to mark crucial life events – such as marriage and divorce – can help the psychological adjustment of those concerned. From this kind of perspective, a divorce hearing could serve as a formal mark for the end of a marriage. In contradiction to the claim that private agreements are more likely to be kept, some proponents of public ordering suggest that a decision handed out with the authority of a court may persuade reluctant spouses to come to terms in situations where it seems impossible to get an agreement through negotiations or conciliation.

It is easy to overestimate the part that court decisions can play in matters such as divorce. It is common for those involved to feel that the court should 'sort everything out'. In fact, at best, a judicial decision can only provide a very bare framework within which individuals have to reorder their lives and come to terms with the inevitable pain and confusion. Ultimately, a court is not able to force a reluctant father to see his children or an angry mother to welcome access visits. While we may believe that modifying court proceedings and moving towards some particular form of private ordering may be more likely to achieve the resolution of the conflicts at divorce, we have to recognize that such behaviour between individuals can never be fully regulated or controlled by such means.

THE GRANTING OF A DIVORCE

The combined effect of divorce for irretrievable breakdown and the special procedure by which uncontested divorces are dealt with on paper (and by post) by registrars, has been to reduce the role of the court in dissolving marriages to a pure formality, but with unpleasant overtones arising from the necessity to specify in writing the details of adultery or, more painful perhaps, of 'unreasonable behaviour'. This benefits nobody and costs a considerable amount of money.

It would be sensible to accept that the court now has no useful function in this respect, and to consider a simpler alternative. The concept of marriage as a partnership suggests a solution. Most partnerships can be dissolved by written notice of an appropriate length. Rather than serve a petition for divorce which, in practice, is not resisted in any but the most exceptional cases, the marriage could be dissolved by a formal notice in writing after, say, the expiry of twelve months waiting period, either on terms agreed between the parties or determined by the court. This would emphasize that divorce is essentially a dissolution of partnership by the act of the parties themselves or one of them, and leave the court to its fundamental role of settling disputes in as fair and just a manner as possible. It would also make much clearer to people that, when they embark on marriage they are entering upon a partnership that has far-reaching financial consequences that will have to be dealt with if the partnership ends, not in the traditional way by payment of maintenance by one to the other under a legal duty, but by a division of assets, compensation for loss of earning capacity and economic disadvantage, and payment for child care. It would also emphasize the duty of both parties to make full disclosure both of their assets and their intentions if these have financial consequences, as would, for example, immediate plans to remarry.

All these matters might be settled *before* the divorce becomes effective, probably in the form of a deed of divorce similar to a deed of separation which was often used in the past. However, it would be important for the court to retain its powers to intervene to prevent injustice because agreements made in the emotional turmoil may give one party an unfair bargaining power. As a result it is conceivable that in some marriages the parties would wish to define their rights and liabilities on divorce before they marry. At present, agreements made before marriage that contemplate divorce are held to be contrary to public policy and therefore legally unenforceable. But there is a case for permitting a new form of marriage contract of this kind.

Little change would be required to the existing law on financial arrangements. The provisions of the 1973 Act dealing with these arrangements are very broad. The court's powers over property and money are virtually complete and the guide lines in Section 25 would serve satisfactorily in this context of a dissolution of partnership. Even a pre-marriage agreement could be fitted into this scheme which requires the court to take into account 'all the circumstances of the case'.

The Booth Committee report, as we shall see, does not go quite as far as us in the matter of divorce. While retaining the various 'facts' that are required to substantiate the irretrievable breakdown of marriage, they do suggest a spouse should be allowed simply to state their grounds without giving any details of what has happened. Of course, the Booth Committee was charged with the task of looking at procedures under the present law rather than the law itself. The logic of the Booth argument would be to modify the law in the way we have suggested.

MATTERS RELATED TO CHILDREN

If the divorce itself were to become a simplified matter of public notice of a private decision, courts would be free to devote their full attention to the settlement of disputes and, perhaps, to safeguard the position of children in other ways. Before discussing disputes we should consider the role of the courts in cases where the parents are in agreement about their children. At present in such cases the petitioner parent is required to give the court a brief outline of what is planned for the children and then to appear before the judge at the so-called children's hearing (also called Section 41 hearing after the relevant section of the Act) so that the court can certify that it is satisfied that the arrangements for the children are the best that can be made in the circumstances. It is a condition of divorce that the court shall be 'satisfied' with the arrangements for the children. As we have mentioned already, there are those who believe that hearings such as these are an unwarranted and undesirable intrusion into the lives of parents and children and should be abolished. Certainly on the face of it their functions seem very limited. Studies[8] have shown that it is unusual for a hearing to take more than a few minutes so that any examination of the situation must be very superficial, and it is very rare for courts to do anything but accept what is proposed. There are indications that judges are reluctant to start searching lines of questioning for fear that the discussion might be prolonged or they might expose a problem for which there is no obvious solution. Parents who have tried to raise questions about the current arrangements and care of their children are not uncommonly dismayed to discover that the points they are trying to raise are brushed aside.

There are practical issues too. Many of the problems that are likely to emerge when the questioning is a little more thorough are those beyond the powers of the court to do much about, concerning such matters as housing, social security benefits or schooling. There seems little point in discussing them. Furthermore, such an approach would be time-consuming, as more judges would be required to operate the system and, of course, costs would rise.

Thus it seems that the present system is unsatisfactory and we must move in one direction or another. We could abolish these hearings and rely on the usual protective services and legislation that operate during marriage to continue to look after the interests of children at divorce. This would also have the merit of being consistent so that the situation would be akin to that when a child is orphaned, when there is no particular requirement for the courts to examine arrangements made for the child. Such a move might also serve to remove a false sense of security that the present system provides adequate protection for children and might encourage the health and social services to take greater interest in children at divorce.

At present, one of the protective mechanisms available to courts is to make a supervision order. This places a responsibility on either the probation or social work service to take a continuing interest in the child. Such orders are very rarely made unless a dispute exists over a child, so abolishing children's hearings in undisputed cases would have little effect on such orders. But even if they did, it might be of small consequence as there is little evidence that supervision orders are very effective or add much to the child protection system that exists independently of the divorce legislation.

Despite these powerful arguments we would, on balance, like to see the system move in the opposite direction and to strengthen the role of the children's hearing. Here again we are in agreement with the conclusions of the Booth Committee[9] which we will consider below. We take this view because we believe that the role of the court is much wider than as a potential protective system for children. Hearings could become of much greater symbolic importance for children and parents if they were seen, in part, as a public confirmation of the continuing role of both parents as parents after the ending of their marriage. This could be an important way of indicating to parents that parental obligations and duties are not interrupted by divorce and, in line with the arguments advanced in chapter 4, that continued contact is usually in the best interests of the child. At present in most cases the mother, as petitioner, attends a children's hearing. For the hearing to perform the role we indicate here, it would be appropriate for *both* parents to be required to attend.

Searching questioning about the ways in which parents intend to look after their children is probably not only ineffective but inappropriate in such a situation. However, there seems every reason to encourage some discussion with a view to referring parents to a court welfare officer if they indicate any problems. It could also provide an occasion when parents could be given information about such things as single-parent benefits, perhaps in the form of a booklet with addresses and phone numbers of appropriate statutory and voluntary organizations. Again, this is a suggestion that the Booth Committee has adopted though they seem to favour rather less specific information being included in a booklet than we believe would be desirable.

By the same token, it might be appropriate for joint custody orders to become the norm at divorce (see pp. 138–41): we would like to suggest that they become the usual arrangement rather than as at present where they are only made in a small minority of cases. Indeed, were parents to ask for any other custody arrangement, this could be taken as sufficient reason for a court to investigate the matter even in the absence of a formal dispute about the children.

FAMILY COURTS

The creation of a family court is widely canvassed as the answer to many of the present difficulties in settling disputes at divorce. The idea is for a specialized court that would move away from the traditional adversarial model and place much greater emphasis on conciliation. But while many people, both professional and lay, seem to favour a family court of some kind there are many varied and sometimes contradictory ideas that have been described by that term. Many of the proposals that have been put forward are very vague about many of the practical details.

The present debate has its origins in the proposals of the Finer Committee on One-Parent Families which advocated a family court based on six principles. These are:

1. It must be an impartial judicial institution, regulating the rights of citizens and settling their disputes according to law.

2. It will be a unified institution in a system of family law which applies a uniform set of legal rules, derived from a single moral standard and applicable to all citizens.

3. It will organize its work in such a way as to provide the best possible facilities for conciliation between parties in marital disputes.

4. It will have professionally trained staff to assist both the court and the parties before it in all matters requiring social work services and advice.

5. It will work in close relationship with the social security authorities in the assessment of the needs and liability in cases involving financial provision.

6. It will organize its procedure, sittings, administrative services and other arrangements, with a view to gaining the confidence and maximizing the convenience of citizens who would appear before it.

While broad principles of this kind meet with wide approval, it is quite another matter to turn them into a practical working system. We also have to consider how such change should be brought about: for some, slow evolution is the preferred route, while others favour an overnight replacement of the present system. We will open our discussion by looking at a number of basic issues or principles that have been part of some, or all, of the proposals for a family court and then describe one example of a family court system in practice. We will then conclude this section with a discussion of the extent to which matters might be improved without adopting a family court.

Perhaps the most limited version of a family court is one that calls for a unification of the various systems of law and courts that apply these. At present, problems relating to the ending of a marriage may be dealt with in a magistrate's court, a county court, a county court sitting as a divorce court, and the Family Division of the High Court. These courts operate a complicated and confusing system of overlapping law. While very few people would defend the present system without any changes, the obstacles to revision are more formidable than might appear at first sight.

To a lay person, the reform of a law might seem a fairly straightforward matter of sitting down and writing something better than exists already, but there are two main difficulties in the case of family law. The law is complicated not simply because it has grown up over a long period of time and has gone through repeated additions and modifications as its scope and purposes have altered, but also because it deals with complicated human affairs that have ramifications through almost all other aspects of life and, therefore, other parts of the law. For example, changes in the way in which property is divided at divorce are likely to have consequences for the law of property itself. The second reason concerns the principle, or principles, on which any law is based. We have already quoted Finer who talked of law derived from a single moral standard. But what is that standard? It is clear that in a great many of the issues there is wide disagreement about what the basic principles should be. Without agreement, or at least a reasonable degree of consensus, fundamental law reform is not feasible. For example, there is clear disagreement about the extent to which the history of a marriage and, in particular, the conduct of the spouses should influence decisions at divorce. If conduct is to play a significant role, there must be a process by which each party states what has happened (in their view), and which allows these accounts to be open to challenge by the other party. Any such system is going to require an elaborate set of rules and procedures. However, if, on the other hand, conduct is deemed to be of no importance, it would be possible to devise a very much simpler system whereby the basic 'facts' of the marriage – its date, number of children and so on – are presented to the court.

Another example concerns the position of children. At present children are not represented independently of their parents at divorce. There is a good historical reason for this, in that matters concerning children at divorce are ancillary to the basic proceedings in which the divorce itself is granted to the two parties to the original marriage. There are those who believe that children would be better protected if they were represented independently but this would require a basic change in the nature of the proceedings so that they could become parties to it. Others argue that parents are in a much better position than an outsider to protect the interests of their own children, so making independent representation, except in the exceptional circumstances that it can be arranged at present, unnecessary and undesirable.

As well as a unified system of law, most proposals call for a single court to administer it: a family court together with a family appeal court. Any such change would, of course, require that present courts give up some of their functions which would be resisted in some quarters. Most magistrates, for instance, do not wish to give up their domestic jurisdiction. They feel that they are particularly well placed to exercise it and also that removing it might alter the role of the magistrate in a way that might be damaging for all their work. Others present a contrary argument and say that because the magistrate's court (formally known as the police court) deals with criminal matters, it carries a stigma for those who go to it for domestic matters. In addition, others have criticized the kinds of assumptions about parenthood and family life made by some magistrates, recruited as they still are from a relatively narrow stratum of British society.

It is also important to recognize that the administration of the present system continues to make changes very difficult. Currently, it falls under three different government departments, the Lord Chancellor's Department, which administers the Divorce and High Court, the Home Office, which carries responsibility for the magistracy and the Probation Service (which provides court welfare officers), and the Department of Health and Social Security, which is concerned with local authority care for children. One weakness of our system of government is that issues which fall between departments are particularly difficult to change because this involves altering delicate balances of power within the governmental system itself.

A second feature common to many family court proposals is that they should move the system away from the adversarial style of procedure. The usual argument here is that while the adversarial procedure is appropriate in criminal cases where each side presents its evidence and the court decides between them, the nature of family disputes is such that adversarial proceedings only serve to increase anger and bitterness.

It is also argued that issues being dealt with are not of the same nature as in criminal law so that the same procedures are not necessarily appropriate. As we saw in chapter 2, much of the work of the court at divorce involves the exercise of discretion on the basis of information provided by the parties and perhaps independent professionals such as court welfare officers. While a criminal court must decide which version of the 'facts' is supported by the evidence, in a divorce court there may be little agreement about what information is relevant to the case and the 'facts', such as they are, may be open to a number of different interpretations.

The usual alternative proposed to the adversarial system is the inquisitorial model in which the judge takes a much more active role in the questioning of the parties. This shifts the balance as the judge, not the parties or their representative, decides what the important information may be and how far the proceeding will range. At present in a custody dispute, a parent may produce an affidavit in which they may describe at length what they believe to be the moral failings of the other parent, and numerous incidents of the marriage itself. In court it is very likely that the judge will ignore all or most of such information. However, its presence in the affidavit is likely, to say the least, to upset the other parent, who may well retaliate with similar accusations. Under an inquisitorial system a judge could avoid the whole area and stick to much more practical questions about childcare and plans for the future.

It is certainly true that many adults find the mud-slinging that the adversarial system encourages a very upsetting part of the divorce system. This is not only because it often involves the exposure of very private aspects of married life but it also constitutes a breach of the trust that existed between the spouses in the marriage. Couples have unwritten rules about what is private to them and what may be shared with others. Not only are these rules broken in affidavits but the information is taken out of context and often given a slant that makes it particularly offensive to the other partner. While it has been said by some that the ritualized slanging matches of the divorce process serve a beneficial purpose in that they allow people to express their anger and get it out of their system, few of those who have experienced it see it in such terms. They are much more likely to feel that it was an unnecessary part of the whole process that increased and prolonged the bitterness and anger and prevented them from making the fresh start they so much desire.

As well as a less adversarial style, many advocates of family courts suggest that their proceedings should be relatively informal so that people may feel more at ease and able to express themselves clearly. Those who have had experience of the present system often complain that they have not been able to say what they feel and that much of the business has gone on over their heads, as most of the discussion was about legal issues and took place between the lawyers and the judge. The argument here is partly one about private ordering and a call for a system that allows the participants greater control of the proceedings. We should note two potential difficulties for a family court. The first is that unless the judge exercises a close control, the participants may find themselves getting into just the kind of claims and counter-claims that can make the adversarial proceedings so upsetting. To avoid this the agenda of the court may have to be set by the judge, but when this is done participants may again feel that they have not had a real chance to express themselves properly and their arguments have not been listened to.[10]

The problem is probably insoluble. It is in the nature of formal proceedings, such as courts, that participants may feel that their private world has not been adequately represented because part of what is at issue is competing versions of reality. A totally informal court controlled by the participants might avoid this difficulty but at the same time might forfeit the power to make decisions and would not constitute a court at all.

The second difficulty concerns the relative power of participants. It has been suggested that as systems of justice move towards private ordering they disadvantage those who are already in a weak position. Informal justice systems may favour those who are confident, can express themselves clearly and are generally articulate. For example, a man is more likely to develop the relevant skills as he may use them in the course of his work. Women, on the other hand, may have less experience in presenting a case for themselves in any context and may suffer in proceedings which depend on skills of this kind. At worst this could lead to a situation where someone who has dominated and bullied their way through a marriage continues to exercise their power in divorce proceedings.

Of course, even under the present system legal aid has not abolished all differences of power. Knowledge, for instance, can lead to one party receiving better advice and support in pursuing their case. But the point remains that when we consider any family court system we have to think how changes in procedures may shift the balance between those in conflict who may use it. It is also necessary that justice is seen to be done and due process is followed. To serve any judicial function, a court must have some formality of procedure – indeed that is what a court is, a formal system of procedures for deciding issues in conflict – so while it may well be that much can be done to make courts more approachable and less remote for those who use them, there are limits to this process.

Another feature of many family court proposals is that those who work in them should specialize in family matters. This is only true at the moment in the Family Division of the High Court. There is a strong case for specialization. In so far as the issues under discussion in a court concerned with domestic matters are different from those in other branches of the law, specialist knowledge and experience are desirable. The skills that make a good County court judge may not be the same as those that would be appropriate in divorce work so that some selection of those who have appropriate interests and knowledge might be very desirable. There is, however, a counter-argument which says that family work is both depressing and emotionally taxing, dealing as it does with the failure of relationships and other highly emotive matters. Judges, it is suggested, should be encouraged to have some respite from such work. However, it would be quite possible to devise a system that would allow both specialization and selection as well as a chance to 'dilute' family work with other branches of the law.

The other main points against specialization come from people who believe that lay magistrates would be much better at dealing with domestic matters than professional judges. They suggest that a panel of three magistrates (with both sexes represented) is likely to reach more satisfactory decisions than a single judge. In addition, there is the claim that magistrates, because they are lay, are in some way closer to domestic life, and therefore in a better position to reach decisions concerning it. However, it is our belief that a degree of professional detachment is essential in family work. We all have experience of close social relationships and our own feelings are likely to influence how we see the social relations of others. While we can never totally rule out such personal bias, it would seem that professional training of some kind is the best way of minimizing it.

On the other hand, while efforts to expand the social groups from which magistrates are recruited have only been partially successful, judges still come from a narrow stratum of society and must in some part reflect the values of that group and the professional world in which they operate. This can be seen in statements in reported judgements which sometimes express the values and social position of those who make them.

Mediation and conciliation

The final feature of family court proposals we shall consider is the use of conciliation and mediation procedures. While these already exist in the current systems, most plans for family courts involve a considerable extension of their use. These were mentioned in the last chapter but we need to consider them in rather more detail here. As with the term 'family court', reconciliation, conciliation and mediation can mean different things to different people, so we must begin with some more precise definitions.

Reconciliation is the provision of support and counselling which has the aim of bringing estranged spouses back together again. Traditionally this is represented by the 'marriage-saving' activities of marriage counselling agencies such as the Marriage Guidance Council. *Conciliation* is defined by the Finer committee as

> assisting the parties to deal with the consequences of the established breakdown of their marriage whether resulting in divorce or separation, by reaching agreement or giving comments or reducing the area of conflict upon custody, support, access to and

education of children, financial provision, the disposition of the matrimonial home, lawyer's fees and every other matter arising from the breakdown which calls for a decision on future arrangements.

It is not always possible to draw a line between these two activities as one may lead to the other. A couple seeking help with a marital problem from, say, a marriage guidance counsellor, may reach the point where they decide to separate. From then on, reconciliation may become conciliation. The reverse is also true, as a proportion of couples who have gone to a conciliation service because they believed their marriage was over have, in fact, been reconciled.

Traditionally, English law has emphasized reconciliation rather than conciliation. There is the provision, for instance, which allows broken periods of separation to be added together to make up the time required to obtain a divorce, so permitting couples to cohabit for experimental periods of reconciliation. And at present, a solicitor acting for the petitioner is required to state whether he has discussed with the petitioner the possibility of reconciliation and informed him or her of the appropriate agencies. Provisions such as this seem little more than empty gestures and their origin has more to do with a political price paid for a reformed divorce law than a carefully planned attempt to modify the behaviour of divorcing spouses. These same pressures may help to explain the absence of a nationwide conciliation service. In an atmosphere where there was disquiet about 'easier' divorce, attempts to set up divorce conciliation were thought likely to damage the chances of changing the divorce law itself by those interested in divorce law reform.

Counselling is essentially similar to conciliation or reconciliation except that it may only involve one of the parties. It may vary in the extent to which it is directive or otherwise. Non-directive counselling may consist of an opportunity to talk things over and the counsellor may point out things that had not occurred to the client, or help them to explore contradictory feelings and confused emotions. Directive counselling has a much more specific and explicit aim which might be reconciliation or conciliation.

Mediation is the process of providing a link or channel of direct communication between the spouses so that they may discuss their

differences. Examples of mediation are the joint judicial appointments that some courts are experimenting with where both parties
are brought together and asked to state their differences and the
areas of common ground. Unlike conciliation which may take many
sessions, this kind of mediation is usually attempted at a single
session. Where parties have not been in direct contact and perhaps
have felt that the position reached in the negotiations between solicitors does not entirely fit with their wishes, this form of mediation
can produce significant results. Another form of mediation is the
joint meetings sometimes held by court welfare officers in the course
of making a report in a disputed custody case. Sometimes this process
is referred to as conciliation. However, by the definition we are
using here it is mediation as it is brief, and because the mediator is
often involved in the decision making (i.e. the writing of a welfare
report which in a majority of cases makes a recommendation which
the court is very likely to follow).

At present there are probably about fifty conciliation services
working on a voluntary basis in various parts of Britain. The best
known of these is the Bristol scheme which was set up very much
along the lines suggested by the Finer Committee. There have been
some attempts to evaluate this scheme in terms of the number of
disputed issues that have been resolved during conciliation and on
these measures it appears to be very successful. But the process of
evaluation is a very difficult one because there are many sorts of
outcome we might consider. For example, we might think it is less
important to know how many issues are resolved at the time than to
see how far any agreements that were made are being kept at some
later date. Is it the case, as has been claimed, that an agreement, say
about access, that has been worked out by a process of conciliation
is more likely to be kept than one handed down by a judge after a
court hearing? As yet we do not know, as the necessary follow-up
studies have not been carried out.[11] Recently, the Lord Chancellor's
Department has set up a research project to evaluate the present out-
of-court conciliation services and the in-court mediation schemes.
When this has been completed the general picture may become
clearer.

Gwynn Davis[12] has set out very clearly the potential advantages
of conciliation:

1. It can enable the parties to retain greater control over the conduct and outcome of their own case.
2. It can allow their individual interpretations of their differences to be taken into account.
3. It can provide a degree of emotional support which may enable them to shift their view of what is fair.
4. It may encourage them to focus on the interests of family members as a whole.
5. It may assist them to develop a pattern of communication which will serve them in good stead in future negotiations.

One important factor that must be considered in any evaluation is the variety and variation in conciliation practice. For example, some schemes try to put pressure on clients to reach agreement by setting limits on time available for negotiation and by the conciliator adopting a relatively active role. In this they approach the model of the in-court services where time is very limited and there is the ever-present threat of the stresses and uncertainties of a court hearing if an agreement is not reached. Others take the view that such pressures can be counter-productive or may lead to ill-considered agreements and that a more relaxed approach is more effective. Perhaps particular people or particular problems would be better with one or other style so that there may be no single best system and a good conciliator would need to be able to adjust their strategy to suit each case.

There is also the important question of who should be conciliators – what kind of training or selection is required? Should it be open to anyone or is a previous qualification in social work, psychology, counselling or a related discipline necessary or indeed desirable? At present, attempts are being made to impose some basic training requirements, though others believe this to be premature and likely only to inhibit experiment and development. The matter has been complicated by the very rapid acceptance of the idea of conciliation. This has led the three professional groups who might seem most appropriate to provide conciliators to begin to compete for control over the field. It is hardly surprising that, at a time when social and welfare budgets are being cut, the professions involved should seek new outlets for their members. The three groups involved are social workers, marriage guidance counsellors and probation officers. Not surprisingly, the latter group, in their role as court welfare officers, has largely been concerned with in-court schemes. But while members of any of these three groups may make excellent conciliators, the skills required in conciliation are not identical with those needed for the other activities these professions undertake.

As Gwynn Davis[13] summarizes them, the elements involved in conciliation are:

1. never giving emotional support to one party to a dispute at the expense of another;
2. encouraging both sides to express their true feelings and ensuring that the points made by each are listened to and understood;
3. ensuring that the discussion remains focused on the issues;
4. controlling and limiting heated exchanges so that, while anger and distress are acknowledged, they are not allowed to overwhelm and dominate the proceedings;
5. adhering to the parties' understanding of their differences rather than imposing an interpretation upon them;
6. willingness to offer clarification and reinstatement of respective positions.

At present the relationship between conciliation and the courts is neither formal nor legally binding. A court cannot force people to go to conciliators, nor are they bound to accept any agreement made during conciliation. But, in practice, courts are unlikely to upset an agreement that has been made. This raises the question of who is to protect the interests of those who might be affected by an agreement but who are not party to it, principally children. As we mentioned in the last chapter, there can be pressures on the parties and the conciliator to reach an agreement so a deal may be struck concerning the children. The court, not wishing to upset things, does not enquire too closely into its consequences and simply writes it into a court order. Who then protects the children?

While it is reasonable to expect that a conciliator will ensure that the children's interests are protected, conciliation services are still developing appropriate procedures and practices in this area.

A point often made about conciliation (but not mediation) is that it is able to reach people earlier than the court system and that problems are usually more soluble the sooner they are tackled. It is not simply that people's positions consolidate over time but it may become increasingly difficult to change established arrangements and re-lationships. As we saw in chapter 4, courts seldom change arrange-ments for children that have been in operation for some time; they usually confirm the status quo. This means, of course, that as it is often many months before a court hearing takes place, courts have less influence in determining what happens to children than the parents have through the arrangements made in the heat of the moment when they first separated. Conciliation could lead to a review of such arrangements at a time when change is still possible. However, there are also disadvantages as the long waits for a court hearing also operate as a kind of rationing system. It is not so much that the problems go away, but that life cannot be suspended while waiting for the courts, so that some sort of arrangement may be made. This can mean that by the time the court sitting is reached, a solution of some kind has been found. Couples are under pressure to reach some measure of agreement so that things are sorted quickly. This can happen, for instance, when one, or both, of the spouses is keen to remarry as they want the divorce settled as soon as possible. If access to the system were to be made easier and without any delay, it seems likely that the calls on it would increase and that problems that people are forced to solve for themselves at present would be taken to conciliators. It is very difficult to know whether this is to be welcomed or not. But in any event it does remind us that the demand for a system is not a fixed quantity but is determined, in part, by its accessibility.

As well as the difficulty with conciliation we have already con-sidered – that it can favour the articulate and powerful – it has been suggested that it is a form of dispute-resolution that will only work effectively for those used to solving differences by negotiation. Class differences could be important here. It is probably true that at present those who go to conciliation (who represent a very small proportion of those in dispute at divorce) are more likely to be middle class. We do not know what might happen if the clientele were broadened to other social groups.

Those who are now using the service do so quite freely. If con-ciliation were tied more closely to the court system the pressure to take part is likely to increase which might lead to rather different results, both in terms of the success rate and of the structure of the conciliation itself.

It is often claimed that conciliation is much cheaper than the settlement of disputes in court and by solicitors paid for out of the legal-aid fund. Though work is under way, we do not as yet have any good estimate of the costs of conciliation or, indeed, of the proposals for family courts. Clearly, cost is not the only consideration – we might feel it was well worth spending a bit more if the general level of unhappiness and distress were reduced – but is likely to be the major consideration in the present political climate. In assessing costs we must consider the system in broad terms. We need to look beyond the legal system to assess the cost implications of changing legal practice in the light of social costs in other areas such as the provision of health and welfare services, for example. If conciliation is successful in reaching its aim of providing support for parents and minimizing avoidable pain among children and their divorcing parents, then this could result in a decrease in the need for other counselling, support and health services.

The family court in practice

We turn now from theoretical considerations to an example of practice. Over the last decade or so family court systems have been set up in several parts of the world. While American practice is probably most discussed in Britain, it is a less helpful example than some of those provided by Commonwealth countries, as the latter have developed from a legal system closer to our own. The case we have taken is New Zealand. This example has the further advantages that its courts serve a country with a very similar divorce rate to our own and where beliefs and values about family life are also close to those in Britain. A big difference, however, is the size of the country. New Zealand's population is not much more than a twentieth of that of Britain. This means that by our standards, the judges, lawyers and other professionals concerned with divorce are a very small group of people who are in close contact with each other, which makes change much easier to accomplish and allows continued discussion to iron out problems as they arise. This, of course, not only applies to the legal system and may be why New Zealand has so often been in the vanguard of change in the social and political spheres. As Asquith once remarked, New Zealand is a 'laboratory in which political and social experiments are every day made for the information and instruction of the older countries of the world'.

In its organization, the New Zealand family court recognizes that people who have recently experienced the end of their marriage are often in a vulnerable and emotional state and that feelings run high. Therefore, there is an informal and sensitive first point of contact with the court. For the same reasons, judges in their family courts are specialists chosen not only for their knowledge of the law but also for their experience and knowledge of the social and psychological aspects of family life, and their commitment to conciliation and non-adversarial resolution of family disputes. Nearly all the initial appointments were made from the ranks of the New Zealand equivalent of County court judges, but several subsequent ones have come directly from the legal profession. All family-court judges are qualified to do other kinds of County court work but, in practice, spend a high proportion of their time in the family court so ensuring a genuine degree of specialization. The New Zealand family-court judges come together as a team from time to time to discuss aspects of their work and to learn from other professions whose expertise is related to the work of the courts. Throughout the system there is a very strong emphasis on this kind of inter-professional collaboration.

In New Zealand, children are represented by lawyers appointed by the court and chosen from a pool of experienced people, some of whom have undertaken additional instruction to prepare them for the special nature of the work. The family court deals with marriage, marital separation, domestic violence and molestation, maintenance, matrimonial property, divorce, status of children, paternity, custody, access, guardianship and adoption. The original New Zealand proposal went further than this to include such things as juvenile delinquency and criminal matters arising within families such as incest and assaults. As yet, these latter areas have not been included, partly because there are disagreements about whether it is appropriate to include criminal matters, and also because there was a desire not to overwhelm the courts just as they were becoming established and gaining experience.

The key person in the New Zealand family courts is called a counselling co-ordinator. These people (they are at present all women) are responsible for the organization of all the conciliation referrals, as well as for the assigning of custody and access cases to appropriate professionals when specialist assessments and reports are required, and for the arranging of post-decision counselling, which is sometimes ordered or recommended by the court. This is the person seen by anyone coming to the court for the first time, who may well on that occasion offer information and crisis counselling. When a problem arises – let us say a mother has decided to leave her husband but there is a dispute over their child – she may go straight to the court or first to a solicitor. The solicitor, having explained the procedure to the mother and answered any immediate questions, will refer her to the counselling co-ordinator. She may explore the issue with the mother and try to define the areas of agreement and disagreement, and will contact the father and seek his views. In other cases, the solicitor will make a request for counselling on behalf of the client and the co-ordinator will arrange a referral without meeting the party (or parties) themselves. Perhaps things go fairly well and rather than there being a basic disagreement, it turns out that the spouses were simply very anxious about the future and uncertain about what arrangements to make. At this stage, they could agree to separate and their lawyers would make any necessary arrangements about maintenance. After two years' separation (in New Zealand, this is the only basis for ending a marriage) they can make a joint application to end their marriage. At this time the court would review the situation of the child and, assuming all is well, will formally divorce the couple.

Perhaps things are not quite so straightforward and the couple cannot agree on terms for a separation. It this event, they will return to their lawyers who will make a simple formal application to the court. The counselling co-ordinator will then refer the couple to a conciliator. If this conciliation succeeds, consent orders (i.e. court-approved agreements) will be made and the couple agree to separate as before. However, if agreement cannot be reached over the child, a counsel for the child will be appointed at this stage and the court may request various special reports. Perhaps a child psychiatrist will be asked to see the child, if the counsel for the child believes that such a specialized assessment is appropriate, or a clinical psychologist might be asked to advise on the child's feelings about access visits.

The next step is a mediation conference. For this the two parents with their solicitors, the child's counsel and the judge sit in an informal setting. The judge as chairman, having read the appropriate reports, explores the issues in dispute with the parents and tries to find common ground. The counsel for the child will put what he or she feels is most important from the child's point of view. If there is agreement, consent orders will be drawn up. If not, the judge can order more conciliation, new reports or more or less anything else he thinks might help. There may be a further mediation conference. When the judge feels that mediation has no more to offer then, and only then, do things proceed to a formal court hearing, and it is only then that each party with their solicitor can begin drawing up their affidavit and move into the adversarial phase. But even at this point in the proceedings the hearings do not usually have the strongly adversarial style of the English court. This is partly because un- necessary cross-examination is discouraged, and also because the court does not rely solely on the two parties and their representatives for the main body of evidence. Other reports that the court has had prepared play an important part in the proceedings. While extensive evidence is not yet available, it is generally believed that the system has led to a considerable reduction in the number of contested hearings.

The final part of the system is appeals. In New Zealand these go to the High Court which does not have specialized family judges. This is a matter of concern to some people because it is felt that it is essential to have a Court of Appeal which is fully knowledgeable about family matters and shares the orientation of the family court. In England, our situation is rather reversed and, as we have seen, we have no specialized judges in the bottom tier(s) though we have the Family Division of the High Court.

Much of the conciliation for the New Zealand Family Court is provided by their Marriage Guidance Council (a body very similar to our own) which is the only organization that has been approved generally to take court referrals. This means that referrals can only be made to other counsellors with the approval of the judge in individual cases. In practice, however, the judges leave this decision to the counselling co-ordinator and a good number of non-Marriage- Guidance-Council referrals are made. The great skill of the coun- selling co-ordinator is to refer couples to appropriate conciliators.

Over time, the co-ordinators have built up a detailed picture of the variety of conciliation and counselling available in their community so they can, as far as possible, match the couple and their problem to a particular counsellor. The counselling co-ordinator also acts as a quality control for conciliation. If certain people seem less than helpful they get no further referrals.

There are frequent meetings between the various professionals who work within or for the courts at which knowledge and experience are shared and these help to develop a consistent approach to problems. There are clear guidelines for the various tasks that a court may assign so that, unlike in Britain, it is quite clear what is required if, for example, a psychologist is asked to prepare a report. The role of counsel for the child can be important in ensuring that reporting professionals know just what is expected of them. It may be, for example, that a report has been requested for a specific purpose or in relation to one specific issue, rather than an overall assessment: counsel should ensure that the reporter knows their brief and does not exceed it.

Meetings are also held with pressure groups in the community and other interested people. It is strongly believed that the function of the court should be understood by the community it serves and must have the confidence of that community.

The New Zealand system is only a few years old and formal evaluation has just begun. It has its critics but it is unclear how far these people are objecting to the principle of a family court *per se* or to how this system is run. For example, some feminists in New Zealand complain that the courts are too favourably inclined towards fathers' claims for custody. If this is the case, is it because fathers are favoured in any system that emphasizes private ordering, or because the values of those who work in the New Zealand courts tend to favour fathers? Others complain that the courts do not serve the Maori population adequately, but, again, that could be true of any court system. It is not obvious why a family court would be especially unlikely to meet the needs of a minority group.

Many women and New Zealanders in general seem to regard their courts with pride; those who have experienced them at first hand seem to feel that they are supportive and helpful, a view that is not very widespread among those who have experienced divorce courts in Britain.[14] Could it work here? That question cannot be answered until we make some experiments.

IMPROVING THE PRESENT SYSTEM

While plans for family courts are still being formulated in Britain, specific proposals have been made for simplifying divorce proceedings, and for attempting to make them less contentious, by the Committee chaired by Mrs Justice Booth. The Committee was set up by the Lord Chancellor to consider changes that might 'mitigate the intensity of disputes, encourage settlements, and further the welfare of the children' and cut costs. As its Report[15] shows, there is indeed considerable scope for improving matters without changing the law. This is as far as some people think reform should go – to make the present system work better and reduce the figure of nearly £100 million which is spent annually on legal aid for matrimonial cases. For others, this is at best a stop-gap before we move to more fundamental reform and at worst a way of buying off the pressures to create a family-court system. Our own view is that most of the Booth proposals would be desirable and ought to be introduced as soon as possible. However, to introduce them would not, by definition, change the present system fundamentally and cannot be seen as the last word in divorce reform. The Committee was specifically barred from considering the law itself so the proposals do little to reduce the complexities of it and the several courts that operate it.

The Booth Committee makes eighty proposals for change, many of them concerned with very detailed and technical aspects of court procedure. Most of the recommendations can be seen as part of an attempt to push the present law as far as possible towards private ordering. As the Committee states, the aim is for couples to 'be encouraged and assisted to settle matters themselves, with the benefit of full legal advice and, where appropriate, the help of a conciliation service'. 'We are firmly of the view that the primary decision-making responsibility should rest with the spouses themselves and that they should be given all necessary help in deciding for themselves what should happen to their children, their property and their marriage.' It is only when after all encouragement and support for a couple to reach an agreement have failed to produce the desired results that the court would take over and determine the issues 'expeditiously and inexpensively'.

The key to the proposals is an initial hearing early in the proceedings for all couples with children. Both parties would be encouraged to attend and would provide factual information about the children, financial circumstances and so on. As with the family courts we have just described,

> The hearing will be essentially inquisitorial in its nature, will give the parties themselves not only a better understanding of the questions to be resolved but also a stronger sense of participating in and controlling the litigation so that they will be less willing subsequently to accept any undue delay. With encouragement to reach their own solutions about their own affairs we think that some of the intensity and bitterness of the dispute will be mitigated.

Under the new proposals it would become possible for the parties to make a joint application to the court, and in all cases specific details about the children – where they live, who looks after them, etc. – would have to be given. In the case of an application being made on the grounds of the spouse's unreasonable behaviour, no details of the behaviour itself would be given; instead it would be stated that 'The respondent has behaved in such a way that the applicant [the report recommends that the present petitioner should become an applicant] cannot reasonably be expected to live with him (her).'

Three outcomes would be possible from the initial hearing. Where there is a full agreement between the parties, perhaps after some in-court mediation, the court, in the person of the registrar who would conduct these hearings, could make all the necessary orders including the granting of a decree and a declaration that the arrangement for the children is satisfactory. This declaration would therefore abolish the need for a later children's hearing before a judge.

If there is partial agreement, consent and interim orders would be made and the remaining issues in dispute would be defined so that mediation* can take place and dates set for a future hearing. An

---

* The Report calls it conciliation but, by the definition we have been using, it is mediation.

important part of the recommendations is that the responsibility for setting the timetable for hearings would pass from the parties to the court in order to avoid delays and to prevent the tactical use of hearing dates by parties in attempts to gain an upper hand.

When disagreement is complete, interim orders would be made at the initial hearing, and a timetable would be set for mediation and a future hearing.

In general, the Report gives strong support to conciliation and mediation but the Committee's brief limits it to the consideration of court-based schemes. It makes the sensible suggestion that where a court welfare officer has been involved in mediation, the same officer should not then be responsible for a report to the court, should continuing disagreement make this necessary.

As far as children are concerned, the Report emphasizes the continued joint responsibilities of parents, but they retreat from the view expressed in their earlier consultation paper that joint custody should become the norm to a position where they suggest it should be encouraged but that there should be no presumption in its favour. We feel that it is a great pity that the Committee did not follow the logic of its own arguments about joint parental responsibility and come out in favour of a system whereby joint custody would be granted unless in a particular case specific reasons were brought forward against it. Rumour has it that there was considerable opposition from the legal professions (which appears to have won the day) to the suggestion that there should be a presumption in favour of joint custody.

Another suggestion of the Booth Committee, which we strongly endorse, is the provision of an information booklet for parents that describes some of the difficulties children may face at divorce and the ways in which parents can provide support. Research studies have documented the need that many parents have for factual information and a booklet is a cheap and easy way to provide it.

The Booth Committee Report is, of course, merely a set of recommendations and there is no guarantee at all that they will be accepted. Much may depend on the resource implications, which are very difficult to estimate. If a high percentage of all cases is settled at the initial hearing as the Committee hopes, the overall cost of the full scheme might not be above the present, as the increased resources needed to support the initial hearing might be more or less balanced by the savings produced through avoiding contested cases. Where cases continue to be contested, the costs might be reduced as the proposed power for the court to control the procedures should simplify things and reduce legal aid costs and court time.

But the more fundamental issue is whether it is worth proceeding with what are, in effect, some tidying-up measures of the present system or whether we should not first decide whether the system itself requires change – here we refer both to the law itself and to the court structure. To take an example: Booth recognizes, correctly in our view, that the long recitals of evidence of unreasonable behaviour that appear not infrequently in affidavits may lead to unnecessary ill feeling and conflict. Therefore, the Committee recommends, as we have noted, that the papers for the initial hearing should simply record that unreasonable behaviour has occurred. At this point, however, should we not go the whole hog and examine the basis on which a divorce is granted? Our view, as we explained earlier, is that a divorce should be granted after a formal notice by a spouse and a twelve-month waiting period. While the Booth Committee was limited to a consideration of the working of the present law, we should perhaps be less circumscribed in assessing its Report. We should not allow the many very sensible recommendations of the Report to prevent consideration of the more fundamental issues.

FINANCIAL MATTERS

Surveys of divorced people show that money and property are even more likely to be the cause of disputes than children. Not surprisingly, such disputes are most common in middle- and upper-class families where there is more income and property to fight over. For those without capital – the majority of divorcing couples – the question of occupation of the matrimonial home, usually a council house, is the prime issue. In theory, matters to do with money and children are separate at divorce. In practice, they are closely linked as decisions about where the children will live and who will look after them have obvious implications for any financial settlement. We know[16], for example, that about half of all children who were living in an owner occupier matrimonial home move out at divorce, either because the house is sold or is occupied by the non-custodial parent. Surprisingly perhaps, matrimonial homes are sold at divorce as frequently when a couple have children as when they are childless, but more predictably, the only cases when a non-custodial parent remains in the old family home seem to be those when that parent is the father. Mothers remain in the home only when they are the custodial parent.

Courts face a number of difficulties in trying to settle financial disputes. As with matters related to children, they are operating largely in the area of discretion but here the indications from society at large about how discretion might be exercised are very confused and deeply divided.

One issue is whether or not maintenance payments should be subject to modification according to the conduct of the spouse or, to put it in terms often heard in public discussions: why should blame-less men support guilty wives who have run off with someone else? Parliament has recently reaffirmed the principle that, in more serious cases, conduct should be taken into account. However, the courts have tended to apply such a principle only in very rare cases and there is, as yet, little indication that things have changed since the new Act came into force. The reluctance of judges to enter into discussions about conduct, which is shared by many in society, is based on a number of reasons. Making conduct a more central issue would mean that each party would, in arguing its case, produce just the sort of inflammatory material that increases anger and bitterness at divorce. Also what should the modulus be? At what point does conduct reach a point of seriousness, become sufficiently 'gross and obvious' – to use the original legal phrase – that it should be con-sidered? If a wife has had an affair, would that always lead to a reduction? If she has had two affairs should the reduction be doubled? Should we expect a husband who has been violent to his spouse to pay more? We will return to these questions.

At divorce the workings of private law, concerning how couples divide their property, and income, and public law – affecting such matters as income tax and social security payments – are often unrelated and sometimes contradictory. In theory, when a court is calculating the amount of maintenance an ex-husband might reasonably pay, they do not look at the consequences of their decision in terms of the state benefits each party may receive. Each spouse is equally liable to maintain the other, but in practice virtually all maintenance is paid by husbands to ex-wives. However, state benefits rather than maintenance payments are the major source of income for most divorcees and their children. Probably about 60 per cent of mothers with children become dependent on supplementary benefit for at least a period of time after separation.

It is also difficult to find a system which can deal equally fairly with a couple whose considerable financial resources mean that payment of substantial maintenance would have little if any influence on the payer's standard of living, and the much more common situation where the couple have little or nothing by way of savings and a single income hardly adequate to maintain the marital household, let alone the two that may be produced after the divorce.

Initially, discussion of these complex issues may be simplified by drawing a distinction between marriages with and without children. For marriages without children, the issues are much more straightforward and less controversial. Few would argue any longer for an automatic principle of long-term support for spouses where no children are involved. Instead, it seems reasonable to have a principle of equality modified by such factors as compensation for any loss of career opportunity arising out of domestic work, or loss of pension rights. Where appropriate, especially where marriages have lasted less than, say, ten years, settlements should be made on the clean break principle, i.e. a once and for ever settlement rather than continuing payments. A clean break settlement should not then be open to review in cases where either party undergoes an unexpected change in fortunes. Often there will be little or nothing in the way of property to divide, and in such cases a period of compensatory payments – say, for a spouse who had kept house and wishes to undergo a period of training before seeking employment – might be appropriate. For the remainder of our discussion, we will be concerned with divorces that involve children.

Let us begin with some broad principles. Our society is one where the basic assumption has been that a man will earn and support his wife and children. Money earned by men is a 'family wage' and is regarded as being sufficient for him, his wife and children, and taxation allowances are structured accordingly. In addition, other benefits for women, such as pension rights, depend, at least in part, on the husband's earnings. Although the majority of married women with children undertake waged work for significant periods during their 'married life', this is often regarded as an extra to the men's income and, of course, women's average income levels are a good deal lower than those of men. However, it is still the norm for most women to give up work outside the home if they have children, at least for a time. Given that most child care continues to be provided by women in the absence of satisfactory day care, the possibilities for mothers to pursue a lifelong career are still greatly reduced when compared with those of their male partners. However, underpinning the wage market is a system of state benefits which are intended – at least in theory – to provide support for those unable to work, or those whose earnings are below a minimal level.

Thus, it has been traditionally assumed that if there is a divorce, the husband, as wage earner, will continue to support his wife and children. Responsibility for children lasts until they leave home and for the wife endures for life unless she remarries and is supported by another man. Until the law was changed in 1984, the principle intended to guide financial provisions was that a settlement should leave the wife and children in the position they would have been in had the divorce not taken place (modified, if necessary, by a deduction for gross misconduct). As the recent change in the law has recognized, such a principle is quite unworkable and unhelpful as there is seldom sufficient money available to make this a feasible goal. Like much of divorce law it was a hangover from the days when divorce was confined to the relatively well off.

It has been estimated that a parent with two children needs about 75 or 80 per cent of the money that is required by a couple with two children for the basics of food, housing and so on. Courts with their usual pragmatism have tried to use other rules of thumb such as the 'one-third rule', to guide decision making about money. However, decisions would seem to vary widely from court to court and the system makes it hard for couples and their advisors to know what might happen in a particular case, so bargaining in the shadow of the law is particularly uncertain leading to increased conflict and bitterness. For the majority who have little to argue over, what is at stake in court settlements is the extent to which state benefit will make up the income of either party, though this is not how cases are argued overtly. As we have mentioned already, it is state benefits and not ex-spouses that provide most of the support for women and children after divorce.

Maintenance orders are frequently in arrears or not paid at all. Estimates suggest that as many as 80 per cent may be seriously in arrears or unpaid. Because it is a relatively cumbersome procedure to alter orders to keep pace with inflation, many orders are long out of date. If men do not pay, repeated (and expensive) legal action that is frequently ineffective is the only course open. The ultimate sanction for the non-payer is prison.

At any one time about 2,000 men are in prison for non-payment of maintenance, a procedure which ensures that their own maintenance, as well as that of their wife and children, will fall on the state. Studies of men imprisoned for this reason suggest that they are much more likely to be the very poor, for whom courts have set maintenance at an unrealistic level, than the better off who could well afford to pay but choose not to. Wealthy defaulters find it easy to avoid anything as drastic as prison. In the majority of poorer families, which are largely dependent on state benefits, there may be very little incentive for a man to pay because any maintenance received by the mother would simply be deducted from what she receives from the State.

So far in this discussion we have assumed the traditional pattern of the mother looking after the children. Of course, some men have custody of their children, but in these cases it is extremely rare for them to receive financial support from their ex-wives. This is partly explained by generally low levels of female income but also because it is still seen to be 'unnatural' for men in this position to receive support from a woman.

Given the basic principle of the family wage, it is clear that many mothers will require support either from the ex-husband or from the state or both. At present, state support is so far from adequate for many households that not only does the lone parent experience considerable financial and emotional stress, but the children's development is also significantly impaired. According to one recent survey, 80 per cent of divorced single parents were living below the poverty line – defined as 140 per cent of supplementary benefit entitlement.[17] There are three ways, in theory, in which the position of such households could be improved: the ex-husband could pay more; the mother might earn more; state benefits could be increased. At present, the state tends to favour husbands (and their second families if they have them), especially at the lower income levels. In assessing his ability to pay, the state will not reduce an ex-husband's income below a point representing his supplementary benefit entitlement, including household costs, plus one-quarter of his net disposable income or £5, whichever is the greater. By contrast, his ex-partner and child(ren) will be assessed at the supplementary benefit level without this extra entitlement.

As we have seen, maintenance orders are often not paid in full. The financial position of many mothers and children would be improved if maintenance were paid at the level set by the court and if levels were regularly updated to keep pace with inflation and the changing needs of growing children. There is evidence to show that men who are in regular contact with their children are more likely to pay maintenance. In addition, this contact may lead to the provision of other resources: pocket money, toys and clothes for example, as well as other unpaid services such as babysitting or childminding, which may help to reduce the mother's financial outlay. As a result, any attempt to encourage continued contact between parents and children might also improve the financial situation for some as well, of course, as offering the other advantages we discussed in the last chapter. One suggestion for increasing the efficiency of payments is Finer's recommendation that the state should take over the collection of money from the father, or other 'liable relative', to use the official term, perhaps in the form of an addition to income tax which would automatically be adjusted each year to allow for inflation on the same basis as already happens to some other benefits. The mother would then receive her maintenance from the state and where the father was unable to pay or for any reason the state could not collect the money from him, the state would automatically make up the difference. Such a system not only has the advantage of ensuring regular payments for the mother, but would help to avoid direct confrontation over money between parents.

For many single parents, working outside the home is something that they choose to do for more than financial reasons. The workplace can provide companionship and social support. This is re-flected, for instance, in the results of studies of social isolation and depression in mothers of young children, which show that those who have jobs outside the home are less likely to be depressed. But the ability of parents to work is dependent on the availability of adequate child-care facilities as well as the state of the employment market. In fact, employment levels for divorced women with the care of children are higher for those with professional work. This seems to be partly because they are better able to keep the jobs they had during their marriages because they have the resources to pay for child care. For other social groups, the absence of a partner in the home, who perhaps provided child care while the mother worked on evening shift, for instance, reduces the possibility of finding outside employment. Given the lack of child-care facilities, as well as of suitable jobs, it is unlikely that the employment level for single parents can increase very much in the near future. In addition, we should remember that the poverty trap means that for many, earning a regular income may make no difference to their financial position because of the consequent reduction in state benefits. We will discuss state benefit levels further below.

Maintenance and 'conduct'

The argument that a sense of justice has to be preserved by imposing financial penalties on those whose conduct is felt to be unacceptable has been put forward most forcibly by middle-class men through an organization called Campaign for Justice in Divorce, which has had an undoubted influence on the Matrimonial and Family Proceedings Act 1984. Certainly, there are cases that affront the sense of justice of the husband involved. Take, for example, a professional man in his thirties who is beginning to feel established in his career and financially confident. The wife begins a relationship with another man and eventually the couple reach the divorce court. The mother gets custody of the children, maintenance and the matrimonial home – having bought out the husband's interest – and the husband moves into a flat feeling deeply hurt and angry. He feels that he has lost everything – wife, children, house. The final blow comes when he discovers that the new lover has moved into his old home. It is very tempting to feel that in such a case the 'blameless' husband deserves some kind of compensation; thus the pressure for conduct to be taken into account. Our belief is that if we wish to improve the overall situation of those going through a divorce, we should resist the temptation to use any notion of conduct in such instances for three main reasons.

First, the concept of conduct is in itself a difficult one. Not only does the judge or registrar have great difficulty deciding the kind of conduct which is sufficiently outrageous that it would be 'inequitable to disregard it' but such judgements are also certain to vary from court to court making justice less than uniform. In addition, the argument tends to be one-sided: it is generally concerned only to distinguish 'blameless' men from their 'guilty' wives and is used to reduce maintenance payments. Surely, if conduct is to be taken into account it should apply equally to all parties? Not only would this mean increasing maintenance for a spouse in appropriate cases as well as decreasing it in others, but also increasing payment to children who had suffered particularly from their parents' behaviour. Justice should also demand that fines for bad conduct are available to all. However, in most cases there is precious little income or property to redistribute at divorce. How, for instance, would we provide justice for a 'blameless' husband who is unemployed and therefore not paying maintenance? In effect, the current use of conduct means that the remedy is only available to affluent middle-class men and as such does not meet any reasonable test of justice.

Our second argument concerns the effects that the use of a conduct provision may have on the process of divorce itself. It perpetuates the notion of guilty and innocent spouses, which, in theory at least, was set aside when the idea of irretrievable breakdown was introduced. The reason for that change was to prevent long and bitter post-mortems about marital behaviour. There is also a difficulty in principle. In relationships such as marriage both parties have the responsibility for whether it continues or ends. It might seem obvious to blame the wife in the example we cited earlier, but we have to ask why she chose to enter a new relationship. In such situations there is usually an infinite regress of action, or its absence, on both sides that make any notion of innocence or blame inappropriate. Perhaps the wife was driven into the new relationship because she felt abandoned by the husband who was always entirely preoccupied by his work. He might well say that this was essential as his career was at a crucial point and his preoccupation was caused by his concern to have an adequate income for his wife and children. And so the circle goes on. If it is accepted that a major aim of any divorce system should be to reduce bitterness and recrimination and to encourage spouses to look forward rather than back, we should not allow the use of any evidence about conduct in the determination of financial affairs.

Our final point concerns the welfare principle. The line between the maintenance paid to a parent and that paid to children is more theoretical than real. Therefore, the reduction of maintenance to a spouse on the grounds of conduct is likely to have a negative effect on the children. Why should they suffer in an attempt to placate their aggrieved father? One can make the argument more abstract. Why should any welfare payment be made subject to somebody's judgement of the morality of the recipient? Even in the rather murky area of state benefits, the principle, if not the practice, is not based on the idea of reducing payments on the grounds of the sexual or other moral conduct of the recipient.

However, to remove this recourse to arguments about conduct will eliminate a significant outlet for the expression of the anger and frustration felt by some divorced men. While we believe that this avenue *should* be closed, we should also recognize the existence of this kind of anger and provide more constructive ways of dealing with it. Here follows a powerful reason for extending the various counselling and other supportive services.

The impact of remarriage

Views about finance and remarriage are perhaps even more deeply divided than those about the conduct issue. About half of the divorcing population remarry in the first five years after divorce. In financial terms, women with children who remarry are much better off than those who do not, partly because of their new partner's income and partly because remarriage increases the probability of them working outside the home. For men, remarriage does not change their obligation to support children of their first marriage but, in practice, their support is more likely to be given to their second, rather than their first family. While public opinion seems to support this practice rather than the theory, courts often try to maintain the other position. Typically, when a remarried man with a new baby applies to the court to have his maintenance payment reduced on the grounds that his income is not sufficient to support his new and growing household and keep up the payment to his first wife and children, he will be told by the court that having made his bed, he must lie on it. The fact that he has taken on new obligations is no reason for his first family to suffer. Such decisions create understandable bitterness among second wives, who often feel that their marriages can never escape from the shadow of their husband's first marriage. Such feelings may well contribute to the stresses of second marriages and their relatively high divorce rate. These antagonisms can also undermine the relationship between the father and the children of his first marriage, and, as we have already noted, contact between fathers and their children tends to fall off after the remarriage of either partner. Children of a first marriage may well resent preferential treatment being given to children of a second marriage. They may well connect inadequate maintenance with what they may feel as inadequate love and attention.

However, as long as we accept that parents have a continuing responsibility to support their children, such conflicts will occur. We suggest that the only fair principle to apply to such situations is that parents' resources should be divided equally between their children, and that this principle should only be modified when the needs of the children vary. Of course, this means that if a man marries several times and has children in each marriage, the children of his earliest marriage will receive a declining proportion of his resources as more children arrive. But it should be noted that this is exactly what happens to children born within a first marriage. With each additional child born into the family, each child receives a declining proportion of the household's resources. It is partly for this reason that the life chances of children in very large families are slightly less than those in smaller ones.

The underlying principles of maintenance

Before leaving the issues concerning financial settlement, we must return to some of the underlying principles. We have seen that the whole system is based on a notion of the family wage. Whether consciously expressed or not, marriage involves a contract in which the husband undertakes to maintain his wife and children. The same principle is applied to unmarried fathers with respect to their children. Although marriage has come to be regarded as more of a partnership and the husband's obligation to maintain has become theoretically a mutual one for both spouses, men still carry most of the responsibility for maintenance. This is because the overwhelming majority of child care is still provided by women both within and after marriage and the majority of women earn a great deal less than men. We have seen that poverty for women and children is the common result of divorce but given the poverty trap and the assumptions of the principle of the family wage, almost the only way of escape for divorcees is remarriage.

Thus, policies based on the principle of the family wage continue to make women dependent on men for income, both within marriage and after divorce. Although our society espouses a notional commitment to the principle of equal pay and opportunity for men and women, it is constantly and inevitably thwarted by the assumption that women should, and will, provide unpaid child care. Support systems for women after marriage – maintenance and/or state benefits – are thus connected in a way which inevitably perpetuates the dependence of women on men.

Let us look at it from a child's point of view. The emotional and material provision made by *both* parents help to determine their children's life chances. However, the welfare system provides support for children in a number of different ways. These range from direct money support like child benefit to specialized paediatric medical services and the education system. Because these are paid for from tax revenue, there is, in effect, a net flow of resources from earning individuals without children to those with them. The net amount of benefit a family will receive from this transfer will depend, in part, on the number of children they have. The costs to the non-childbearing population are increased as more children are born.*The tax and welfare systems are organized, at least in theory, so that these benefits are proportionally more valuable for those in the lower income groups than upper. We have created a system which enjoys wide popular support, whereby society as a whole undertakes to underwrite some of the costs to parents of bringing up children.

Thus, the answer to the poverty that follows divorce must be seen more broadly than simply increasing the income levels of divorced women with children. We need to take a radical look at the basis on which the state provides benefits. If benefits to lone-parent households were seen less as a replacement for the lost family wage and more as a payment for child care and as a benefit for the child, it might be possible to begin to find a way out of the present tangle. If the state were to mediate between divorced parents by providing an adequate level of support for all children and their custodian parents and undertake the collection of the appropriate contribution from liable relatives (most often the father) this itself would be a significant step in the right direction. It would ensure that the caretaker parent received a regular and predictable income without being subjected to the whims of ex-partners, who, as we have seen, are often extremely unreliable in their support. Furthermore, it would remove one potential battlefield and cause of bitterness between ex-spouses. Given the role that maintenance payments appear to play in access problems, such a move would support our stated principle that encouragement should be given to the continuing relationship of both parents with their children. The direct result of paying child benefit of this kind at a reasonable level, coupled with better child-care facilities, would be to reduce the poverty already experienced by a large number of children and their caretaker parents. It would also reduce the financial dependence of women on men, more generally. One of the many benefits that might follow would be a reduction of the pressures on divorced mothers to remarry for purely financial reasons.

Public discussion of the social consequences of current divorce trends frequently provokes questions about how children born in

* We are simplifying matters here. It must not be forgotten, for example, that the production of children provides a labour force who in the future will pay taxes, which in turn are used for health and welfare services for those beyond retirement whether or not they have produced children earlier in life.

recent decades, who are much more likely to have experienced a parental divorce than those of earlier generations, have been affected in the longer term. Inevitably, evidence about the longer term comes from earlier generations. Some recently published research based on a sample of children born in 1946[18] indicates that by early adulthood their chances of gaining the qualifications, occupation and standard of living that they might otherwise have been expected to enjoy had been affected by their parents' divorce. Presumably this is partly because, like other poor children, the divorce-related adversities they had experienced had undermined their capacity to benefit from educational opportunities and also because they were much less likely to have received direct cash gifts to set up a home. Thus, a more equitable system for distributing resources at divorce, which also focused more directly on the needs of children, would help to reduce some of the long-term disadvantages experienced by them. It is our view that the encouragement of systems and practices which raise and secure the domestic living standards of such children will do more than anything else to make their welfare paramount in both theory *and* practice.

CONCLUSION

On several occasions we have taken issue with the view that changes in divorce and its procedures inevitably affect levels of *actual*, as opposed to *legal*, marriage breakdown. Nevertheless, we would like to conclude by suggesting that the kinds of social arrangements made to terminate marriages will continue to expose many of the assumptions, implied exchanges and unspoken contracts on which the partnership itself is based. Earlier in this chapter we suggested that one way forward would be to consider divorce as the termination of a *domestic partnership*. A very significant potential benefit of such a change might be its eventual effects upon popular beliefs and assumptions about marriage itself. If, as a society, we became used to the idea that, romantic love apart, choosing a partner and creating a home together is as much about material as emotional considerations and that in daily life these are usually closely interwoven, then it might be easier for those contemplating marriage to consider the terms of the contract more carefully. Although there is a great deal of evidence that material considerations do impinge upon the choice of a partner, or indeed on the decision to marry at all, these are rarely discussed explicitly. This is partly because of the popular belief that we should marry 'for love'. If public images of marriage, and the value structure built round it, were based on marriage as a mutual commitment to a domestic partnership 'of bed and board', this might seem mundane, even cynical to some, but it would encourage potential partners to reflect more upon the economic and material commitments and exchanges on which it is inevitably based. Thus it might be that wherever education or preparation for marriage occurs, whether formally in schools, in the media, in vicars' studies or informally among friends and family, there might in future be much more open discussion of how jobs, money and the entire unpaid household and domestic economy underpin marriage. Hopefully, such a change in consciousness would encourage potential husbands and wives to consider how their individual visions of the future – domestically and occupationally – are to be fitted together. While discussions of this kind at the beginning of a marriage would be no proof against 'growing apart' later on, they might help to establish that each partner's balance of 'inside' and 'outside' commitments, responsibilities and investments will inevitably affect their partnership over time.

Furthermore, far from devaluing the idea of marriage as a relationship based on mutual love and trust, we believe that an open and honest recognition of the ways in which our personal lives are affected by material considerations and public structures is an important source of liberation for both sexes. To expose the economic foundations of marriage for what they are may, in fact, do a great deal to enable individuals to create and sustain partnerships that more adequately express their differing – and changing – circumstances, needs and aspirations.*

---

* Since this chapter was completed two important discussion documents have appeared: Law Commission Working Paper No. 96, *Family Law. Review of Child Law: Custody*, (London, H.M.S.O., 1986); and *Review of Family and Domestic Jurisdiction*, The Lord Chancellor's Dept, London.

NOTES

I DIVORCE IN ITS SOCIAL CONTEXT

1. Here, as elsewhere in the book, we are referring to England and Wales. The law is often different in Scotland and Northern Ireland. In Scotland, for instance, divorce is possible immediately after marriage, whereas in England and Wales it is now necessary to wait for at least one year.

J. Haskey, 'The proportion of marriages ending in divorce', *Population Trends*, 27 (Spring) (1982), p. 4; Family Policy Studies Centre, *Divorce: 1983 Matrimonial and Family Proceedings* (London, 1983).

2. R. Leete, *Changing Patterns of Family Formation and Dissolution in England and Wales 1964–76*, Studies on Medical and Population Subjects No. 39 (London, H.M.S.O., 1979).

It is important to note that these historical trends are by no means unique to Britain. Most industrialized societies also experienced a similar post-Second World War peak, a levelling out in the 1950s and then a sustained increase through the 1960s and 1970s. See R. Chester (ed.), *Divorce in Europe* (The Hague, Martinius Nijhoff, 1977).

3. O.P.C.S Population Monitor, *Divorces 1984*, FM2, 85/1 (London, H.M.S.O., 1985).

4. See, by way of example, Society of Conservative Lawyers, *The Future of Marriage* (London, Conservative Political Centre, 1981).

5. *Marriage Matters* (London, H.M.S.O., 1979).

6. Quoted in M. Green, *Marriage* (London, Fontana, 1984), pp. 29, 61.

7. A survey of family beliefs carried out in Sheffield and Aberdeen with the aid of a grant from the Medical Research Council by David Clark and Jacqueline Burgoyne, with fieldwork conducted by Social and Community Planning Research.

8. J. Burgoyne and D. Clark, *Making a Go of It: a study of stepfamilies in Sheffield* (London, Routledge and Kegan Paul, 1984). This research was completed with the aid of a grant from the then Social Science Research Council.

9. See J. Klein, *Samples from English Cultures* (London, Routledge and Kegan Paul, 1965), chapter 1.

10. W. Bagehot, *The English Constitution* (London, Fontana, 1963).

11. Burgoyne and Clark, op. cit., chapter 6.

12. See, for example, R. Fletcher, *The Family and Marriage in Britain* (Harmondsworth, Penguin, 1971); J. Dominian, *Marriage, Faith and Love* (London, Darton, Longman and Todd, 1981); J. Burgoyne, 'Contemporary expectations of marriage and partnership' in *Change in Marriage* (Rugby, National Marriage Guidance Council, 1982).

13. This tension between family ideologies, systematic explanations offered about family life generally, and the evaluation of behaviour of known individuals was first observed by E. Bott in her classic study of marriage, *Family and Social Networks* (London, Tavistock, 1957).

14. M. Anderson, *The Family: Conference Papers*, British Society for Population Studies, Occasional Paper 31 (London, O.P.C.S., 1983).

15. R. Chester, 'Divorce in England and Wales', in R. Chester (ed.), *Divorce in Europe* (The Hague, Martinius Nijhoff, 1977).

16. R. Chester, 'Divorce and legal aid: a false hypothesis', *Sociology* 6, 2 (1972), p. 214.

17. B. Ineichen, 'Youthful marriage: the vortex of disadvantage' in R. Chester and J. Peel (eds.), *Equalities and Inequalities in Family Life* (London, Academic Press. 1977), pp. 53–70.

18. B. Thornes and J. Collard, *Who Divorces?* (London, Routledge and Kegan Paul, 1979).

19. D. Leonard, *Sex and Generation* (London, Tavistock, 1980).

20. This was also true of a sample of divorced people interviewed in 1980 for the *Daily Mail*.

21. K. Dunnell, *Family Formation 1976* (London, H.M.S.O., 1979), Table 12.12.

22. J. Martin and C. Roberts, *Women and Employment: a lifetime perspective* (London, H.M.S.O., 1984).

23. See A. McRobbie, 'Working class girls and the culture of femininity' in Women's Studies Group (eds.), *Women Take Issue* (London, Hutchinson, 1978); V. Walkerdine, 'Some day my prince will come' in A. McRobbie and M. Nava, *Gender and Generation* (London, Macmillan, 1984); M. Brake, *The Sociology of Youth Culture and Youth Subcultures* (London, Routledge and Kegan Paul, 1980), chapter 5.

24. For example, A. Pollert, *Girls, Wives, Factory Lives* (London, Macmillan, 1981); S. Westwood, *All Day, Every Day* (London, Pluto Press, 1984).

25. P. Willis, *Learning to Labour* (London, Saxon House, 1981).

26. J. Burgoyne, 'Cohabitation and contemporary family life'. End of Award Report to the Economic and Social Research Council (1985).

27. See *Social Trends*, 15 (London, H.M.S.O., 1985), Table 2.11.

28. P. Willis, 'The Docile Generation', *The Times*, 31 July 1984, p. 11.

29. Service for the Solemnization of Matrimony, Book of Common Prayer.

30. Of the sample, 39 per cent thought cohabitation before marriage was a good idea; 36 per cent a bad idea; as an alternative to marriage the percentage giving approval fell to 15 per cent with 45 per cent thinking it a bad idea. See note 7.

31. See note 26.

32. R. Chester, 'Is there a relationship between childlessness and marriage breakdown?', *Journal of Biosocial Science*, 4 (1972), pp. 343–454.

33. J. Haskey, 'Children of divorcing couples', *Population Trends*, 31 (1983).

34. Thornes and Collard, op. cit., p. 92.

35. See A. Oakley, *From Here to Maternity* (Harmondsworth, Penguin, 1981).

36. C. Clulow, *To Have and To Hold: marriage, the first baby and preparing couples for parenthood* (Aberdeen, Aberdeen University Press, 1982).

37. G. Brown and T. Harris, *The Social Origins of Depression* (London, Tavistock, 1978).

38. O.P.C.S. Population Monitor, op. cit., Table 5a.

39. Leete, op. cit.

40. Although there was a sharp increase in the number of divorce petitions filed in 1984 as a result of the implementation of the Matrimonial and Family Proceedings Act 1984, it is too early to estimate the longer-term effects of the reduction of the time-bar.

41. R. Chester, 'The duration of marriage to divorce', *British Journal of Sociology*, 22 (1972).

42. Unpublished data from a survey of *Woman* readers carried out in 1982.

43. See J. Burgoyne, *Breaking Even: divorce, your children and you* (Harmondsworth, Penguin, 1984), Chapter 7.

44. O.P.C.S. Population Monitor, op. cit., Table 9.

45. See note 46.

46. Leete, op. cit.

47. Cited in M. Borkowski, M. Murch and V. Walker, *Marital Violence: the community response* (London, Tavistock, 1983).

48. J. Haskey, 'Social class and socio-economic differentials in divorce in England and Wales', *Population Studies*, 38 (1984).

49. D. Marsden, *Mothers Alone* (Harmondsworth, Penguin, 1969).

50. For, as John Eekelaar points out, maintenance payments are deductible against income for tax purposes so that the higher a man's income the greater benefit he derives from this exemption. See *Family Law and Social Policy* (Weidenfeld and Nicolson, London, 1978), pp. 192–5.

51. c.f. G. Runciman, *Relative Deprivation and Social Justice* (Harmondsworth, Penguin, 1972).

52. See Burgoyne and Clark, op. cit., pp. 190–200.

53. Leete, op. cit., p. 41.

54. See J. Burgoyne and D. Clark, 'Family reconstitution: remarried parents and their children' in R. Rapoport, Rh. Rapoport and M. Fogarty (eds.), *Families in Britain* (London, Routledge and Kegan Paul, 1981), pp. 286–302.

55. Burgoyne and Clark, op. cit., chapter 6.

56. J. Haskey, 'Remarriage of the divorced in England and Wales – a contemporary phenomenon', *Journal of Biosocial Science*, 15 (1983), pp. 253–71.

57. J. Haskey, 'The proportion of marriages ending in divorce', *Population Trends*, 27 (1982).

2. DIVORCE AND THE COURTS

1. Morley, *Life of Gladstone*, Vol. 1 (London, 1903), p. 567.

2. Foljamb's case. 3 S.A.L.K. 138.

3. J. Roberts, *Divorce Bills in the Imperial Parliament* (Dublin, 1906).

4. See R. E. Megarry, *Miscellany at Law* (London, 1955), for the full citation.

5. [1981] A.C. 487.

6. [1973] Fam. 72.

7. Perhaps we should note that very little information is available about the financial position of spouses after divorce and that little is known about the longer-term effects of court orders. While a couple of small-scale studies have recently been completed, we still feel it is highly undesirable that public policy should be made and modified in this area in the absence of firm information.

8. [1970] A.C. 688.

3. ADULTS AND DIVORCE

1. Many of the studies to which we refer most frequently in this chapter are based upon small samples of couples and individuals who have experienced marital problems or who are divorced. It is ironic that despite the rise in the divorce rate, researchers working on low budgets that preclude the costs of survey techniques necessary to contact a large and representative sample of couples or individuals of differing marital statuses often experience difficulties in 'finding' suitable informants or are forced to recruit via inevitably partisan sources. See J. Burgoyne and D. Clark, *Making a Go of It; a study of step-families in Sheffield* (London, Routledge and Kegan Paul, 1984).

2. J. Bernard, *The Future of Marriage* (New York, Yale University Press, 1982).

3. B. Thornes and J. Collard, *Who Divorces?* (London, Routledge and Kegan Paul, 1979).

4. D. Sanders, *The Woman Book of Love and Sex* (London, Sphere Books, 1985).

5. J. Burgoyne, 'Marriage on the dole', *Listener*, 13 June 1985, p. 10.

6. J. Martin and C. Roberts, *Women and Employment: a lifetime perspective* (London, H.M.S.O., 1984)

   S. Westwood, *All Day, Every Day* (London, Pluto Press, 1984)

7. R. Jowell and S. Witherspoon, *British Social Attitudes: the 1985 Report* (Aldershot, Gower Press, 1985).

8. See S. Edgell, *Middle Class Couples* (London, Allen and Unwin, 1980).

9. See, for example, M. Davidson and C. Cooper, 'Women managers: work, stress and marriage', *International Journal of Social Economics*, 112 (1984), p. 17.

10. J. Brannen and J. Collard, *Marriage in Trouble* (London, Tavistock Publications, 1982).

11. Sanders, op. cit. These findings are confirmed in a recent, parallel survey of men readers. See *Woman*, 14 September 1985, pp. 18–21.

12. For a specific example of such a study see D. Clark, K. McCann and R. Taylor, 'Work and marriage in the offshore oil industry', *International Journal of Social Economics*, 112, 2 (1985).

13. Potential sources of stability in marriage are also discussed in chapter 5.

14. See P. A. Hunt, *Clients' Responses to Marriage Counselling* (Rugby, National Marriage Guidance Council, 1985).

15. M. Murch, *Justice and Welfare in Divorce* (London, Sweet and Maxwell, 1980).

16. Burgoyne and Clark, op. cit.

17. See the survey carried out for the *Daily Mail* by N.O.P. (1980) for further confirmation of this point.

18. C. Smart, *The Ties that Bind* (London, Routledge and Kegan Paul, 1984).

19. See, for example, P. Ambrose, J. Harper and R. Pemberton, *Surviving Divorce* (Brighton, Wheatsheaf Books, 1983).

20. See also G. Davis, A. MacLeod and M. Murch, 'Divorce: who supports the family?', *Family Law*, 13 (1983), p. 217; J. Eekelaar and M. Maclean, Maintenance After Divorce (Oxford, Oxford University Press, forthcoming); M. Maclean and J. Eekelaar, *Children and Divorce* (Oxford, Centre for Socio-Legal Studies, 1986).

21. See Martin and Roberts, op. cit.

22. See T. Hipgrave, 'Lone fatherhood: a problematic status' in L. McKee and M. O'Brien (eds.), *The Father Figure* (London, Tavistock Publications, 1982); V. George and P. Wilding, *Motherless Families* (London, Routledge and Kegan Paul, 1972).

23. N. Hart, *When Marriage Ends* (London, Tavistock Publications, 1976).

24. Ambrose *et al.*, op. cit.

25. R. M. Blackburn and M. Mann, *The Working Class in the Labour Market* (London, Macmillan, 1979).

26. R. Weiss, *Marital Separation* (New York, Basic Books, 1975). This is an excellent account of divorce as an emotional transition.

27. See Burgoyne and Clark, op. cit., chapter 3; and J. Burgoyne, *Breaking Even: divorce, your children and you* (Harmondsworth, Penguin, 1984).

28. Burgoyne and Clark, op. cit.

29. Quoted in M. Green, *Marriage* (London, Fontana Books, 1984).

30. See J. Burgoyne and D. Clark, 'Why get married again?', *New Society*, 52, 913 (1980), p. 12. See also article by C. Smart and H. Land in M. D. A. Freeman (ed.), *State, Law and the Family* (London, Tavistock Publications, 1985).

4. DIVORCE AND CHILDREN

1. For a general account of the legal aspects of the position of children at divorce, and discussion of custody, care and control, and access, see B. M. Hoggett and D. S. Pearl, *The Family, Law and Society* (London, Butterworth, 1983); S. Maidment, *Child Custody and Divorce* (London, Croom Helm, 1984).

2. Effects of divorce on children are described by J. Wallerstein and J. Kelly, *Surviving the Break-up* (London, Grant McIntyre, 1980); E. M. Hetherington, 'Children and Divorce', in R. W. Henderson (ed.), *Parent–Child Interaction* (New York, Academic Press, 1981); M. P. M. Richards and M. Dyson, 'Separation, Divorce and the Development of Children: a Review' (London, unpublished report for the Department of Health and Social Security, 1982); D. A. Luepnitz, *Child Custody* (Lexington, MA, Lexington Books, 1983); Maidment, op. cit.; A. Mitchell, *Children in the Middle* (London, Tavistock, 1985).

3. Not all studies agree that the children of divorced parents are themselves more likely to divorce than children of 'intact' marriages. It is likely that the connection has become less strong as divorce rates have risen. The link was clear for the children of the post-Second-World-War divorce peak.

4. See Richards and Dyson, op. cit., and Maidment, op. cit.

5. This is suggested by findings of the higher incidence of problems requiring clinical intervention in boys. However, when children in mid- to late childhood are asked, girls report more upset than boys. See Mitchell, op. cit.

6. M. E. J. Wadsworth and M. Maclean, *Parents' Divorce and Children's Life Chances* (in press, 1985); M. E. J. Wadsworth, *Roots of Delinquency* (Oxford, Martin Robinson, 1979).

7. M. E. J. Wadsworth, 'Relationships between parents and children', in M. P. M. Richards and P. Light (eds.), *Children of Social Worlds* (Cambridge, Polity Press, 1986).

8. See Richards and Light, op. cit.

9. These studies are discussed in M. P. M. Richards, 'Children, parents and families', in J. Burgoyne and M. P. M. Richards (eds.), *Public and Private Lives*, in preparation.

10. For example, M. Rutter, *Maternal Deprivation Reassessed* (Harmondsworth, Penguin, 1984). See also R. E. Emery, 'Interparental conflict and the children of discord and divorce', *Psychological Bulletin*, 92 (1982), p. 310.

11. R. D. Hess and K. A. Camera, 'Post-divorce family relationships as mediating factors in the consequences of divorce for children', *Journal of Social Issues*, 35 (1979), p. 79; M. Lund and J. Riley, *Children's Adjustment after Marital Separation: the importance of parental harmony and non-custodial parental involvement* (unpublished paper, 1984).

12. J. W. B. Douglas, 'Broken families and child behaviour', *Journal of the Royal College of Physicians*, 4 (1970), p. 203.

13. E. Ferri, *Growing Up in a One-parent Family* (Windsor, N.F.E.R., 1976).

14. See Hess and Camera, op. cit.

15. For example, J. Eekelaar and E. Clive, *Custody after Divorce*, Family Law Studies, No. 1 (Oxford, Centre for Socio-Legal Studies, 1977).

16. Ferri, op. cit.

17. Maidment, op. cit.

18. Booth Committee Report, *Report of the Matrimonial Causes Procedures Committee* (London, H.M.S.O., 1985).

19. F. W. Ilfield, H. Z. Ilfield and J. R. Alexander, 'Does joint custody work?', *American Journal of Psychiatry*, 139 (1982), p. 62.

20. A. Anbabanel, 'Shared parenting after separation and divorce', *American Journal of Orthopsychiatry*, 49 (1979), p. 320; C. R. Ahrons, 'Joint custody arrangements', *Journal of Divorce*, 3 (1980), p. 189; S. Steinman, 'The experience of children in a joint custody arrangement', *American Journal of Orthopsychiatry*, 51 (1981), p. 403.

21. Eekelaar and Clive, op. cit.; Maidment, op. cit.

22. M. P. M. Richards, 'Post-divorce arrangements for children', *Journal of Social Welfare Law*, 133 (1982).

23. For example, M. Kirkpatrick, M. Smith, C. Roy and R. Roy, 'Lesbian mothers and their children', *American Journal of Orthopsychiatry*, 17 (1981), p. 317.

24. For example, R. Chester, 'Health and marital breakdown', *Journal of Psychosomatic Research*, 17 (1973), p. 317.

5. WAYS FORWARD: THE PURSUIT OF PARTNERSHIP

1. J. Martin and C. Roberts, *Women and Employment: a lifetime perspective* (London, H.M.S.O., 1984).

2. As we have already noted, the experiences of the Swansea working-class couples studied by Leonard contrast very markedly with many of the now-divorced informants in Thornes and Collard's study (see chapter 1).

3. J. Haskey, 'Social class and socio-economic differentials in divorce in England and Wales', *Population Studies*, 38 (1984).

4. L. Fagin and B. Little, *The Forsaken Families* (Harmondsworth, Penguin, 1984); A. Coyle, *Redundant Woman* (London, Women's Press, 1984); J. Popay, 'Women, the Family and Unemployment', in P. Close and R. Collins (eds.), *Family and Economy in Modern Society* (London, Macmillan, 1985).

5. Finer Report, *Report of the Committee on One-Parent Families* (London, H.M.S.O., 1974).

6. J. Goldstein, A. Freud and A. J. Solnit, *Beyond the Best Interests of the Child* (New York, Free Press, 1973).

7. See, for example, A. Bottomley, 'Resolving Family Disputes: a critical view' in M. D. A. Freeman (ed.), *The State, the Law and the Family* (London, Tavistock Publications, 1984).

8. G. Davis, A. Macleod and M. Murch, 'Undefended divorce; should Section 41 of the Matrimonial Causes Act 1973 be repealed?', *Modern Law Review*, 46 (1983), p. 121; M. Dodds, 'Children and divorce', *Journal of Social Welfare Law* (1983), p. 13.

9. Booth Committee Report, *Report of the Matrimonial Causes Procedures Committee* (London, H.M.S.O., 1985).

10. There is an interesting discussion of these issues in the context of the Australian family courts: J. Wade, 'The family court of Australia and informality in court procedure', *International and Comparative Law Quarterly*, 27 (1978), p. 820.

11. More generally, very little is known of how far court orders are kept. Some cases come back to court because orders have been broken, but in others the parties may simply give up, feeling that further court orders are unlikely to work. In other situations, the parties may agree between themselves to vary the order and may not feel it necessary to obtain formal approval. For instance, as a child gets older a different pattern of access visits may evolve or informal transfers of custody are made. Until we have some longer-term follow-up studies our knowledge of how court decisions may influence events is very limited.

12. G. Davis, 'Conciliation and the professions', *Family Law*, 14 (1984), p. 6; see also S. Roberts, 'Mediation in family disputes', *Modern Law Review*, 46 (1983), p. 537.

13. Davis, op. cit.

14. M. P. M. Richards, 'Divorce, Some Attitudes of Divorced Parents and the Children of Divorced Parents', unpublished paper (University of Cambridge, 1984).

15. Booth Committee, op. cit.

16. M. Southwell, 'Children, divorce and disposal of the matrimonial home', *Family Law*, 15 (1985), p. 184.

17. See G. Davies, A. Macleod and M. Murch, 'Divorce: who supports the family', *Family Law*, 13 (1984), p. 217; M. Maclean and J. Eekelaar, *Children and Divorce: Economic Factors* (Oxford, Centre for Socio-legal Studies, 1983).

18. M. E. J. Wadsworth and M. Maclean, *Parents' Divorce and Children's Life Chances* (in press, 1986).

FURTHER READING

Throughout the book we have given references to the sources of the more significant and controversial evidence we have used. In many cases these would serve as a starting point for further exploration of the evidence. To help the reader who wishes to go further we are also providing a selected list of other books which we have found helpful. The ones which are starred (*) are titles intended primarily to give advice and information for those experiencing a divorce at first hand.

S. Atkins and B. Hoggett, *Women and the Law* (Oxford, Basil Blackwell, 1984)

*R. Brown, *Breaking Up: a practical guide to separation and divorce* (London, Arrow, 1980)

*J. Burgoyne, *Breaking Even: divorce, your children and you* (Harmondsworth, Penguin, 1984)

J. Burgoyne and D. Clark, *Making a Go of It: a study of step-families in Sheffield* (London, Routledge and Kegan Paul, 1984)

A. J. Cherlin, *Marriage, Divorce and Remarriage* (Cambridge, Mass., Harvard University Press, 1981)

R. Chester (ed.), *Divorce in Europe* (Leiden, Martinius Mijhoff, 1977)

*Consumer Association, *Divorce: legal procedures and financial facts* (London, Hodder, 1984)

*D. Davenport, *One Parent Families* (London, Sheldon Press, 1979)

J. Eekelaar, *Family Law and Social Policy* (second edition), (London, Weidenfeld and Nicolson, 1984)

*W. Harper, *Divorce and Your Money* (London, Unwin, Paperbacks, 1983)

*E. Hodder, *The Step-parents' Handbook* (London, Sphere Books, 1985)

B. Hoggett and D. Pearl, *The Family, Law and Society* (London, Butterworth's, 1983)

*A. Hooper, *Divorce and Your Children* (London, Unwin Paperbacks, 1983)

*B. Maddox, *Step-parenting* (London, Unwin Paperbacks, 1980)

S. Maidment, *Child Custody and Divorce* (London, Croom Helm, 1984)

* A. Mitchell, *When Parents Split Up: divorce explained to young people* (London, Macdonald, 1982)

M. Murch, *Justice and Welfare in Divorce* (London, Sweet and Maxwell, 1980)

M. P. M. Richards, *Parents, Children and Divorce* (London, Cambridge University Press, in press)

* P. Rowlands, *Saturday Parent* (London, Unwin Paperbacks, 1980)

* G. Search, *Surviving Divorce: a handbook for men* (London, Elm Tree Books, 1983)

C. Smart, *The Ties that Bind* (London, Routledge and Kegan Paul, 1984)

* J. Swihart and S. Brigham, *Helping Children of Divorce* (London, Scripture Union, 1982)

E. B. Visher and J. S. Visher, *Stepfamilies, Myths and Realities* (Secaucus, New Jersey, Citadel Press, 1979)

J. Wallerstein and J. Kelly, *Surviving the Break-up* (London, Grant McIntyre, 1980)

R. Weiss, *Marital Separation* (New York, Basic Books, 1975)

* A. Willans, *Divorce and Separation: every woman's guide to a new life* (London, Sheldon Press, 1983)

INDEX

A CHOICE OF PENGUINS

Castaway Lucy Irvine

'Writer seeks "wife" for a year on a tropical island.' This is the extraordinary, candid, sometimes shocking account of what happened when Lucy Irvine answered the advertisement, and found herself embroiled in what was not exactly a desert island dream. 'Fascinating' – *Daily Mail*

Out of Africa Karen Blixen (Isak Dinesen)

After the failure of her coffee-farm in Kenya, where she lived from 1913 to 1931, Karen Blixen went home to Denmark and wrote this unforgettable account of her experiences. 'No reader can put the book down without some share in the author's poignant farewell to her farm' – *Observer*

The Lisle Letters Edited by Muriel St Clare Byrne

An intimate, immediate and wholly fascinating picture of a family in the reign of Henry VIII. 'Remarkable . . . we can really hear the people of early Tudor England talking' – Keith Thomas in the *Sunday Times*. 'One of the most extraordinary works to be published this century' – J. H. Plumb

In My Wildest Dreams Leslie Thomas

The autobiography of Leslie Thomas, author of *The Magic Army* and *The Dearest and the Best*. From Barnardo boy to original virgin soldier, from apprentice journalist to famous novelist, it is an amazing story. 'Hugely enjoyable' – *Daily Express*

India: The Siege Within M. J. Akbar

'A thoughtful and well-researched history of the conflict, 2,500 years old, between centralizing and separatist forces in the sub-continent. And remarkably, for a work of this kind, it's concise, elegantly written and entertaining' – Zareer Masani in the *New Statesman*

The Winning Streak Walter Goldsmith and David Clutterbuck

Marks and Spencer, Saatchi and Saatchi, United Biscuits, G.E.C. . . . The U.K.'s top companies reveal their formulas for success, in an important and stimulating book that no British manager can afford to ignore.

A CHOICE OF PENGUINS

Adieux: A Farewell to Sartre   Simone de Beauvoir

A devastatingly frank account of the last years of Sartre's life, and his death, by the woman who for more than half a century shared that life. 'A true labour of love, there is about it a touching sadness, a mingling of the personal with the impersonal and timeless which Sartre himself would surely have liked and understood' – *Listener*

Business Wargames   James Barrie

How did BMW overtake Mercedes? Why did Laker crash? How did McDonalds grab the hamburger market? Drawing on the tragic mistakes and brilliant victories of military history, this remarkable book draws countless fascinating parallels with case histories from industry world-wide.

Metamagical Themas   Douglas R. Hofstadter

This astonishing sequel to the best-selling, Pulitzer Prize-winning *Gödel, Escher, Bach* swarms with 'extraordinary ideas, brilliant fables, deep philosophical questions and Carrollian word play' – Martin Gardner

Into the Heart of Borneo   Redmond O'Hanlon

'Perceptive, hilarious and at the same time a serious natural-history journey into one of the last remaining unspoilt paradises' – *New Statesman*. 'Consistently exciting, often funny and erudite without ever being overwhelming' – *Punch*

A Better Class of Person   John Osborne

The playwright's autobiography, 1929–56. 'Splendidly enjoyable' – John Mortimer. 'One of the best, richest and most bitterly truthful autobiographies that I have ever read' – Melvyn Bragg

The Secrets of a Woman's Heart   Hilary Spurling

The later life of Ivy Compton-Burnett, 1920–69. 'A biographical triumph . . . elegant, stylish, witty, tender, immensely acute – dazzles and exhilarates . . . a great achievement' – Kay Dick in the *Literary Review*. 'One of the most important literary biographies of the century' – *New Statesman*

A CHOICE OF PENGUINS

An African Winter   Preston King   With an Introduction by Richard Leakey

This powerful and impassioned book offers a unique assessment of the interlocking factors which result in the famines of Africa and argues that there *are* solutions and we *can* learn from the mistakes of the past.

Jean Rhys: Letters 1931–66
Edited by Francis Wyndham and Diana Melly

'Eloquent and invaluable . . . her life emerges, and with it a portrait of an unexpectedly indomitable figure' – Marina Warner in the *Sunday Times*

Among the Russians   Colin Thubron

One man's solitary journey by car across Russia provides an enthralling and revealing account of the habits and idiosyncrasies of a fascinating people. 'He sees things with the freshness of an innocent and the erudition of a scholar' – *Daily Telegraph*

The Amateur Naturalist   Gerald Durrell with Lee Durrell

'Delight . . . on every page . . . packed with authoritative writing, learning without pomposity . . . it represents a real bargain' – *The Times Educational Supplement*. 'What treats are in store for the average British household' – *Books and Bookmen*

The Democratic Economy   Geoff Hodgson

Today, the political arena is divided as seldom before. In this exciting and original study, Geoff Hodgson carefully examines the claims of the rival doctrines and exposes some crucial flaws.

They Went to Portugal   Rose Macaulay

An exotic and entertaining account of travellers to Portugal from the pirate-crusaders, through poets, aesthetes and ambassadors, to the new wave of romantic travellers. A wonderful mixture of literature, history and adventure, by one of our most stylish and seductive writers.

A CHOICE OF PENGUINS

The Book Quiz Book   Joseph Connolly

Who was literature's performing flea . . .? Who wrote 'Live Now, Pay Later . . .'? Keats and Cartland, Balzac and Braine, Coleridge conundrums, Eliot enigmas, Tolstoy teasers . . . all in this brilliant quiz book. You will be on the shelf without it . . .

Voyage through the Antarctic   Richard Adams and Ronald Lockley

Here is the true, authentic Antarctic of today, brought vividly to life by Richard Adams, author of *Watership Down*, and Ronald Lockley, the world-famous naturalist. 'A good adventure story, with a lot of information and a deal of enthusiasm for Antarctica and its animals' – *Nature*

Getting to Know the General   Graham Greene

'In August 1981 my bag was packed for my fifth visit to Panama when the news came to me over the telephone of the death of General Omar Torrijos Herrera, my friend and host . . .' 'Vigorous, deeply felt, at times funny, and for Greene surprisingly frank' – *Sunday Times*

Television Today and Tomorrow: Wall to Wall Dallas?
Christopher Dunkley

Virtually every British home has a television, nearly half now have two sets or more, and we are promised that before the end of the century there will be a vast expansion of television delivered via cable and satellite. How did television come to be so central to our lives? Is British television really the best in the world, as politicians like to assert?

Arabian Sands   Wilfred Thesiger

'In the tradition of Burton, Doughty, Lawrence, Philby and Thomas, it is, very likely, the book about Arabia to end all books about Arabia' – *Daily Telegraph*

When the Wind Blows   Raymond Briggs

'A visual parable against nuclear war: all the more chilling for being in the form of a strip cartoon' – *Sunday Times*. 'The most eloquent anti-Bomb statement you are likely to read' – *Daily Mail*

A CHOICE OF PENGUINS AND PELICANS

Adieux   Simone de Beauvoir

This 'farewell to Sartre' by his life-long companion is a 'true labour of love' (the *Listener*) and 'an extraordinary achievement' (*New Statesman*).

British Society 1914–45   John Stevenson

A major contribution to the Pelican Social History of Britain, which 'will undoubtedly be the standard work for students of modern Britain for many years to come' – *The Times Educational Supplement*

The Pelican History of Greek Literature   Peter Levi

A remarkable survey covering all the major writers from Homer to Plutarch, with brilliant translations by the author, one of the leading poets of today.

Art and Literature   Sigmund Freud

Volume 14 of the Pelican Freud Library contains Freud's major essays on Leonardo, Michelangelo and Dostoevsky, plus shorter pieces on Shakespeare, the nature of creativity and much more.

A History of the Crusades   Sir Steven Runciman

This three-volume history of the events which transferred world power to Western Europe – and founded Modern History – has been universally acclaimed as a masterpiece.

A Night to Remember   Walter Lord

The classic account of the sinking of the *Titanic*. 'A stunning book, incomparably the best on its subject and one of the most exciting books of this or any year' – *The New York Times*

FOR THE BEST IN PAPERBACKS, LOOK FOR THE 🐧

A CHOICE OF PENGUINS AND PELICANS

The Informed Heart   Bruno Bettelheim

Bettelheim draws on his experience in concentration camps to illuminate the dangers inherent in all mass societies in this profound and moving masterpiece.

God and the New Physics   Paul Davies

Can science, now come of age, offer a surer path to God than religion? This 'very interesting' (*New Scientist*) book suggests it can.

Modernism   Malcolm Bradbury and James McFarlane (eds.)

A brilliant collection of essays dealing with all aspects of literature and culture for the period 1890–1930 – from Apollinaire and Brecht to Yeats and Zola.

Rise to Globalism   Stephen E. Ambrose

A clear, up-to-date and well-researched history of American foreign policy since 1938, Volume 8 of the Pelican History of the United States.

The Waning of the Middle Ages   Johan Huizinga

A magnificent study of life, thought and art in 14th and 15th century France and the Netherlands, long established as a classic.

The Penguin Dictionary of Psychology   Arthur S. Reber

Over 17,000 terms from psychology, psychiatry and related fields are given clear, concise and modern definitions.

FOR THE BEST IN PAPERBACKS, LOOK FOR THE 🐧

A CHOICE OF PENGUINS AND PELICANS

The Literature of the United States Marcus Cunliffe

The fourth edition of a masterly one-volume survey, described by D. W. Brogan in the *Guardian* as 'a very good book indeed'.

The Sceptical Feminist Janet Radcliffe Richards

A rigorously argued but sympathetic consideration of feminist claims. 'A triumph' – *Sunday Times*

The Enlightenment Norman Hampson

A classic survey of the age of Diderot and Voltaire, Goethe and Hume, which forms part of the Pelican History of European Thought.

Defoe to the Victorians David Skilton

A 'Learned and stimulating' (*The Times Educational Supplement*) survey of two centuries of the English novel.

Reformation to Industrial Revolution Christopher Hill

This 'formidable little book' (Peter Laslett in the *Guardian*) by one of our leading historians is Volume 2 of the Pelican Economic History of Britain.

The New Pelican Guide to English Literature Boris Ford (ed.)
Volume 8: The Present

This book brings a major series up to date with important essays on Ted Hughes and Nadine Gordimer, Philip Larkin and V. S. Naipaul, and all the other leading writers of today.